My China Diary
1956–88

*Let a hundred flowers bloom and
let a hundred schools of thought contend.*

– Mao Tse Tung

My China Diary
1956–88

K. Natwar Singh
External Affairs Minister (2004-05)

Rupa & Co

Copyright © K. Natwar Singh 2009

First Published 2009
Second Impression 2009
Third Impression 2009

First in Rupa Paperback 2011

Published by
Rupa Publications India Pvt. Ltd.
7/16, Ansari Road, Daryaganj,
New Delhi 110 002

Sales Centres:

Allahabad Bengaluru Chennai
Hyderabad Jaipur Kathmandu
Kolkata Mumbai

All rights reserved.
No part of this publication may be reproduced, stored in a retrieval system, or transmitted, in any form or by any means, electronic, mechanical, photocopying, recording or otherwise, without the prior permission of the publishers.

The author asserts the moral right to be identified as the author of this work.

Photo credit: Hari Krishna Katragadda

Typeset by
Mindways Design
1410 Chiranjiv Tower
43 Nehru Place
New Delhi 110 019

Printed in India by
Rekha Printers Pvt. Ltd.
A-102/1, Okhla Industrial Area, Phase-II,
New Delhi-110 020

To the Memory of My Brother
Bhagwat Singh
1926-2010

Deng Xiaoping and Rajiv Gandhi, Peking, 1988

Contents

List of Illustrations xi
Preface xiii

Part One
1956–58

Diary—1956	3
Diary—1957	46
Diary—1958	80

Part Two
Premier Chou En-lai's Visit to India, 20-26 April 1960

Prefatory Note	85
Meeting with Vice-President Dr S. Radhakrishnan	89
Meeting with Pandit G.B. Pant	94
R.K. Nehru's Meeting with Premier Chou En-lai	97
Finance Minister Morarji Desai's Meeting with Premier Chou En-lai	104

Part Three
Prime Minister Rajiv Gandhi's Visit to China 19-23 December 1988

Prefatory Note	113
Prime Minister's Meeting with President Yang Shengkun	122
The Climax: Meeting with Deng Xiaoping	126
Appendices	141
1. Dr S. Radhakrishnan's Speech on Leaving Peking, 27 September 1957	143
2. Prime Minister Nehru's Speech at the Banquet Held in Honour of Chou En-lai, 20 April 1960	147
3. Talks between Prime Minister Nehru and Premier Chou En-lai, 25 April 1960	149
4. Prime Minister Rajiv Gandhi's Speech at Qinghua University, Beijing, 21 December 1988	163
5. India-China Joint Press Communique Issued on 23 December 1988	176
6. Concordance of Chinese Names and Places	179
Endnotes	181
Who's Who	195
Acknowledgements	197
Index	199
Also by the Author	206

List of Illustrations

1. 1st row: Premier Chou En-lai, Marshal Chu Teh, Dr Radhakrishnan, Chairman Mao Tse Tung, Ambassador R.K. Nehru, President Liu Shao Chi.
   2nd row: V.V. Paranjpe, K. Natwar Singh, J.S. Mehta, I.J. Bahadur Singh, September 1957.
2. The Summer Palace, Peking
3. Dr Radhakrishnan with Chairman Mao Tse Tung
4. My house in Tung Sung Pu Hutong, Peking
5. Prime Minister Nehru, Premier Chou En-lai, Marshal Chen Yi, Sardar Swaran Singh, New Delhi, 20 April 1960.
6. The author with Chih Pai Shih in 1956.
7. Prime Minister Jawaharlal Nehru speaking at his banquet for the Premier Chou En-lai, in a grim mood, seated next to Indira Gandhi, 20 April 1960.
8. The author with Madam Soong Ching-ling, also known as Madam Sun Yat-sen in December 1955, New Delhi.
9. Deng Xiaoping with the author while P.V. Narasimha Rao and Dinesh Singh look on.
10. Invitation card to the banquet at Rashtrapati Bhavan.
11. Invitation card from Premier Chou En-lai.
12. Chairman Mao welcoming President Voroshilov of the USSR, Peking 1957.
13. Han Suyin, Peking, 1956

14. Mela Chang, Peking, 1957
15. K. Natwar Singh with Prime Minister Rajiv Gandhi, Mrs Sonia Gandhi and Mr P.V. Narasimha Rao in fur-cap, Peking, 1988.
16. Chairman Mao Tse Tung

Preface

This book is divided into three sections. The first covers the years 1956-58. The second deals with Prime Minister Chou En-lai's[1] visit to India in April 1960. The third describes Rajiv Gandhi's[2] path-breaking passage to China in December 1988. He succeeded where his grandfather, Jawaharlal Nehru,[3] faltered and failed.

I belong to the 1953 Indian Foreign Service (IFS) batch. I opted for Chinese as my foreign language – the first IFS entrant to do so. Why Chinese? Why not French or Russian? Here's why. In those remote, almost prehistoric days, Prime Minister Jawaharlal Nehru met new entrants to the IFS individually. He gave each of us no more than ten minutes. It was, for young men in their twenties, a very special occasion. To pretend that one was not nervous or tense is to give oneself retrospective airs. Of course, one was nervous.

My ordeal began with the prime minister asking me in Hindi, '*Kya humae Cheen se koi khatra hai?*' (Do we need to fear the Chinese?) I replied, '*Jee, hai bhi or nahin bhi* (sir, we do and do not) because one's closest neighbour is one's closest enemy and one's closest friend'. The great man's response was, '*Mujhe Chanakya niti sikha rahe ho*' (Are you trying to teach me Chanakya's philosophy?). He smiled, asked one or two more questions on the Five Year Plan, South Africa, etc. The *agni pariksha* (trial by fire) was over.

On 14 April 1953, I joined the IFS and IAS batches at Metcalfe House in Old Delhi for training. Our training was not strenuous. One peculiarity sticks in my mind. The principal and the vice-principal,

M/s Bapat and Shukla, both ICS men were not on talking terms. So much for esprit de corps.

At Cambridge, I had been doing history for my tripos. After getting into the IFS, I switched to Chinese. A benign follower of Marshal Chiang Kai-shek[4] attempted to teach me Mandarin. Neither of us succeeded.

On his return from the successful China tour of 1954, Prime Minister Nehru spoke to the officials of the ministry—IFS probationers included—about his impressions of China and its leadership, particularly his discussion with Chairman Mao Tse Tung[5] and Premier Chou En-lai. Incidentally, his first letter on his China visit was written to Lady Mountbatten[6] from Raj Bhawan immediately after his landing in Kolkata on 2 November 1954.[7] The record of his discussion with Chairman Mao Tse Tung and Premier Chou En-lai in October 1954 makes it clear that no real meeting of minds occurred. The Chinese leaders spoke as communists and Nehru, as a genuine democratic socialist, was strong on generalities and less so on specifics.

In December 1954, I was attached to a Chinese cultural delegation which performed in Delhi, Mumbai, Chennai and Kolkata. It was my first exposure to Chinese dance, music and state-controlled culture. The dance I loved; the music I loathed.

In Chennai, after the show, Vice-Minister Chen Chen Tho[8] garlanded K. Kamaraj Nadar,[9] the then chief minister, who, imagining that all Chinese look alike garlanded the interpreter, whose vigorous protests made the chief minister even more determined! In Delhi, at the beginning of the show, I gave Jawaharlal Nehru a copy of the programme adding, 'One rupee, Sir.' He took out his purse and gave me a rupee. T.N. Kaul,[10] the joint secretary roundly ticked me off for my impertinence.

In December 1955 came Madame Soong Ching-ling[11] (Mrs Sun Yat-sen). I was attached to her. She knew English, but spoke only Chinese in public. She stayed with the prime minister at Teen Murti House and charmed everyone. I gave her the alarming news that I would soon be posted in the Indian Embassy in Peking (now Beijing) and hoped to see her there. She graciously said, 'Yes, do contact me,' and I did.

Before leaving for China in June 1956, S. Gopal, director of the historical division, Ministry of External Affairs asked me to read Edgar

Snow's *Red Star Over China*. It immediately made me an admirer of Mao Tse Tung and his formidable Long Marchers[12]. Thus equipped, I embarked on my not-so-long march to Mao Tse Tung's New China. It was June 1956. My lowly status as third secretary in the embassy ensured my non-involvement in high-level diplomatic deliberations or writing dispatches for the enlightenment of our mandarins in South Block back home. I made no contribution to policy making or policy implementation. No one in particular was passionately interested in my evolution as a worthwhile diplomat. This was a blessing in disguise. I was left to myself and that suited me. Both time and space were available to me. But the latter was limited. Peking offered no hedonistic outlets. It was not a place for sowing your wild oats or burning your bridges and any such attempts would have resulted in personal disaster. I had no intention of tempting fate. Austerity and a Spartan lifestyle confronted one on arrival in Beijing which suited me.

I was then going through a period of ostentatious puritanism. I had an instinctive aversion to bourgeois comforts. Beijing was an ideal place for this unexciting pursuit. Here, a sybaritic interlude of even a minor character was inconceivable. Peking of that era was a good place to have a rendezvous with oneself. This I often did. My underemployment continued till I started attending Peking University in 1957. In the meanwhile, I did not go to seed.

My diary from 1956-58 I hope, gives some idea of the texture and tenor of life in the Chinese capital, and the temper of the times more than fifty years ago. It makes no claim to literary excellence. The recurrent trivialities of diplomatic existence, the verbosity, the repetitions, the callow judgments needed drastic weeding out. Personal references have been minimised. Pretentious passages have been given the red pencil treatment. Freshness has not been sacrificed.

As a period piece it may have some value. A diary can be a tyrant. It can enslave the diarist. This did not happen with me. I did not live for the diary; weeks passed when I did not even go near it.

The China of the late 1950s was still a nation in the making. It was not a world player in any field. In many countries the notice boards read – China: No Entry. The diplomatic corps was small – less than thirty missions. All socialist (read communist) countries were represented at high levels. From Asia, the prominent ones included India, Indonesia, Burma, Ceylon, Vietnam and Pakistan. Only Egypt from West Asia was represented. From Europe – Norway, Holland and Sweden. The UK had a chargé d'affaires. The press corps came mostly from the socialist countries. Reuters and AFP have their correspondents.

China, as I said, was not then a world power. Its leaders, however, were of world stature. After the death of Stalin[13] in 1953, Mao Tse Tung was the numero uno communist leader in the world. Chou En-lai was a man of immense charisma, ideological stamina, vision, diplomatic astuteness and supple negotiating brilliance.

It was a heaven-sent opportunity and I made the most of it.

Part One

1956–58

Diary—1956

24 June

While I was on district training in South India from 1 January to 1 May 1956, my father[1] suffered a heart attack. Neither he, nor anyone else informed me about it. I learnt of it only when I went to Bharatpur on 3 May. I immediately postponed my departure for Peking by a month.

25 June

Arrived in Hong Kong at 1:00 pm. Frightening approach to the runway. Pilots have to be extra careful. Hong Kong looks lovely from the air. But all things look nice from above. It is warm with high humidity. The blessings of a diplomatic passport – cleared by customs in no time. Staying at Hotel Miramar in Kowloon. Did not know of the existence of Kowloon and never realised that Canton was more than a hundred miles away from here. Room no. 232. I like Hong Kong. Aden and Port Said no match. Have not seen Singapore. Hong Kong is fabulous and fantastic. Perhaps the best place in the world for shopping, dissipation and burning your earnings. A paradise for hedonists. Licence and freedom seem to go together. I must come here again. Visited the Hari Lila tailoring shop. He himself took the measurement for my suits. Told me that they would be ready the next day. Bought cuff links. HK $2.

Gossi Sotto[2] also in Hong Kong. Staying at Hotel Peninsula. Our date in HK could not be kept. She is too busy and I have to leave tomorrow morning. When will I meet her again? Mexico is so far away.

Crossed over to Hong Kong in a ferry. A sea of cars. Went to the Indian Commission. Not overworked. Adarkar, the head of mission, has transparent gay bush shirt on. Spoke to me paternally, condescendingly. Excessively complained almost about everything. Some confusion about arrival of the courier from Peking to collect the 'A' diplomatic bag. Lovely view of the harbour from the commission.

Shopping was both cheap and expensive. Any amount of choice and quick service. Attractive shop girls, fashionably and elegantly dressed. Most looked gorgeous.

27 June

Contacted John Swaine. He was at the London course for Commonwealth Foreign Service probationers in the summer of 1954. He came over and we went out for dinner. Saw him after two years. Talked of Cambridge friends. John not changed much. He is no revolutionary, but soft, polite and correct. Ate at the Princess Garden Restaurant. Authentic Chinese food—very tasty—but had too much of it. Upset my stomach. Then went to the Oriental ball room. Extraordinary place. For HK $10, you get a hostess who entertains you. Met a woman called Lam Yee. Good-looking but terribly business-like. Smoke filled the room.

28 June

Left Hong Kong for Sum Chun. Filthy place, public toilet even worse. Took train to Canton. Chinese travel agency made the bookings. Spent night at the Masses Hotel. Foul. Felt completely cut off. Pearl River, not pearly at all.

I have a compartment to myself. Train spotlessly clean. No overcrowding. The Chinese attendant spoke broken English. A flask of hot water and mug on the small table. First taste of green Chinese tea, no milk and no sugar. Ordering food created a comic situation. Finally got through to the waiter. Music played at all times – sounded too shrieky. Frequent stoppages. Stations not crowded like ours.

Reached Wuhan after twenty-four hours. Crossed the river by ferry. Barely one or two cars, but lots of bicycles and animals. It was hot. Ferry without hood. The mighty Yangtse River has no bridge over it.

4 July

I'm in the process of settling down. Everything is novel. The Hsin Chiao Hotel, where I am staying is meant only for foreigners. It's not glamourous like the Hong Kong hotels.

I have been in this hotel for nearly three days. Today, for the first time I went to the dining room, hoping to have a proper breakfast. Easier said than done. The menu was in Chinese. The waiters did not know English. My Chinese was confined to only thank you, *'hseai hseai ni'* and sorry, *'tuai pu chi'*. I was beginning to despair. Then walked in a lady, with a colourful Chinese dress. She sat three tables away from me. Looked stunning. She wore lipstick and short hair. I kept looking at her every now and then. Having recently read *A Many Splendored Thing* and seen her photo, I was certain that she was Han Suyin.[3] I sent her a note. She confirmed. She was indeed Han Suyin and asked me to join her. I was thrilled. 'So many people seem to know me, it's really dreadful,' she said. However, she made me feel comfortable. I did not know that she was half-Chinese.

8, 9, 10 July

The embassy is still deciding what to do with me. Ashok Bhadkamkar[4] gave me a table and chair in his room. He is the first secretary and head of Chancery.

Han Suyin and I meet every day. I asked, 'When were you in China last?' She replied that it was her first visit to the People's Republic. She is a doctor and still a practicing one. She told me that her father was

Chinese, mother was Belgian. Father lived in Peking and her mother was dead. She was impressed with Mao's China. We talked about E.M. Forster.[5] On the importance of personal relationships and loyalty, she asserted that, 'The world never changes whatever the system.' (How wrong she proved.)

I'm learning. She is a good teacher. I enjoy being with this likeable celebrity. She told me about the glaring problem of the conflict between the Communist Party and the intellectuals, on the latter's re-education programme. The party thought it has lost touch with the people. They produced sensitive but not 'living literature'.

She gave me a guided tour of parts of the Forbidden City. We walked together. She floored me when she said that she has fallen in love with an Indian Army officer,[6] whom she met in Kathmandu not so long ago. She obviously has more time on her hands than me. She said, 'I'm at a great advantage. I know the people and the language. I ask simple and stupid questions.'

I have now met all my colleagues in the embassy. All have been exceptionally nice. The ambassador[7] and Smt Rajan Nehru invited me for tea. Some pep talk. The ambassador's wife – very talkative. Asked me where I was staying. Hsin Chiao Hotel, I replied. The office day usually begins with an 'officers' meeting' in the ambassador's office.

Back to Han Suyin. Her next book is called...*And the Rain My Drink*. It is about Malaya. I mentioned C.R. Mandy, the editor of the *Illustrated Weekly of India*. She asked, 'Is this the man who liked the picture better than the book?' She herself thought the picture, *Love Is a Many Splendored Thing* 'lousy'. I politely disagreed. She forecasted that her book on Malaya would annoy many people: 'It upholds the under dog. Malaya is a backwater.' She came to China with our help. I knew. We facilitated her visa. The Chinese took their time over it. I did not tell her this.

My education continues. It's quite something having such a lively and beautiful person giving so much time to a callow non-entity. I discover she is forty. Looks thirty. I am twenty-five. Forty is too old! When I told her I had read her *Chunking Dairy*, she was a bit startled. She told me about her early life. She was very forthright. 'I'm married to an English police officer. But I no longer love him.' I said nothing.

I took photographs of her in front of the Nine Dragon Screen in Peihai Park, a part of the Forbidden City open to the public. She asked me about my camera. I told her it was a Russian Zorki, given to me by Nikita Khrushchev[8] after his visit to India in December 1955. 'Don't be so impressed. He did not give it to me personally. I was only a liaison officer – my job was to ensure that the baggage of the Soviets was not lost.' She laughed.

26 July

The Chinese literary world is celebrating the centenary of George Bernard Shaw.[9] He died aged ninety-four in 1950. Several of his plays have been published in Chinese for his 100th birth anniversary. A Chinese edition of some of his writings has been published.

Met Ahmed Ali[10] at the ceremony held at Peking Hotel. I told him that Forster had spoken about him to me at Cambridge. He was friendly in a formal way. He was representing some Pakistani organisation. I could recognise no one else.

15 August

Independence Day reception. Well-attended.

The Chinese government has issued a strongly-worded statement on the Suez Canal question. Part of it read:

'The Egyptian people built the Suez Canal on their own territory with their own sweat and blood. All international treaties concerning the Suez Canal cannot but recognise that the Suez Canal is an integral part of Egypt, and that the Suez Canal company is an Egyptian company. . . . The Asian and African countries declared unanimously at the Bandung Conference that colonialism in all its manifestations was an evil which should speedily be brought to an end. . . .'

Our prime minister has been praised for his stand on Suez.

20 August

The prime minister of Laos, Prince Souvanna Phouma[11] arrived on a state visit. Received by Chairman Mao. Chou En-lai hosted a banquet. The joint statement that was issued emphasised the importance of the Five Principles of Peaceful Co-existence. SEATO* was condemned. M/s Nixon and Dulles severely criticised, especially Dulles for calling non-alignment, 'immoral'.

Fascinating to see comrades Mao and Chou receiving Prince of Laos. The usual banquet for him. Both leaders looked very impressive. Mao was taller. Chou was better looking, better turned out. Everyone in the crowd was shouting, 'Mao Chusi, live ten thousand years.'

2 September

I have been here for two months now. Still living in Hsin Chiao Hotel. The Chancery is not far; the staff car picks me up and drops me back. I have placed an order for the small Volkswagen – the Beatle.

I have been sightseeing. Took a pedicab to get around. Didn't have much work. We had the morning meetings in the ambassador's office. V.V. Paranjpe,[12] our Chinese pandit gave summary of the day's news from the *Peking Daily* and one or two other newspapers. No foreign English newspaper available in Peking. Ours come by bag once a week from Delhi. Indian news not frequent in Chinese papers.

So far I have only seen the Forbidden City. The official name now is the Imperial Palace. The place is breathtakingly beautiful. Only a part of the Forbidden City is open to the public. In the same compound live the top leaders of China. No entry there. The most impressive part of the Forbidden City is the Tien An Man – Gate of Heavenly Peace. It is a massive building and Mao Tse Tung's huge portrait in the centre of the front wall can be seen even from a distance of hundreds of yards.

---

*Southeast Asia Treaty Organisation was planned to be a Southeast Asian version of NATO (North Atlantic Treaty Organisation) in which the military forces of each member would be coordinated to provide for collective defence of its members.

There is an Indian silk shop on Wang Fu Chin Street. There I met a stunningly beautiful girl who spoke English. Her name is Mela Chang.[13]

5 September

I'm beginning to like Chinese food. The restaurants are messy but the food is superb. Not fattening. I'm far from being fat.

Mela unexpectedly dropped in at my hotel. She is half-Chinese, half-Russian.

Played tennis at the International Club. Three hard courts. One or two good players. Also a swimming pool.

Slight nip in the air.

18 September

My Chinese teacher, Dean Chang (sixty-five), with exquisite manners is certainly no communist. He is immensely patient with me. I'm not good at languages. Chinese is not an easy language to learn. But I was the first IFS officer to study Chinese. Dean Chang, before taking up this job, had to be cleared by the Wai Chio Pu – the Chinese foreign office.

I had some preliminary thoughts on Indian and Chinese view of history; the Chinese is linear. I may be wrong on China; I know so little. But one thing I do know. Unlike the Chinese, the Hindus have no sense of history. Even today the historical sense has just begun to be aroused. It is more jingoism.

Nothing exciting happened today. The National Congress has been on in Peking and delegates from forty-six countries have arrived. For all we know, they might be meeting in Lhasa! I could not think of a similar gathering going unnoticed by the populace in most other countries.

Why is this atmosphere of hush-hush and mystery? Perhaps they are able to transact more business as they are not disturbed by any press men, visitors or public opinion! I have only the experience of living in India and the UK. I'm just learning how a communist state runs. Liu Shao Chi[14] is very much alive. When I was in HK early this month, his disappearance was the main topic of interest in the papers besides the Suez issue.

In the morning meetings, Pai read out from *The Peoples' Daily* and *Ta Kung Pao*. Lots on Suez. Some tension on the Formusa front. It's called Taiwan on the mainland. The Patil[15] delegation has its farewell party today. D.K. Barua[16] is the most amusing member.

Some progress in Chinese. I can now write my name and date in Chinese. The Chinese cannot pronounce 'r', so Natwar Singh becomes 'Na Hua Singh'.

19 September

Today is the Autumn Moon festival. As I type this, I can see a glorious full moon staring at me from the window. Not a speck of cloud in the sky. A cool and really silvery evening. It was Han Suyin who said that the moon looked bigger in Beijing than anywhere else. I'm moonstruck, not sunstruck. Like in the old days, today is a day of festivities in China. People worship moon cakes. The only time I ate one was with Han Suyin at the Peking airport when I went to see her off. I liked them. Not bad to taste. Not enough sugar for my liking. Chinese food is fabulous but no sweets, no puddings, no desserts. No milk products, except yoghurt.

The weather changes with phenomenal speed here. I had to go back to the hotel to get a coat. Bought a coat for *masi* Hutheesing.[17] Good stuff. Pity, Rana & Co could not take it. They are leaving tomorrow. Patil – honest, simple, humble, efficient and sound. A rare bird, that's why I suppose he left the ICS.

M/s Sundarayya,[18] Namboodiripad[19] and P.C. Joshi[20] called at the embassy. Glad that the boss saw them. I also had a word with E.M.S. Namboodiripad. He stammered, but was not self-conscious at all. They were received at the highest level.

P.N. Sharma, the well-known photographer is here. Had himself photographed with Mao, Chou En-lai and Liu Shao Chi. Took a photo of mine also.

Shaun Mandy's[21] letter. I wonder if I can send him something. This may amuse him, but it cannot possibly be allowed to get into print.

Miss Lee: 'I'm very keen to learn English.'

MP: 'Then you must go to England; that is obviously the best place to learn that language.'

Miss Lee: 'I cannot go to England just now.'

MP: 'When will you go?'

Miss Lee: 'After (the) liberation of England.'

This is a good example of thought control; or is it brain washing?

20 September

Went to see off the Patil delegation. At the airport, D.K. Barua pointed to the western hills and asked the lady interpreter, 'What are those hills?' She replied, 'Western hills.' Barua asked in return, 'Before or after liberation?' He was fed up with being repeatedly told that everything he saw was made after liberation.

Had a talk with Malviya at the airport. Said he was deeply impressed with the Chinese experiment. The change that has been brought in the *manavta* of this country was something remarkable. The enthusiasm was infectious and he felt it was genuine. It was not possible to collectivise land holdings on such a vast scale without the support of the people. He said that people have been forced to do all sorts of things.

The Chinese peasants are of course so badly off, that collective farming really means liberation for them. The Chinese regime has bumped off a hell of a lot of people, but that is inevitable. China needs a major operation to cure her of her chronic ailments. India cannot repeat what China has done. Malviya said, 'In China they do not allow grass to grow under your feet. They don't mind if it grows on the roofs of their houses. In India it grows all over the place.'

The differences in the Patil delegation are evident even on the surface. Some are less enthusiastic than others on the Chinese revolution. The ambassador has not taken to them. Tarlok Singh,[22] an ICS officer is with the delegation. An expert on agriculture, modest and soft spoken as well.

Dean Chang arrived late due to the incessant rain. He is such a likeable old man. I wonder what he thinks of New China. People like him have definitely been badly hit. I must read Chou En-lai's report on the intellectuals.

My Chinese is getting on. Did over four hours today. Exhausted and forgotten most of it. By the end of the year I should be speaking more fluently. I feel so diffident speaking the little Chinese I know. Not shyness. Just ego. I don't want to look inept. In Chinese I'm San Dang Misu – third secretary. The ambassador is called Ta She.

The Hsin Chiao Hotel is getting fuller by the day. Delegations are arriving for the 1 October celebrations.

21 September

Ran into the Bradsdorff.[23] Hsin Chiao Hotel is something like Trafalgar Square; if you wait long enough, the man you are waiting for will turn up. Bradsdorff and I were learning Chinese at Cambridge three years ago. He is much older than me, and a distinguished Danish author. I still remember my treating him casually and in a most off-handed undergraduate manner, until I discovered who he was. He is here with his wife, writing a book on China.

The morning meeting went on rather aimlessly for an hour and a half. The chief's mannerisms reminded me more and more of the Maharaja of Bharatpur. Lots of news in the papers about the arrival of delegations. At lunch met Juan A. Parrochia[24]—the first Chilean I have known—globe-trotter and architect. Introduced to me by Gossi. Juan considered modern Chinese architecture poor and inferior. Said they were only creating new slums, no floor space in labourers' houses. Talked on South American architecture. Some of the world's best architects are in Venezuela, Columbia and Brazil. Said the Rashtrapati Bhawan was badly planned. It gets cut off in the middle, when you see it coming up from India Gate. Not so the Arc de Triomphe in Paris. I never thought of that.

Discussion on China's population. Strength of a nation? He said that one New Zealander was worth twenty Chinese at the moment. Machine vs man. I said that it was because of their population that China and India were so important. More hands, more production. He said that we would be better off if we had half the people we actually have.

Met the Changs. Chinese with American wife, working in the UN as simultaneous interpreter. Discussed Han Suyin. I asked him about my age. He said thirty-seven. When I told him that I was twenty-five he felt like a heel. Good lesson for me. Never ask other people to guess your age and never hazard to guess other peoples' ages. Certainly not in China. All Chinese look much younger than they are. 'What are so many Englishmen doing in the British Embassy here?' he asked. I said, 'They are looking before and after and pinning for what is not.' Well-received.

The spitting habit of the Chinese is comparable with ours of scratching our private parts in public. Both are disgusting. Take your pick on which is worse.

I am surprised to know that the people of Peking will only get limited facilities and opportunities for witnessing the 1 October parade. A superficial visitor to China will not know this. The parade is meant for foreign consumption and making films which will be shown all over China and the world. In the People's Republic, the people are not allowed to see it.

I'm gradually realising that Mao's China is a tough place to live in if one is not a diplomat. He is trying to create a new human being and a New China. At what price? I have as yet, no idea. I have a lot to learn, see and read.

22 September

The charms of domestic felicity and its wrangles. Medha Bhadkamkar cut her son Nilu's hair and Ashok did not have his lunch. Said he was far too upset. Something so touching; Nilu is not quite three. Only speaks Chinese.

Preparations for 1 October. Painting of houses and shops. More goods visible in the markets. Wang Fu Ching, Chang An Ta Chea all looking spic and span. Road building at a remarkable speed. The Chinese work round-the-clock. The profit motive is absent, yet the best is done.

If the budgeted expenditure is crossed then they have a meeting. *Khai Huai*.[25] Idleness is not permitted.

Some days ago Bradsdorff said that he was impressed with Kuo Mo Jo's[26] article, 'Let a Hundred Schools of Thought Flourish'. I have not seen it. Kuo Mo Jo is a well-known author and court poet. He is not a party member.

Party at home of Robert Ellis.[27] He is our cipher man. A remnant of the Raj. My refusal to learn dancing is perhaps a handicap in the IFS. I think ballroom dancing is not Indian and we can do well without it. When will I stop being self-righteous? Short story ready. Shall send it to Mandy.

Dean Chang very diffidently asked me if I could get him a stethoscope when I go to Hong Kong next time. I asked what he would do with a stethoscope? 'It is not for me, it is for a doctor friend of mine.' I assured him I would certainly bring one. Had no idea that even a basic item was unavailable for a doctor.

24 September

Lunch at Pai's. Bradsdorffs unable to come. They were suddenly called up for an interview with one of the ministers. This happens all the time here. The Chinese send for one at any time they like, and what is strange is that people cancel all other appointments and rush to meet them. The Wai Chiao Pu also follows the same routine. They send for ambassadors at all hours. Pai speaks better Chinese than any other person in the entire diplomatic corps. He also enjoys his drink.

Another thing, which annoys one in Peking is that no Chinese replies to your invitation. You invite five and eight may turn up. For their own functions they send invitations almost a few hours before it is about to start. They must be having a hell of a laugh to see all of us running to their functions. I wish diplomats would have a showdown on this and tell the Wai Chiao Pu to follow international practices. I'm perhaps being naïve. After all, this is my first posting.

Pai came up with the charming story of a Chinese artist who used to give expensive dinners. He had no money to pay for his dinners;

so he used to present the owner of the restaurant with one of his paintings. How wonderful! Before liberation, Peking used to be home to eccentrics and odd characters.

Preparations going at breakneck speed for 1 October. In China, the year is divided into two parts. All works begin and finish either on 1 May or 1 October. The Chinese, unlike us, like to finish things before schedule. They have few holidays. They work even on Sundays.

26 September

Cold has set in. I'm already wearing my overcoat in the evenings. The worst is yet to be. Drove to the airport to receive the Nepali Prime Minister Tanka Prasad Acharya.[28] The Chinese gave him a welcome, which I would call, an organised spontaneous one. The right number of Buddhist monks, the right number of girls, the right number to give bouquets to the right people. The crowds were far too well-disciplined, far too well-organised. We too can do with a little bit of discipline. But it is only a short step to regimentation. Diplomats were allowed on the tarmac, no confusion about photographers, no noise, band played lively music, goose step by the Guard of Honour. Chou En-lai – handsome, charming and fresh as ever. He got a cheer from the crowd. The Nepali national dress is a sartorial monstrosity. Even the smartest of them looks as if he is either got out of bed or is just about to do so. Some even resemble coat hangers.

I'm all for having a sensible national dress. The slogan should be 'Down with the Dhoti.' It is the most impractical garment. The Chinese have been more practical about dress. Men and women all wear coats and trousers. The emancipation of women is one of the most significant and mighty reforms carried out by New China. In India, we have given our women constitutional freedom but not economic freedom. All other freedoms lose much of their attraction.

For the next few weeks, there will be a string of delegations coming here. Ahmed Soekarno[29] will be the next one. Saw a huge portrait of him going up in the city. Stalin has also been put up for the 1 October parade in front of Tien An Man.

27 September

For the president's visit, the road builders are having a race with time. The poor fellows are working relentlessly for days and nights. I understand that many of them are not used to road-making; they are counter revolutionaries and they have to pay for their misdeeds through hard labour.

In the evening, I saw the dreadful Indonesian documentary on President Soekarno's visit to the USA. The film was badly edited. If one were to judge people by their looks, then I think the Indians would definitely stand out, especially the women. Soekarno, the showman he is, was nonetheless overwhelmed by what he saw in the USA.

28 September

Military delegation led by Lt Gen J.N. Chaudhuri[30] of Hyderabad fame has arrived. Nothing much to write home about the Peking airport. No proper place to sit, no restaurant, no book shop, no nothing. In any case not too many flights come to Beijing. The Chinese as usual turned up in ill-fitting clothes. But they are better soldiers and clothes alone don't make a soldier. They do, however, need to have a smarter turnout.

Banquet in the evening for the Nepali prime minister – a total fiasco. The Nepal PM gave the impression of being in a state of continuous confusion. The guests went away most disgruntled. But Chaudhuri was in good form. He was lively, with an army sense of humour. He looked grand in his uniform. The others were completely overshadowed by him. Military Attaché Brig Malik, made himself look useful.

29 September

The parliamentary delegation led by the Speaker, Ananthasayyanam Ayyengar[31] arrived today. If Mavlankar[32] had been alive, he would have led this delegation. I remember his discussing this trip with Soong Ching-ling when she was in India last December. The delegation was received by Liu Shao Chi. He is younger than Chou but did not look so. He seemed intellectual with a stern expression. The professional welcomers are perhaps permanently housed at the airport. As usual, our delegation arrived in the most varied clothes. I wish our MPs would realise that dress too has a place in a goodwill mission. A closed collar coat and trousers would do very well. Dhoti is no dress for any occasion. With J.B Kripalani[33] dropping out of the delegation, it lost some of its weight. The rest of the MPs were really ordinary blokes. Lakshmi Menon[34] was an exception.

Drove back from the airport with David Chipp. Discussed Soekarno with him. 'He is the Nehru of Indonesia and he can do no wrong. Only he could have survived (politically) after marrying a prostitute.' He continued, 'But he can also be the Hitler of Asia when it comes to eloquence.' Chipp spoke of colour bar in Indonesia.

There are at the moment three thousand foreign visitors in Beijing. Almost the whole lot are state guests. How the Chinese manage to look after them is remarkable. But China is a big show window and the Chinese are adept at showing off when occasion demands. They do so much for delegations, that one cannot but go back impressed. The delegations always meet the right people and see the right places. A short visit succeeds to create the right impression. I'm not minimising the achievements of the regime; they are both impressive and spectacular. Nothing like this has ever been done in the world in so short a time. But what depresses is the manner in which it has been done. No one can step out of line. No freedom of expression at all. No free press. Even in the party, it is limited, disagreement may lead to oblivion. The top people are Marxists, but also very Chinese. The important thing for us is to realise that what happens in China today, is going to have a profound influence on India in times to come. We have no fear of any kind of crude expansionism, but infiltration of ideas is a distinct possibility. Impossible for Indian ideas to penetrate into this country though.

30 September

I'm completing three months in Peking today. It would be trite to say, 'How time flies.' But I have not discovered any original way of expressing the same feeling in fewer words. I have, for the first time, lapsed into a brief depression. Mostly due to my conjunctivitis which I caught in Cambridge in May 1954. No sign of it disappearing.

Peking is all set for the great day tomorrow. Delegations are pouring in. Our parliamentary delegation is staying in Hsin Chiao. Lunch for them – the usual mess and chaos. The big event has been the arrival of President Soekarno of Indonesia. We raced to the airport after lunch. Large turnout. Welcome party headed by Chairman Mao Tse Tung. Lovely day.

Mao got a big cheer. My second look at him. I was rather excited. Shamelessly, I ran all over the place with my camera taking pictures. Mao looked fatherly and dignified. Slow of pace. He was the man who mattered the most. Tall for a Chinese, his mole below lower lip, visible. Mao's suit was brownish. Receding hairline. Did not look his age, but all Chinese look ageless. Soong Ching-ling, also Liu Shao Chi, Chu Teh, Chou En-lai all were present. All in blue Mao suits. They stood at a discreet distance from Mao. I got some close shots of Mao and the others. I got within a foot of Mao. Secret service men in plenty, but difficult to make out. All wore similar clothes. People shook hands with Mao as he strolled around. All eyes on him.

Soekarno got out of the plane in military uniform, medals, baton and black Indonesian cap. I first saw him in Delhi in 1950, when he came to Delhi University with Nehru. He has an aura around him.

Mao and he drove back to Peking in an open car. The crowds on the road were so close to the cars passing, that they must have literally touched Mao and Soekarno with their hands. The general public was as usual well-behaved, no breaking of cordons and no rowdyism. Almost the entire way from the city to the airport was lined with people two or three deep. It is breathtaking to see how well the Chinese organise things. Their machinery must be vast and efficient.

1 October

What a day! The sky developed a major leak in one of its mighty water reservoirs. It rained the whole day. What a perversity of nature! Yesterday was such a fine day. This is the day for which everything has been done for the past so many months, everything has been focussed on this day and it nearly all got washed away, but for the superb and unbeatable will and discipline of the Chinese participants in the Tien An Man (TAM) parade.

The parade began at 10:00 am. Ended at 2:00 pm Half a million men, women and children marched past Chairman Mao, who was on Tien An Man, along with all the other top leaders of China. Soekarno and Tanka Prasad were also up there. What a contrast – the glamorous Indonesian and the not-so-glamorous Nepalese. Everybody in China knows how to march in step and walk straight. The parade must have been an eye-opener for these two.

Tien An Man lends itself to a parade on this scale. The sheer size, extent, beauty and magnitude of the place are meant to impress, and they succeed as well. Our parade is chicken-feed compared to theirs. I have never seen anything like this. In spite of the rain it was a memorable sight. The marching was spectacular and the cultural part, even more. Air Commodore Pratap Lal[35] of our Air Force said that it was as good as anywhere in the world. It was a pleasure to see thousands of women in swimming costumes participating in the parade. The dragons were the most ingenious of all. The fly past had to be cancelled because of the frightful weather.

Tien An Man is the most well-known and visible structure (except the Great Wall) in China. It was built by a Ming Emperor in 1420. In Imperial China, royal edicts and proclamations were read out from Tien An Man. On 1 October 1949, Mao Tse Tung standing on the balcony of the Gate of Heavenly Peace, proclaimed the establishment of the People's Republic of China. Now back to the parade. The diplomats were all made to stand in the two-tier stands on the right of Tien An Man. No chairs, but refreshments were available. Bathroom facilities were adequate. Umbrellas were provided. I still have mine with me. The organisation and planning that must have gone in producing anything so vast, was indeed laudable. Hats off to the Chinese. A pity that the people of Peking did not get to see this fantastic event.

Chou En-lai attended our afternoon reception for our military delegates. I could not help feeling that he came a bit too often to our embassy. Poor speeches on both sides. Communist condemnatory political vocabulary is rich. Peng Te Huai[36] spoke. The usual clichés and abuses of the Imperialists (right at that moment Air Marshal Mukerjee[37] was partaking of US hospitality in Washington). Marx had a sharp, extensive and invective vocabulary for his opponents. Oratory and eloquence are unknown in China.

Rain stopped by the evening. Fireworks at Tien An Man at night. The whole space in front of it was packed to the last inch, a sea of men and women in holiday mood, dancing and cheering. Mao was sitting immediately above his enormous portrait at Tien An Man Gate. It was really spectacular.

2 October

This day, eighty-seven years ago, was born Gandhi. We had a function in the embassy to mark his anniversary. The function was saved by Lakshmi Menon who asked us not to have dual standards of thought. 'You praise the Chinese in China for emancipating women but in Delhi you oppose it.' The Buddhist monk also made an interesting speech in very chaste Hindi. All the other MPs were very disappointing. What a poor lot, intellectually.

Lunch at Hsin Chiao Hotel for the parliamentary delegation. Liu Shao Chi and Chou En-lai came. Lunch at 11:30. Too many people in the reception room. Our Speaker Ananthasayyanam made an ordinary speech and messed up the toasts; he mispronounced Liu Shao Chi's name. Liu and Chou paid tributes to Gandhiji. The vegetarian MPs were a nuisance. Chen Chen Tho, the vice-minister of culture was on my table. I got to know him well during his visit to India in 1954. The man is without airs – immensely learned. Has read Kalidas[38] and Tagore.[39] Told me they would stage *Shakuntala* in Chinese the following year.

Picnic in the Summer Palace. An atmosphere of relaxation, fun and gaiety. The government has picked up the good-lookers to be at the picnic. Lovely day. Boating, music and dance, games and acrobatics. The MPs seemed to be enjoying themselves. The Chinese do not consider pleasure evil, though they have so little of it. The picnic idea has been obviously imported from Moscow. But it is a good idea and I hope it will be kept up. Some of us got prizes at the shooting game. Medha, and other ladies were in great demand by the photographers.

Ran into David Marshall[40], the Singapore leader at the picnic. Tall, dark and conscious of his importance. Almost everyone was provided with a guide and interpreter. Free boat rides. Chou En-lai and other leaders present. How good of these leaders to attend! How do they find the time? The other diplomats were thrilled to shake hands with the prime minister.

The Summer Palace is beautiful. Eight hundred and twenty-three acres, four-fifth taken by the lake. Here the wind and water sing. What poetic names of buildings, Lou Shou Tang (Hall of Delight in Longevity) Ten Ho Yuan (Hall of Virtuous Harmony).

3 October

We must have some sort of an institution in Delhi where politicians spend sometime to learn how to talk, eat, dress; how to keep their mouths shut and to read something about the country they are to visit; and not to belch during meals. Speaker Ananthasayyanam is of the opinion that all the MPs should be in dhotis and Gandhi caps, 'I want all of them to look Indians.' What an extraordinary thought!

The cold is really on us. I hate to think what it would be like in December and January. Our MPs have all been provided with fur-lined coats by the Chinese. I hope they return them. My overcoat is not a very great success as far as the Peking winter goes.

4 October

This morning, I told the ambassador that U.Nu[41] was coming here on the 24th.

'Has it been announced?' he asked.

'No, David Chipp told me,' I said.

'Why do you keep contact with David Chipp?'

'We happen to live in the same hotel and he is well-informed,' I replied politely.

Chipp is not on any blacklist; he is a responsible journalist, on an important assignment. He represents Reuters. Ambassador's attitude to the press is bureaucratic. But worse is, not to have any contact with the English and the American journalists. This shall be borne in mind but not followed.

Had an interesting Chinese lesson. Miss Lee explained to me the division of classes in ancient China. Just as bad as ours. It is not possible for a barber to ever get accepted in the top class. She provided further enlightenment. Chinese do not say, 'Darling, I love you.' Nothing demonstrative. It has to be indicated by gesture and behaviour. I told her that the Indian procedure is even more indirect, prolonged and painful. Too much beating about the bush. In Hindi, it is almost impossible to have a realistic love sequence without making one embarrassed.

5 October

President Soekarno's banquet in Peking Hotel. We all got there at 6:00 pm. But the dinner did not start till 7:30 pm. The Indian Embassy, except for the ambassador and Mrs Nehru, all sat at one table not far from the head table, on which sat Chairman Mao, Chu Teh, Liu Shao Chi, Chou En-lai, Soong Ching-ling. Unlike Delhi, the state banquets here are held in hotels. The seating is done on the main table. The first seventeen tables are reserved, the rest hundred or so are on a first-come-first-served basis. There were about a thousand guests.

Soekarno made a short speech (half an hour), beautiful diction. Interpreted in Chinese and English, spoke without a script, but he had obviously thought a great deal over what he would say. This was the crowning point of his visit to China. I think he produced the desired effect, although his theatrics have not gone unnoticed. The Chinese are adept at impassivity, except, perhaps Chou, who is most impressive.

This was my third close look at Mao. He made a characteristically short speech, his voice like Chou's, is also high pitched. Because he appears in public so rarely, he is much sought-after. The photographers, including the German girl, had a feast day. They were allowed to go right up to the main table and did so all the time. The atmosphere at the banquet was informal. People were coming and going, Mao himself left his seat to talk to Chen Yi[42] while Chou talked to the chief of protocol. Soekarno also left his seat, so did Liu Shao Chi but not Chu Teh. The interpreters sat on the main table next to the VIPs and not behind them. This is far more practical.

The dinner lasted till 9:00 pm. There were eleven courses. I'm now quite deft with my chopsticks. I must get to know a little more about Chinese table manners, they are really fascinating. In ancient China, a man's background could be determined by the manner in which he ate his soup or held his chopsticks.

Almost all the visiting delegations for 1 October were invited to this banquet. From the dinner we went to the Drama Hall. I think this was where they had their National Congress meeting. A fine hall. Not a seat was vacant. So we all sat in super seats. Soekarno and Mao and the other leaders sat in the fifth row. The show itself must have lost Indonesia many friends and without doubt, it bored everybody present. The Balanese dance, I think, is hugely overrated. It was monotonous. Yesterday's performance was not a memorable one. It went on for two and a half hours. During the interval, I was introduced by Chen Chen Tho to Mei Lan Fang[43], the legendary Peking opera star. He only plays female roles. Later, I discovered he had met Uday Shankar[44] in New York in 1930.

6 October

President Soekarno left Beijing. Went to Hong Kong. Got good coverage in the party-controlled newspapers.

7 October

German Democratic Republic's National Day. Banquet at the Peking Hotel. It is strange that the word 'democratic' should be thus prostituted. The West Germans say their government is democratic and so do the Eastern ones. The first deputy premier of East Germany, Herr (sporting a Leninesque goatee) Ulbricht[45] is here. On our table sat a German doctor who lived in East Berlin. Said a lot of rebuilding had been done there. It needed to, for when I was there in December 1952, I was very depressed to see things in East Berlin. It compared very unfavourably with West Berlin.

Ashok Bhadkamkar made an acute observation. He told me that I had the bad habit of jumping to conclusions; and even worse – running away with them. This has to be curbed, and curbed soon or else trouble will ensue. This, I suppose, is the direct result of having an imagination that is more than fertile.

8 October

Saw the MPs' delegation off. On the way back from the airport, we visited the Japanese Exhibition in the Soviet Exhibition Hall, a gift from Moscow. Monstrous architecture. Hats off to Japan. Our exhibition would be something of an anti-climax after theirs. They produced almost everything that there was to produce, cheap and good. The hall was too crowded. What lovely children the Chinese have! A batch of students travelling from India was there. The usual round – Prague, Moscow and Peking, and the pilgrimage is complete.

10 October

I went to the Acupuncture Hospital today. They shot into me seven needles – three in the stomach, absolute hell, two above my thumbs and two in the knees, not so bad. That was to get rid of my stomach ailment, which has been going on for too long and I was prepared to try out anything. Acupuncture is a very old Chinese method of curing all kinds of ailments. The idea is to get hold of the right nerve and then stimulate it by needling it. The course was a long one and I didn't look forward to the next session on Saturday. I was told that the cure was permanent. I earnestly hope so. I doubt Indians would have placed themselves in the hands of unknown Chinese doctors and allowed them to play about with their bodies, especially if the doctors did not speak any other language except Chinese. The Russians have got interested in acupuncture. The hospital was spotlessly clean and the staff was very polite. Shades of 'Hindi-Chini Bhai Bhai'. They were curious to look at my hairy chest. Chinese have very little hair on their bodies.

I spent the day doing my normal work. Struggling with Volume One of Mao Tse Tung's collected works. Got Vols. I & II from Hong Kong. Concentrated communist jargon – dialectical materialism without any concession to style. I do not understand dialectics.

11 October

Shopping in Embroidery Street with Mela. One can pick up some very beautiful and useful things for a song and also things for sending as presents to friends in India. The craftsmanship is there but the colour scheme could be better. I do not know if this failing was always there or is one of the blessings of the New Regime. I have little doubt that art and literature have most definitely suffered in New China. But new trends are already in evidence. I'm not sure if the subordination of art to political ideology is at all desirable. Not much sign of 'Hundred Schools of Thought' contending.

Bought a book on Peking. I have been here now for over three months and know so little about this city, when there is so much to know and see. I have also acquired a Mao cap.

12 October

The world famous Mexican muralist David Alfaro Siqueiros[46] and his wife called at the embassy. What an interesting couple! They were on a trip to China and then they would go to India. Told us about his meeting Nasser[47] in Cairo. Full of genuine love for India. I ran into them again in the evening. They have landed with an unsatisfactory interpreter, who knew enough Spanish to make easy things difficult, and difficult things impossible. Had tea and we discussed art.

Siqueiros is an ideological painter, an intellectual and a communist. Fought in the Spanish civil war, friend of Ernest Hemingway and John Steinbeck. Member of the Communist Party (CP) since 1924. Very anti-American. In spite of his politics, a great artist. Left his book with me. Has greatly influenced Satish Gujral[48] whom he knows. Spoke about Gossi Sotto. Extraordinary coincidence that they both are carrying a message from her to me and now they would carry one from me. Her letter also pulled in today.

I am perturbed about not having any news from home. Lathsahib[49] has not written for over a month and the telegram has not been answered. I hope all is well.

The *Quest* has published my article on R.K. Narayan calling it 'Tribute to R.K. Narayan'. It did not read too well. Moreover, the title was mundane.

13 October

It is Dussehra. Invited by the Indian scholars at the university. Peking University has a charming campus. Ranbir Vohra,[50] a language student sent by All India Radio, was amusing, at his best. The rest of the entertainment was very ordinary.

16 October

Reception by Military Attaché at the International Club. An atmosphere of forced jollility. I came away early, but the others stayed on past midnight.

17 October

Opening of the photographic exhibition of India's First Five Year Plan. Ambassador, for a change, made a fluent speech. Much less self-conscious than at any other function. The exhibition itself was nothing much to preen about.

In the evening the China-India Friendship Association gave a reception for the two delegations now in Peking. They gave us all very nice badges; little ways of winning you over. Earlier in the day, we had all been presented with the silk woven pictures of Gandhiji, Nehru, Tagore and President Rajendra Prasad.[51] Another fine example of Chinese tact and craftsmanship. The banquet was followed by a most wonderful acrobatic-cum-conjuring performance. Breathtaking! What supple bodies the Chinese have! The presentation was so good. The whole event had an air of delicacy and effortless ease about it. The Chinese are proverbially well-known for their acrobatics. The item with the plates was amazing; It must have involved a lot of practice. What cannot the human body master, given time, effort and practice? The performing artists were all very young.

18 October

Eid – our national holiday. It has been a chilly and windy day. Prime Minister H.S. Suhrawardy[52] of Pakistan arrived today. Was received at the military airport. Given a cold, but correct welcome. His retinue was rather extraordinary. So many women. Spoke well. No call for world peace. He did some deft tight rope-walking. The Pakistan Embassy crowd at the airport made a nuisance of themselves by shouting slogans. We have hardly any contacts with the Pakistan Embassy here because of the not-so-dormant hostility towards each other.

I played my first round in the handicap tennis singles. Silly to have a 30+30 handicap. I nearly lost the first set but recovered. I might, with some luck go on to win this tournament.

I bought the first volume of Lu Hsun's[53] selected short stories. I must read him. He is the Premchand[54] of China. Both born in 1880.

Both died in 1936. Bernard Shaw met Lu Hsun in the thirties in Peking. So did Tagore.

19 October

Lunch for Siqueiros and his wife – a great success. Anecdote about Charles Laughton, the Hollywood film actor. 'Paid me $1500 when I asked for $1000 for doing his portrait.' He was fascinated by the Indian salutation with folded hands. Fold them on either side of your face and recline your head, suggesting going to sleep. Do this to women. Has great possibilities! Never thought on those lines, about our *Namaskar* though.

Bahadur[55] told me that I would be going with the parliamentary delegation on their trip to the Kuantung Reservoir and the Great Wall. Quite unexpected but most welcome.

Later in the evening (10:30 pm) we were told that Chairman Mao would receive the delegation, at the midnight hour. Something thrilling about the timing of this interview and typical of things here. Mao had been told that some of the members of the delegation would be leaving the next day, so he fixed the midnight hour. The MPs all turned up in ceremonial dress except Sinha who had packed up his things. Haider Hussain[56] did not show up, said he was too tired. I suppose in the late sixties, even an interview with Mao Tse Tung did not really matter or excite, but if I were that age, I would have definitely gone for this historic meeting.

We arrived at the chairman's house a little before twelve. Drove through the entrance on West Changan Boulevard, skirting the waters of the Nanhai. We passed through the two courtyards and then into the audience chamber where Mao received the delegation. It was a spherical chamber—something like the main hall of the Rashtrapati Bhawan in Delhi—but not that large. Flood lit and heavily carpeted. We were all introduced to Mao Tse Tung and shook hands with him; soft pudgy hands. Director Yu introduced me. Mao has soft skin and bad teeth (he chain smokes). Liu Shao Chi also present as was Peng Cheng, the mayor of Peking and several others. Group photograph followed. Then we walked or rather filed into an adjoining room. There we all sat on two sides of a long rectangular table. The speaker sat opposite Mao and for the next ninety minutes, these two did almost all the talking. The speaker talked much more and did more than justice to himself. There was in him a combination of Brahmanical astuteness and earthiness of a lawyer. Mao Tse Tung smoked most of the time. His silences were eloquent indeed. Edgar Snow[57] got his personality on the spot.

The interview started with the usual courtesies. Chinese tea served by young male and female waiters, who did not mind spilling the tea on the interpreter who jerked his hands too much. I was struck by the fact that there was no atmosphere of servility; the interpreter, sitting next to the chairman, was smoking.

Chairman Mao Tse Tung, is said to be the least sophisticated of all the Chinese leaders, but that in no way diminished his stature. He is not one among equals. There are no equals. He is supreme – intellectual, original thinker, ruthless, practical, a good listener, witty and leg-puller. But I think the speaker too put up a good show. This was evident from the length of the interview, and from the obvious interest Mao took in what the speaker had to say. It was something more than courtesy and politeness that made him sit and listen for so long. The speaker, to his credit, navigated the Indian craft through the rapids with great dexterity. Mao seemed to have been well-briefed about India and Indian politics. He had his own digs and invariably gave a monosyllabic answer in the earlier part of the interview. Later he opened up, but he gave little away except on Pakistan, but that came much later.

Mao-Ayyangar exchange

Mao – 'I can see changes on the globe and visualise that the West is withering away. We are not bothered about the UK and Europe, but about the USA. At the moment the USA is not afraid of China but it is afraid of the Soviet Union. At the moment we are far behind USA technically, and it will take us about fifty years to catch up with them. Unlike you, we have made the mistake of having a vast army of nearly three million and that has hampered progress in other fields. Do you think we have too large an army?'

The speaker's reply was tactful and sensible.

Speaker – 'We haven't studied the military aspect and neither have we seen any of your military installations. We went wherever our hosts took us. We didn't wish to embarrass them by asking them to show places that they might not like us to visit.'

Mao – 'No, we wouldn't have been embarrassed and we have nothing to hide from you.'

Speaker – 'Our armed forces delegation that is here, told me that you had not kept anything from them when you received them. They were very satisfied with their visit.'

Mao – 'I asked them the same question, but they didn't tell me if they thought that our army was too large, that's why I'm asking you.'

Speaker – 'We need to defend our territories and that's the main purpose for having an army. India faces no dangers, but your problems are different and as per force, you had to keep this large army. Like us, you too have a large population and it was your manpower that saved the day in the Korea war.'

I was surprised to hear that Mao Tse Tung said that China had been spending thirty-three percent of its budget for defence purposes. This was too much. In the next few years they hoped to bring it to twenty percent and then to twelve percent.

Mao – 'We want peace and development in our country. At this moment, we can produce only medium-sized machinery, not big and precision machinery. This we must build.' He said this in reply to the speaker's remark that India and China lead the world in handicrafts.

Mao not once said that China was on top in anything. This studied modesty is typical of all Chinese leaders, and in contrast to our leaders who all the time pat themselves on the back and throw their achievements in the face of others. The Chinese tone is like, 'we have done little, we wish to learn from you.' Mao listened with interest to all that the speaker had to say, about our Five Year Plan and the freedom movement. Mao said that they had been misinformed about the freedom movement in India and it was only now that they realised that the struggle led by Gandhi and Nehru was a mass movement.

I think he said this tongue-in-cheek. Nehru in 1954 had told him about the freedom movement. He said that they understood the works of Gandhi better today.

Speaker – 'Gandhi believed in soul force and to him, means were more important than the ends.'

Mao – 'Non-violent, non-cooperation were also struggles. Was it a philosophy of revolution?'

Speaker – 'Your progress is so fast that you will soon catch up with us.'

Mao – 'Not necessarily.'

Ambassador – 'We will go ahead together.'

Mao said that they had to win the battle of ideas. The West was losing it. Suez was touched upon. (The Chinese have condemned the British-French-Israeli attack on Egypt. Huge anti-imperialist demonstrations were held outside the British Embassy for several days.)

Mao laughed when the speaker said that in the earlier years of our Independence, India had been like a drum, beaten on both sides by Russia and the USA. Now the world had come to realise that our way was the right way, the beating was much less. Mao agreed.

Mao asked questions about our Five Year Plan. Listened with interest to the story of the integration of the Indian states. The speaker remarked, 'The princes were done away within a few months after 1947, without a civil war. Like your capitalists, they are allowed to exist and are provided for.'

Mao said, 'But our capitalists are allowed to work.'

'So are the princes in India,' the speaker said somewhat incredulously. 'We have given them pensions.'

Mao said the princes of Tibet were alarmed each time reform was suggested. Perhaps the Indian way would help there. (This was an important and significant remark. All was not well in Tibet.)

During the discussion Mao smoked non-stop. So did Liu Shao Chi. Mao paid the Indian ambassador a fine and neat compliment when he got up to light the ambassador's cigarette. Deliberate gesture. Enough to indicate, 'See how much we like you.' Not done patronisingly, but with ease.

Mao said that in the standing committee, he was only a delegate, Liu Shao Chi was the boss. If the speaker invited him to India, Mao would accept. Hope was expressed that more and more people in the two countries would make an effort to learn each other's language. (Not much chance of this happening.)

On the way out, Mao stopped three times to talk to delegates. Had his overcoat and famous cap on. This time he touched on Pakistan. The Chairman Mao said that he had told the Pakistan prime minister now in Peking, that by joining the Baghdad Pact they had lost the friendship of their Middle East friends. By joining SEATO they had lost the friendship of East Asian nations. The Pakistani leader has sought another interview with him. Mao also said he had no faith in the UNO, as it was completely dominated by the USA. Kashmir was discussed.

Mao – 'You must decide it amongst yourselves. I wish to see India reunited. Partition was unnatural.'

The speaker said that by division, 'We have lost our two hands. If Kashmir went, then we would lose our head.' Mao was surprised to know that forty million Muslims still lived in India and were opposed to Pakistan's policy on Kashmir. Earlier Mao had quoted Confucius.

We left his residence at 1:45 am. For me it was a historic occasion. Mao was no ordinary mortal. All the MPs thought it to be the climax of their trip and were impressed by the performance of their leader. So was I. But the speaker was not overawed. I was fortunate to have been present at this meeting. Perhaps I may not get another opportunity to see Mao from close quarters for long. The late hour, the venue, the talk, the proximity to one of the greatest men of our time added to my excitement. The meeting showed that there was a team spirit among the top leaders of China. I was struck by the informal and yet correct manner in which Mao Tse Tung mingled with his other colleagues. No women present. Mao in his grey closed collar suit.

At 2:30 am we reached the station to board the special train that was to take us to the Kuantung Reservoir and the Great Wall. We left at 3 am on the dot. Each one of us had a compartment to ourselves. Most comfortable and luxurious. Women serving tea. I went to sleep almost immediately after hitting the pillow.

20 October

Kuantung Reservoir. A moderate effort, well-located, small, but vital for Peking. Men and women doing manual labour. The MPs asked pointed questions and were most keen to get photographed. I had a talk with Radha Raman[58] of Delhi. The special train took us to the Great Wall in four hours.

The Great Wall was disappointing. Saw it for five minutes and it's all over. For the times when it was built, it was a tremendous feat of labour and engineering; but it failed to enchant me. I felt the same disappointment here as I did on seeing the Waterloo Battlefield in Belgium. Its length was indeed impressive. Not the entire wall was built three thousand years ago. Some portions were built much later.

I was surprised to note that not one MP had taken either a book or a magazine to read on the way; neither did they show any curiosity about the history of the Great Wall. The Chinese for once slipped up. No handouts, no picture postcards of it. The delegation saw Liu Shao Chi in the evening.

21 October

Farewell lunch by the speaker. His speech was too long. Liu Shao Chi and Chou En-lai spoke. In contrast, both were brief. No Chinese leader speaks extempore. Their language precludes any attempt at eloquence.

22 October

The Parliamentary delegation left. The speaker made a most indiscreet speech at the airport. Actually mentioned Formosa, Chiang Kai-shek. All that he could have said was good bye and thank you for everything. He was very sore in the morning about his previous day's speech not being reported in the newspapers. Interestingly, Suhrawardy's speech has been reported.

23 October

The *People's China* has come out with a cover of Lu Hsun, calling him Gorky of China. I have not read Gorky.[59]

In the evening to the Peking Hotel for the Suhrawardy banquet. The earlier coolness has given way to some warmth. Suhrawardy is no angel, spoke well, had no dietary fads. Lady Feroz Khan Noon[60] is having a holiday on the house. Her husband has not come. Round of jokes about Lady Noon and Lord afternoon!

The big surprise of the evening was the appearance of Chairman Mao at the banquet. Not an accident. A subtle, but significant indication of the success of the visit. The Pakistanis were mostly in western clothes including Suhrawardy, who was Napoleonish in height. Mao's speech was a masterpiece of brevity. Just one sentence.

How easy it would have been to have said a little more but that international complication it might have created. It was left to Chou En-lai to hint at foreign policy and his visit to Pakistan. We have to watch these developments very carefully. China was out to get Pakistan out of the US camp. They might well achieve something by being more friendly with Pakistan. This would be at our cost.

The dinner was of poor quality. The music good. Chou En-lai performed deftly with Mao Tai toasts. It's now clear to me that he had a tremendous capacity for consuming the burning liquor.

Shaharyar's[61] mother was also here with the Pakistan prime minister. She told me Shaharyar was marrying the daughter of Pakistan's ambassador to Russia. I first met Begum Sahiba, daughter of the Nawab of Bhopal, in

London in 1954, at Wimbledon. A pleasant surprise to see her here. Asked her to say hello to Shaharyar and to wish him a jolly married life.

24 October

Early morning to the airport. I think we should have a tent or some other arrangement, where we could sleep for the night and meet people when they arrive! Razor-edge cold, wind blowing. A very small crowd to see Suhrawardy off. Took off in an IL-14. Mao's presence at his banquet was of utmost significance.

After lunch, yet another trip to the airport. U.Nu of Burma arrived. I was keen to have a look at him. Have great respect for him. Few people can renounce power once they have got it. U.Nu did it when he was at the zenith of his power and authority. The welcome he got (after all, he was not a prime minister) must have shaken the Pakistanis who were present. Chou En-lai and Chen Yi received him. U.Nu was doubtlessly popular here (if such a thing is possible in a totalitarian state). He got lusty cheers. Buddhist monks were produced to welcome him. He appeared in his national costume and yet looked far from shabby. He had a benign face, a calm on his face, which I have not seen in most leaders. His strength came from inside. His speech made in Burmese was short, simple, friendly and yet open-hearted. Had a winning smile with a soft persuasive voice; was robust and of medium height.

25 October

Had a letter from E.M. Forster. Got here in six days. Bradsdorff gave E.M.F. the gift I sent him. It was a charming letter: 'What a lovely gift, and how kind of Dr Bradsdorff to convey it. He could not stay long, but gave me a little news of you, and I gathered from him and from your letter that Peking is not too bad, and is anyhow interesting. A Hundred Schools of Thought is a cheering edict. Unfortunately, there is always the hundred and first.'

'There are two schools of thought only for your scroll. Dr Bradsdorff maintained it should be hung horizontally. I surely am right in upholding it perpendicular and I shall do so pending your ruling to the contrary. We sought a third opinion from the birds, as to which way they would prefer their heads to hang, but they didn't seem to mind.'

My acupuncture continues. It is helping my stomach. A slow process though.

26 October

Read Mao, without much enthusiasm. Very cold. I have acquired a polar cap with flaps to cover my ears. The Mao cap was okay for the summer. I have a nasty cold. Went to meet Dr Petigura – the only Parsi living in China. Married to a Chinese. Spoke the language fluently.

27 October

A fresh bunch of language students has arrived in the British Embassy. We have only me. Meera Malik[62] was expected soon. Then Darshan Bhutani.[63] They have thirty-nine people who knew Chinese in their office. We made all efforts to make friends with the Chinese, but none to learn their language in earnest.

Medha told me the priceless story about the lunch, ambassador had given for Jainendra Kumar,[64] the Hindi novelist.
Ambassador: 'What paper do you write for?'
Jainendra: 'I'm not a newspaper correspondent.'
Mrs Rajan Nehru: 'Ratan, Jainendra Kumarji is a very well-known novelist and short story writer.'
A: 'So you told me.'
J to A: 'Can you read and write Hindi with ease or not?'
A: 'Please tell me about the floods in Delhi.'
Jainendra is floored.
Mrs Rajan Nehru: 'Ratan, Mr Jainendra Kumar asked whether . . . '
A: 'I heard him, but I want to know about the floods in Delhi.'

Jainendra says something about the floods when the ambassador informs him that he can write poetry in Hindi. This brings the house down.

Ambassador is very sensitive about his hearing not being hundred percent. In fact it is only seventy per cent.

30 October

I have completed four months in Peking. They have passed fairly rapidly and I have been quite happy. My progress in Chinese has not been as good as I would have liked it to be. I find that I'm extremely reluctant to speak it. I want to be perfect at it.

The Middle East crisis was all over the Chinese press. People's Republic, hundred percent with Nasser.

31 October

Went to see Siqueiros and his wife off. They were happy to see me at the airport. Gossi would get her present soon which I have sent through the great painter. It was fascinating meeting Siqueiros.

1 November

In the evening we all went to the Soviet circus. The diplomatic corps had nothing better to entertain itself with. They were all there that evening; U.Nu also. While we went and amused ourselves, our junior staff had really a thin time in Peking. What were they to do? The circus was good in patches. The wire-dance by the girl (she reminded me of Gossi) was excellent. The speeches took almost half an hour. Chinese clapped all the time. I suppose it helped them keep warm.

I had my tennis match with Addis, counseller at the British Embassy. Won. Marshal Chen Yi was on another court, with baggy shorts. Later I heard, that he had fainted at our embassy lunch. It was because Mrs Nehru told him that she would also be in India at the same time. That was too much for him, he passed out hearing this. I have cooked this up!

2 November

Diwali. The highlight of the day has been a massive protest by the citizens of Peking against the British on Suez. I most strongly denounced the British doings in the Middle East. Thousands marched past round Legation Street, shouting slogans, carrying denunciatory posters which had obviously been most painstakingly prepared. Official photographers were there; journalists had tape recorders. It was all done with great precision and frightening discipline. All organised and instigated by somebody powerful. School and colleges and factories must have been closed to bring out such large number of people. Movement in the city was difficult.

3 November to 15 December

First the typewriter got damaged and could not be repaired in Peking. I had to send it to Hong Kong. When it came back, I got ill and had to go to the Russian Hospital.

After October, November was an anti-climax in many ways. Life is quieter. The flood of tourists has stopped. Suez and Hungary made up for the loss of excitement. The local reaction to both has been most revealing. The British and the French asked for it and I have no sympathy for them. But the Chinese reaction to happenings in Hungary is entirely different. The hush-hush gossip is that Mao is not happy at Soviet intervention, but publicly China is with the USSR. Chou En-lai may go to Moscow and Hungary to cool things. Only rumours. They are not neutral in any sense. Hungary showed that the Panchsheel went far, but no further. China and India have fundamentally differed over the Hungarian question. Not publicly. I'm deeply grieved by our official reaction to the Hungarian tragedy. In the earlier weeks we came out badly, it was the limit of double-thinking. We did not know the facts. This was a lame excuse. Krishna Menon[65] was the one who misled the prime minister.

17 December

I drove my Volkswagen to the airport early in the morning to see off David de Pury, who resigned from the British Foreign Service over Suez. He was at Cambridge with me.

Read Indian papers on Hungary. Jayaprakash Narayan's[66] voice was like a beacon of light in the surrounding darkness. Yet, it was a cry in the wilderness. On getting to the office, I was informed by Panu[67] that we had to go and see Chih Pai Shih, the ninety-six year old Chinese painter. I was thrilled. Ever since I got to Beijing I have been trying to see him. I like his work. Chen Chen To had given me an address and that worked. We arrived in his house at about 11 in the morning. The government has now taken up the responsibility, to provide him with a house and servants and all other amenities. As late as 1952 they took no notice of him. Then Chou En-lai visited him for his ninety-third birthday on 7 January 1953. Life changed hence for master artist Chih.

Now he is a national figure. We were greeted by a smartly dressed young Chinese (in Chih Pai Shih's house everybody looked young) who turned out to be his son. We were shown into a small room, the master's study. For the first minute or so I did not notice the great artist. He might not have been there. He was crumbled on a sofa with his back to the sun. He was really sweet to look at, just like a baby. We were told he had not been well lately. I was very keen (shamelessly so) to get as much out of this visit as possible.

The old man was not even aware that we had arrived. I asked several questions. The son shouted in his father's ear. For a brief moment the light shone in the eyes, the mind connected, but the body refused to work and the old man sank back, blank. Then he suddenly came to and offered us tea. I asked his favourite contemporary Chinese painter. He answered, Chen Pan Ting. 'Have you seen any Indian paintings?' 'Yes, I have seen Indonesian paintings.' At ninety-six, India and Indonesia are the same. 'What do you think of the Peace Prize you received?' 'I don't know that my paintings have a peaceful content. But I'm happy to know that they thought them peaceful.' I now know enough Chinese to follow what is being said. Recognition has come almost too late. He was a carpenter for the first twenty years of his life. Has lived in Beijing for the last forty years. Has never gone out of China, but within the country has travelled widely. Born in Hunan. Has stopped painting for the past few months. Mixes his own colours, paints direct with a brush on paper, no drawing at all. He is also a master of seal-engraving on ivory. In his youth he wrote poetry. He read the Thang dynasty poets, Tu Fu and Li Po. His style of painting is impressionistic – Hsieh Yi. He paints his shrimps, crickets, fish from real life. According to a critic, 'He has patiently studied the activities of these small creatures, acquired an infinitely sympathetic understanding of their beings and outer forms.'

The meeting was not satisfactory. His son talked too much. One did not have the heart to trouble the old man. He had blackouts every few minutes. But I can never forget his sensitive face, his magnificent beard and whiskers, his beautiful hands, and those piercing eyes.

Panu took lots of pictures. I could not resist the temptation of having one taken with him. We bought two of his paintings. The son was a bit of a crook, he probably was responsible for all the fakes that could be bought in town. He said he had only three paintings of his father. Really! We bought two for 150 Yuans. Expensive? What does an original Picasso 6" x 8" cost? Compared to that this was for a song. Mine was a lovely eagle in black about 24" long.

When we left, Chih Pai Shih got up to shake hands with us and came to the door to say goodbye. This is how I'll remember him, waving his right hand like a little boy.

20 December

Peita will close for a few days before end of the year.

Much progress in spoken and written Chinese. I'm now reading Mao in Chinese. The teachers all reverentially called him Mao Chu Si – Chairman Mao. Today's Mao text had an arresting phrase, 'When necessary bend like a willow. When necessary stand unbending like an oak.'

I have been here nearly six months and how many Chinese friends have I? Only Mela. How many Chinese homes have I been to? None. To how many Chinese will I write, when I leave this country? None. How many Chinese will write to me? None again.

21 December

The bag arrived. No *Quest*. Earlier in the week, I bought some lovely greeting cards, but the strange thing is that you buy envelopes from one shop and cards from another and then discover that the card is too big for the envelope. In dialectical terms, it's an antagonistic contradiction.

22 December

Drove early morning to Tienstin with Ashok Bhadkamkar. I drove all the way. My VW Beatle is a great convenience. Very cold. Temperature -8 degrees Fahrenheit, below freezing point. Tienstin, large industrial city. Once it was a gay, pleasure giving, and lively city. No longer so. The factories worked overtime. No doubt about the positive side. This was the best government China has ever had. But the human spirit was being crushed. That was a negative impact. If you are not a party member you are not counted, you do not get enough coal, which really means that you can freeze to death. The hotel we went to was dreadful, but the Victoria restaurant was a delight. It must have been quite a place at one time. We had excellent fare. Incidentally, it is not possible to buy petrol at the port. Dagoba itself is a tiny little joke of a port – sleepy, cold and dirty. We saw little children diligently picking up coal from the railway line. They collected very little yet, it was something that counted. We got away at about five. Reached Tienstin at 5:30 pm. A traffic muddle. I have not yet got used to the extraordinary system of signalling here. It is most confusing and gives the policeman enormous scope to catch you on the wrong side. One of them asked me to stop. However, when he discovered that we were diplomats, allowed us to proceed. The big thing in Tienstin was the sight of a petrol pump, which worked. In Beijing there is none to be seen. After filling we went to the travel bureau; they wished to check if the newly arrived American car worked or not. Ashok was mildly amused. It did. Then followed a comedy of errors. I lost touch with Ashok for nearly two hours. Drove from one place to another and then again in the dimly lit streets of Tienstin. He was nowhere to be found. I then finally drove back to the travel bureau. Sure enough, he was waiting there in the terrible cold. I thought he had followed me, but he had not. We had dinner at the Victoria. Left at 9:30 pm. Reached Beijing at 12:30. The next ten hours I spent in bed. It was a pleasant drive, no traffic, except occasional mule carts. If your car breaks down, then you've had it. But law and order is so good that no bodily harm can be inflicted by anyone upon you, on a lonely road even in darkness.

25 and 26 December

Christmas day has no significance for me except, that it is an important day in the calendar; and one likes to recollect where one was at last Christmas day and the one before that and again the year before that and so on. In 1952 I was in Belgium, in 1953 I was in Berlin, in 1954 I was in Madras and last year I was in Delhi and this year I'm in Peking, perhaps next too, but one never knows. Weather – bright but numbingly cold.

The more one stays here the more one is amused. The other day a Chinese friend rang up in the organisation concerned and asked if they would welcome her translating the *Ramayana* into Chinese. The man at the other end asked, 'Who is the author of this book, what is his background?' In other words, he wanted to know if he was a progressive, if his thinking was Marxist-Leninist and so on.

Efficiency, increased production, the elimination of counter revolutionaries, (but then who is a counter-revolutionary, anybody who disagrees with the present set up?) uniformity, discipline are all very well, but what about the freedom of thought, press and speech? What about criticism, what about creativity as opposed to ideological art, what about the human spirit, what about thousands of delightful people who can't take care if left to themselves and allowed to lead their lives? If I'm not mistaken, it was the ancient Greeks who said that the best government is that, which rules the least. The communists believe in the opposite political practice. The government is like a big brother, the national income is the national budget and they can do what they like with the money; thousands of doubtful peace doves go about China in expenses all paid by the poor people. There is no milk in the market and yet milk is being sent to Egypt, in the name of the people of China, every citizen is watched, his activities monitored. For everything we have to depend on Hong Kong.

29 December

The *People's Daily* carried an important editorial this morning. Unfortunately, we did not pay much attention to it. I think almost all the other embassies gave it the importance it deserved. (I confess I didn't read it but read Chipp's despatch on it.) In the evening at the British Embassy, Addis, Martin and Evans all asked me about it. They thought it was a landmark in the history of Communism. They might be exaggerating.

I had an interesting discussion with O'Neil, the British chargé d'affaires. We talked about David de Pury. O'Neil said it was a pity he was away when David resigned. 'I am an expert on this, having done the same thing eighteen years ago.' It was possible even as a very junior official to influence policy in London or Delhi. I said nothing. I have no experience. In these days of diplomacy, the diplomat's functions were being curtailed by conferences and high-powered delegations. He said the function of his embassy in Peking was largely journalistic, to report to the Foreign Office in London, things and events which might help them in the future to formulate foreign policies which would be relevant. 'There is nothing else we can do here, we cannot influence the Chinese government one way or the other and we don't try to, as we know it will not carry any weight.' The sun has indeed set on the British Empire.

30 December

I'm completing six months here today. Beastly day, weather-wise. Still living in one room in the hotel and still having lunch and dinner with the Bhadkamkars.

31 December

The mayor of Mumbai dropped in to the office to meet us. I liked him immediately. Frank, jovial and receptive. The usual talk about China and India. He felt that the Chinese were ahead of us (no doubt about that). In China there was enthusiasm, a sense of participation in the national reconstruction. The mayor felt that if our prime minister gave up his office and kept his eye on party reorganisation, much good could be achieved. At the moment, Nehru was out of touch with the masses. I took this with a pinch of salt.

New Year's Eve dinner at the British Embassy. I gave a lift to the three American newspapermen who had come here against the wishes of the State Department. Their passports have been confiscated. They were the first American journalists to come to China after the Korean war. Stevens of *Look* (a Pulitzer Prize winner for his article on life in the Soviet Union) came from Moscow and his colleague Harrington came from New York via Moscow. William Worthy came directly from New York. There is something very attractive and friendly about Americans. I don't know too many though. The US will be popular here if they have the wisdom to recognise Red China. After all, America has been involved in China for decades before 1949. These three have been impressed by what they saw. Stevens said after Moscow this place was a great surprise. 'Moscow is dead, this place is alive, people are willing to talk, get photographed and smile, apparently in Moscow smiles are rare.' They used their cameras furiously and no one objected. The State Department was stupid to ask them to return.

For the first time I had a look at the house of the British Embassy. Huge place with nineteenth century Chinese architecture. They really must have lorded in their days here, dined, wined and concubined. British atrocities in Peking were not forgotten by the Chinese. During the siege of Peking they used Sikh soldiers to repress the Boxer Rebellion in 1901.

Met Two-gun Cohen.[68] Friend of Sun Yat-sen. Till very recently he was the only person who was acceptable to the Taiwanese and Mao, and had a say in both places. But now he is passé. His heart is in China. He thought Americans were stupid not to recognise this country. Made an interesting remark when he said, 'I would like to hear a tape recording of the talks your PM had with Ike and Chou, not what is put out in the paper but what they really talked.'

The new year has arrived. But I do not feel the least excited. But some of the others are, out of habit. I enjoyed bursting balloons and left at 1:00 am.

Diary—1957

1 January 1957

There was a time when I used to be fond of making new year resolutions. I no longer indulge in such pastimes. Those resolutions were never kept, they could not be kept and there was no need to keep them and no need to actually make them. All I do now, is to look back on the past year and hope for the best in the new year.

The year 1956 for me was in many ways significant. To begin with, I had a delightful spell in South India for my district training. It gave me time to travel, to see parts of my country which I had always liked to visit. I saw many new places. Met old friends and made some new ones. I have come to realise that E.M. Forster's personality and his writings influence me, that personal relationships form an important part of my life. I'm, probably, too uncritical of him but he is a great writer.

Father's illness was one of the major shocks of my life. My mother took upon herself all the illnesses of the family. His illness was a realisation that we were so vulnerable, and things at home would crack up in no time. The only thing that made me go to Bharatpur was their presence.

The international situation has been disturbing and at heart I remain a slave to political life and will probably land up in politics. Yet, I must say the IFS offers an exciting career. Since coming to China six months ago I have not kept well, but I have now taken my health into my hands and I'm going to keep myself fit.

As for the new year, I shall try and speak less, compromise less and mind my own business. For India this may well be the decisive year. Either we go ahead on the road to becoming a great nation or we go downhill for Nirad C. Chaudhuri[1] to have the last laugh. I hope he is proved a false prophet.

2 January

Spent time with Mela – my sleeping dictionary.

3 January

Got up late. Snowfall. Premier Chou En-lai returns today from his tour. Oddly enough, the first snowfall last year was on 17 November 1956, the day he left for his Asian tour. Since then we have had no snow, but for today. I wonder what the stars foretell. We went to the airport to receive him. The entire diplomatic corps has been intimated. Chou En-lai arrived punctually at 4:00 pm, looking sprightly as usual. For the first time I saw his wife, Madam Teng Ying Chao.[2] Unobtrusive and dignified. The three Americans were there to meet him. He made no statement. In a day or two he would be off to Moscow and Warsaw. The Suez crises and the Hungarian events have kept Premier Chou fully stretched.

Indonesian cocktails: The Indian Embassy diplomats stayed on and were invited to dinner. I met some of the young Indonesian attachés there. They get twice my salary but no other facilities. They pay for their houses, etc. Their training programme (there is not much of it) is inadequate and haphazard. There is no properly demarcated foreign service. The Indonesian ambassador is an extremely likeable person. Our boss can learn something from him, but he will not.

I hope Vice-President Hatta[3] forms a cabinet in Indonesia. He is the only man who can save Indonesia. I spent a week with him when he came to India on an official visit in 1955. He is a great lover of books. Speaks English very well. He is just over five feet in height.

On coming back to the hotel I ran into Worthy and with him was Mr Hawkins, one of the American Prisoners of War (Korea) who stayed back here. I took them to my room for a drink. Did not get to talk much with Hawkins, except that he liked the Indians he met in Korea. I told him my elder brother too was in Korea with the Indian contingent. Hawkins speeks perfect Chinese, read the *Time* magazine, is in touch with his family in the States, and may go back. He has been produced in Peking for the benefit of the three American journalists.

I have been using my Chinese seal these days. It is much more important in China than one's signature. Every workman has to have it here, so Hawkins told me. Worthy was impressed by the informality at the airport. Said Moscow was a different story. NKVD men all round and very active. I wished the Americans to come and see things for themselves here. Not recognising the existence of Mao's China makes no sense.

4 January

Played my third round table tennis match. Lost. My Vietnam opponent was from a different class. I have given up my membership of the International Club. During winter I would hardly use it and I saw no point in dishing out Rs 50 each month.

Today is Burma's National Day. Peking Hotel, old wing. Bau Maun, the ambassador was the host. He was such an amusing fellow. Chou En-lai came. As soon as he entered the room, everybody was on alert. He was here, there and everywhere. A much better mixer than Nehru. The three American journalists were there too. Harrington told me that the reception was again a different story from the Moscow ones.

I had a chat with Chen Chen Tho. Talked about the late Dr Chakraborty.[4] The late doctor apparently left his library to the Chinese government and Cambridge University. Then we got on to Chih Pai Shih. Vice-Minister Chen Chen Tho said Chih's son had locked up all his paintings and was waiting for the old man to die. I thought the son was a bit of a crook. Raja Hutheesing[5] said that in his book on China.

5 January

Had an interesting day. The American journalists were like a breath of fresh air here. I asked them for dinner, having forgotten that I had to go the wedding reception of Puri, the stenographer attached to me. He has married a Chinese girl. I hope he has done the right thing. I told the girl exactly what she might face in a lower middle-class Punjabi home in Delhi.

Then I took Harrington and Stevens to dinner in the Tung An Tse Chang. They were both Adlai Stevenson[6] men, contemptuous of Dulles.[7] Took a dim view of the new Eishenhower plan for the Middle East. 'By doing this sort of a thing, we are playing into the hands of the Russians.' We then touched upon the question of colour bar in the US.

They agreed that it was terrible but felt that much was being done to get rid of it. I told them that people in Asia and Africa are very sensitive to colour and if the western nations continued the white man's burden nonsense, they would only harm themselves. I did not say anything of our own white skin complex though.

Khrushchev's speech to the twentieth party last year is now doing the rounds in China and Poland, but not in the Soviet Union. The talk here is that, Mao is not amused with what Khrushchev said about Stalin. It is also being rumoured that Khrushchev sent Mikoyan[8] to explain this speech to Mao and other leaders, its timing and rationale. No one knew of Mikoyan's visit last year.

I told them of the national fly eradication campaign in China. They had heard of it and were amused. Stevens came out with the Mussolini story on the Italian campaign against flies, a campaign in which the flies won. In China they lost.

They enjoyed the food and so did I. It was a thrill to cook one's own food, even if partially. The Mongolian restaurant allowed customers to do so.

6 January

Dinner at the Bahadursingh's – Stevens, Harrington, Winnington, also the Israel Epsteins, Worthy, the Guhas and myself. Quite a meal. It was interrupted by Stevens having to leave the house to submit the notes of his interview with Chou En-lai to the Information Department. I brought him back to the hotel and he typed his notes off. Thoroughly decent of him to show me both the questions he submitted to Chou and his answers.

Chou gave nothing away. Chou En-lai said, 'We thought Eisenhower was a man of peace, but his Mid-East plan has shaken our belief.' Worthy said that the hand of Dulles was apparent. Chou laughed. Chou was planning visits to Moscow, Warsaw and Budapest. This was what Worthy gathered. Worthy asked if I knew anything about the Dalai Lama wanting to stay on in India and not return to Tibet. I was a bit taken aback and told him quite honestly that I knew nothing about it. Then he told me if I knew of Chou's meeting with the East European ambassadors. I said I did. On the way to the hotel, Stevens told me that his friend the Yugoslav ambassador (he said that man was so well-informed) told him that due to American stupidity, the Chinese had to depend on Soviet's economic aid. Stevens was not impressed with the western leaders. 'In Europe, England and US there was not a man of the calibre of Nehru and Chou.' He thought Nasser a demagogue, out to make himself a hero. The Aswan dam was not as important to Egypt as it was made out to be. The Arab states were the only countries in the world where slavery existed even today. I put in my penny's worth by telling them that I was a liaison officer attached to Nasser in early 1955, when he was on his way to attend the Bandung Conference. He certainly had a striking personality. Nehru took him under his wings.

8 January

Yesterday my cold was so bad, I rushed to Dr Petigura and asked him to do something to relieve my agony. Yet another snowfall. The temperature was several degrees below zero. It has been so for the past several weeks.

Dinner with the Katamats of the Indonesian Embassy. Bandung crowd. The Egyptians also at the dinner. They were pampered in Peking and they had neither the sense of humour nor the wisdom to take it all with a pinch of salt. Chairman Mao has made much fuss about the new Egyptian ambassador – General Ragab. Katamats' house was extraordinary. It was highly unsuited for winter conditions. For dinner we had to leave the warm room and walk across the snow covered courtyard. Some slides were shown after dinner. Conversation was neither lively nor stimulating. The Indonesians were poor conversationalists. As individuals they were warm and friendly.

In the evening Marc Riboud,[9] the French photographer dropped in to see me. Sushil Mukerjee[10] had spoken to him about me. He is here photographing Beijing to illustrate a Han Suyin article. He is also illustrating her book on Nepal. We talked of Han Suyin. He liked her.

26 January

Our Republic Day banquet caused a minor flurry. We failed to withdraw the old list from the Wai Chiao Pu, and did not send them the new one. We went by the new one and they by the old one. A near catastrophe was somehow avoided. The Pakistanis reacted typically. Not only did they return our invitation cards after having accepted them, but they also sent back the souvenirs.

The Security Council has voted in their favour. Then why this? I suspect there is going to be trouble on the Kashmir question. We are unwise to take a purely domestic issue to the UN. The Chinese delivered a public snub by appearing with their second and third string people for our banquet. Either there may be nothing to it, or it can be a deliberate decision. It probably is.

27 January

Received an unexpected call from Panu Guha to go to the Asian Students Sanatorium with him. None of us were able to go yesterday. I had heard something about this place and developed an instinctive bias against this 'fellow travelling' institution. Having been there I cannot help giving, purely on humanitarian grounds, full marks to the Chinese. The funds poured in from somewhere and they must be considerable as the place was quite swanky.

It is bitterly cold, snow, sleet and slime all the way. Driving is hazardous. The sanatorium is two years old. India has the largest contingent (forty-five at the moment and fifteen more to come). Mostly from Bengal. Almost all Red. The buildings are, what one may call, the bastard style. Yet they look quite pretty in their curved roofs. We were met by one of the officials of the hospital. Greeted politely and shown into a nice little sitting room – one finds this all over China. Visitors don't have to hang about and go into places they are not supposed to. We were expected and treated with excessive politeness. Everything being taped. Tea served. The official told us how 'the Indian comrades had spent their Republic Day, and were most anxious to meet you.' We put on the white gowns and proceeded to meet the Indian lot. We were taken to a wing where our people stayed, two to a room, clean and tidy. We assembled in a lounge from which one got a beautiful view of the western hills. In the spring and the autumn this must be even a more glorious view. In the lounge, I recognised two of Chih Pai Shih's works – the one of three chickens, quite wonderful.

One may question the ethics of our sick students coming here free, living free on Chinese hospitality. From the national point of view this is not a good propaganda for us. But disease shall not be subjected to propaganda one way or the other. Those young men, almost all students, were suffering from TB. In their own land, with all the good will in the world, they would have not got this kind of medical treatment. Firstly, they can not afford it. Secondly, they can not find beds in hospitals. They seemed happy, as happy as a young person suffering from TB can be. I sat talking to them, listening to their songs and their requests for Indian films and newspapers. I was reminded of the Somerset Maugham story, *Sanitorium*. I came back convinced that we should take more interest in these people, whatever their political views be. They were Indians. They were sick and they were in a foreign land. They welcomed company, which made them more cheerful and hopeful. At least once a month, one of us should visit them. Before leaving, we saw their rooms and dining hall and their library. A fair amount of books in Chinese and Hindi, Bengali and English. Portrait of Tagore. We left at 12:30 am, I'm glad I went. I hope to return. To a patient, the visiting hour is the most important. I know. The nagging loneliness is relieved if one knows that some day, someone will come and see you.

International Evening at the International Club. I got my tennis prize today. I'm the singles champion of Peking's diplomatic corps. A formal presentation was made. I forgot how many such prizes I won. Evening was tiresome. The Indonesians surprised us with their excellent performances. Most of their diplomatic officers took part in the show. The Soviet Embassy produced some excellent items. The Pakistanis (who have been behaving so childishly) presented one of their cruder dances, but it was lively, played to Indian records.

30 January

Ninth anniversary of the death of Gandhiji. Not much known about Gandhiji here. Rabindranath Tagore is better known.

I got irritated with the Reuter's man, who talked nonsense on Suez and Kashmir. Our publicity on Kashmir has been so defective that even our best friends doubt our bonafides in Kashmir. I have no doubt that Kashmir is ours and we have a good case. Its remaining with us is not only good for us, but also for Pakistan. If Kashmir goes to Pakistan, then the forty million Muslims in India will have a tough time. Our secularism too would suffer. I don't see how that could be avoided if Kashmir went to Pakistan. There will be such a sorry mess all around. I wish the Security Council realises this.

Today, I completed seven months in China. Interesting months. Still no end to my staying in one room at the Hsin Chiao Hotel. Gets claustrophobic. It's like an overused railway station. All sorts of people turn up. The other day I saw the novelist Graham Greene.[11] We exchanged brief notes. He avoided meeting me. Some talk of his novel *The Quiet American* being translated into Chinese.

3 February

The Chinese new year or the Spring festival as it is called was a very tame affair. I went out this morning for a drive to the Summer Palace. Roads were very treacherous but I managed. The lake was frozen. I never saw such a dazzling sight before. The Summer Palace itself looked like a fairyland with snow all over it. Not many locals present. Had Chinese food in the Golden Auriole restaurant.

Remarkable piece of good luck. I discovered a second-hand book shop at the back of Peking Hotel. Bought the first edition of *Seven Pillars of Wisdom* by T.E. Lawrence. Also *Shui Hu Chuan* translated by Pearl S. Buck. And the erotic *The Dream of the Red Chamber* with a preface by Arthur Waley, the great sinologist. All modestly priced.

16 February

I sold my typewriter and that offered a ready excuse for not writing my diary. How easy it is to be lazy.

My Chih Pai Shih has been mounted and looks grand. I have also acquired another one. He is best known for painting chickens and shrimps. The prints too have been well and inexpensively framed. Some things are incredibly cheap here while others are inexplicably expensive. Most things are just not available. Old-styled furniture with mother of pearl also readily available. The Chiang Kai-shek crowd abandoned their furniture when they left in 1949-50.

The Chinese film on the Korean War was good and gruesome. The response of the audience was most frightening. They cheered each time someone was killed. Puri's newly acquired bride translated for me in whispers. The cinema hall was overheated and in need of fresh air. Towels are passed from row to row to wipe sweat. I declined to use one used by twenty others.

Went out for dinner at the Tung An Shih Chang mutton restaurant. Two Russians dropped into our room and asked us to help them order their food, as they did not know Chinese. Very friendly and pleasant. Drank toasts, Nehru was the magic word. We did not know what the current magic word was in the Soviet Union. Could not be Stalin. So we kept quiet.

Chipp held forth on his Reuters' bosses. Reuters want an article on the private life of Mao. They may as well hope to get an article on the private life of the inhabitants of the moon. Besides what is the importance of an article like that? How the chairman lives is his business.

A minor fire in Wang Fu Ching. No fuss or disorder. Rather a lot of orderly fuss. Kashmir, Menon's nine-hour filibuster at the Security Council was being talked about in the diplomatic corps.

20–30 February

Lot of commotion about fate and future of Let a Hundred Flowers Bloom and a Hundred Schools of Thought contend. Mao Chu Si was reported to have made a forceful and long speech defending the movement. Lot of open criticism of government, in some papers and some universities.

Dean Chang hesitatingly told me that the Hundred Flowers and Hundred Schools is an ancient concept and a part of Chinese thought and philosophy. Chairman Mao was giving it new clothes. The people supported him.

He also explained to me the Yin-Yang philosophical concept – the male-female phenomenon, the negative-positive ever present in life. Yang is light. Yin darkness.

14 March

Dinner with the Warners of the British Embassy. They are both so young and nice. Then the film on Sir Walter Scott, the British explorer. A brave and good man but also a bit incompetent. Then we talked on till the early hours of the morning about China and the Chinese leaders. Even the British agreed that the Chinese leaders were outstanding. We touched upon the new role Chou was playing, not only as the great leader of the communist world but also as the leader and adviser of Asia.

15 March

It's Holi today. Spring in Delhi, but here we shivered and froze. I don't really care very much for this rather rowdy festival.

In the afternoon I tried to visit the Birth Control Exhibition, but the queue was the longest I have seen in recent months (although each evening I see endless queues for buses and trams). The Chinese are serious on the birth control issue. Like ours, their population has to be checked too. They have made abortion legal. The exhibition is being held in the Chun Shan park. There is something going on today in Peking, but one will not know for weeks what actually happened.

Drove round the city. I noticed that portions of the Wall surrounding the inner city are being pulled down. A part of history being pulled down. The bag arrived. My story has appeared in the *Illustrated Weekly*. The illustration shook me a bit. It is so gaudy. But it is good to see one's name in print. The *Encounter*[12] has arrived at last.

16 March

Called at the Foreign Office. The man I had gone to see was doing his morning exercise, and he was a bit embarrassed to see me just at that moment. So was I. In the afternoon went out to the Jen Min Shih Chang. Bought a screen and another iron lamp. The screen was expensive but very soon they might not be available. In my not too fluent Chinese I bargained and got my way. The time to be here was in the early fifties. The rich were selling everything at throwaway prices.

Minoo Masani has got himself elected to parliament. That was his right place. It was, however, a pity that he came the way he did. The PM is not favourably inclined towards the author of *Our India*. I got to know him in 1951, when as president of the St. Stephen's College Union, I went to Bombay to attend a meeting of the All India Student's Federation. Masani was presiding. He was almost roughed-up till some of us got him out through the back door. J.P. Narayan and Pandit Nehru too addressed our meeting at the BCCI stadium.

27 March

Panu Guha passed this on to me: 'The Chinese People's Committee for the Defense of World Peace, the People's Association for Cultural Relations with Foreign Countries, the Sino-Indian Friendship Association, the China Federation for Literature and Art Circles, the China Union of Musicians and the Peking Branch of the Sino-Soviet Association, jointly request the pleasure of your company at the commemorative meeting to mark the 100th anniversary of the death of the Russian composer, M.I. Kelinka at the Tien Chiao Theatre.' Longest invitation card I have ever received. I never heard of the composer but I went and seldom regretted anything more. The Chinese and the Russians have an infinite capacity of praising each other and boring their guests. The function started at 7:30 pm and from then on till 9:30 pm we had to sit and listen to speeches, one in Chinese and another in Russian, which had to be translated into Chinese. Any other audience would have rightly walked out. Mao Tun,[13] the Minister of Culture was presiding and after a while was yawning away.

As if this was not enough, they had the powerful arc lamps switched on right into our eyes every now and then. The newsmen took pictures when the audience clapped at the end of the speeches in thanksgiving. People would see the film and see the honoured guests giving them a 'spontaneous and thunderous applause'. The music programme was all too brief. Yet I must say the New China government is doing a lot to popularise western music. They had a 125 men-women chorus. Earlier in the year the Bolshoi had performed Swan Lake. I had not seen anything so spectacular and artistically satisfying.

30 March

Kamala Lakshman's[14] show was the best of its type I have yet seen. She was absolutely first rate. What a contrast to the Indonesian dancers whose performance was soporific. I think she is assured success here. Mrs R.K. Nehru has been coaching her on how to conduct herself in China. Kamala was married to R.K. Lakshman,[15] the well-known cartoonist and the younger brother of R.K. Narayan.[16]

On getting back I read Charry's[17] letter. Charry said E.M. Forster was dead. My heart sank. I tried to ring up David Chipp to find out if he knew anything about it but I could not get in touch with him. From this hotel one could not even ring up Cambridge. In January, E.M.F. had written that, though depressed he was physically fit. He was at that time seventy-eight. It was strange that in the past weeks or so I was often thinking of him.

I went to bed thinking that if I had not met him, I would have gone through a life having a completely wrong set of values. He opened up a marvellous world of personal relationships, of friendship and love.

5 April

The winter is definitely over but the approach of spring has been marred by a serious and very widespread epidemic of 'flu'. I got a touch of it, but the others suffered much more, especially amongst the staff. In the Peking University about two thousand students were ill.

Today is the last day of the performance of Kamala Lakshman. She has obviously been a huge success, exotic, attractive and pleasant. Prime Minister Chou En-lai found time to see this show and also to invite us all to a reception after the show.

As usual the invitation arrived at the eleventh hour. He had just returned from Kunming where he has been having secret meetings with UN people. We did not get very good seats for the show as the tickets had been sold out weeks in advance. Kamala should have stayed here for months. Chou En-lai and Ho Lung[18] got an ovation when they entered and people rushed to have a look at them. At the reception, I had a few words with Chou En-lai. He looked at me and I bowed and he came over, clinked glasses and then I hazarded the most obvious but safe remark, 'How did you like the show, Sir?'

'Very much,' he said. Then he turned to his interpreter and said to him that it is a pity Kamala could not go to Shanghai and other places. Before the interpreter could translate I said, '*Tung la*' (I understand). The PM looked me up and down. Then said, 'I hope she will come again.' '*Wo Si huan, tha Tsai lai*' (We hope she will come again). I answered in pure Chinese. I said she was a very *Nien Ching jen* – a very young person and she will have plenty of time to come. I was rather pleased with my linguistic self-confidence. I ran into Mei Lan Fang[19] at the reception. How elegantly he spoke. He was full of praise for Kamala. Had photographs taken with Kamala.

Then one of those extraordinary things happened that only happens to me. I quite forgot that the reception was given by Chou En-lai and not by us. Somehow I was so busy talking to people that I did not notice the others leaving and to my horror realised that I was the only guest left in the room. Chou and others were waiting for me to leave. I still did not catch on. I was thinking how the ambassador and the others could have left before the PM. Then the penny dropped.

I ran out. What a bloody foolish and absent-minded thing to do. To keep the great Chou En-lai waiting was some error. But Peng Chen,[20] the mayor of Peking and Marshal Ho Lung had their eyes on me thinking, 'Why is this young fellow not leaving?'

6 April

Saw Kamala and her party off. Lovely morning. The usual crowd from the Chinese side. Kamala has been a huge success in spite of the several hurdles placed in her way, by well-meaning but misguided people.

In the afternoon Ashok and I went and saw the Birth Control Exhibition. As usual there were a large number of people in the queue, but we flaunted our diplomatic identity cards and were let in. The exhibition was something, which only the Chinese could have organised. It was brutally frank, charts, photographs, models and the most vivid illustrations of how to use contraceptives. People went in batches of twenty or so (men and women both) but the lecturing or rather explaining was all done by women. No hanky-panky about it, no smirking or smiling. No inhibitions.

Since early this year the birth control question has been occupying the minds of people in this country. Marx was against it and so all communists were opposed to it. In China once again on a vital matter he has been bypassed and Malthus[21] given a posthumous nod. The question is dealt on a war basis. Prices of contraceptives are reduced by thirty percent and they are readily available in the shops. This is happening all over the country. Why can we not do the same thing?

7 April

Went to the military airport to receive the Polish prime minister and his party. The usual crowd and Chou En-lai. It was a gloomy day and the reception was moderate. Chou made a speech which was unusual.

The communists have formed a ministry in Kerala. There is a subdued but genuine interest here in the Kerala outcome. It is a unique event and a great challenge to all of us in India. It is also a challenge to the Indian communists. The formation of this ministry will, I hope, make the other states pull up their socks and to make efforts to put a stop to inefficiency, corruption and nepotism. When I accompanied the chargé d'affaires for his meeting with Chou, the other day, the Chinese prime minister gave us the details of the Kerala results. We, in the embassy, had no information at all.

8 April

Met Riboud's friends. I like them both. Cameron, a New Zealander, seemed sound and intelligent. Homosexual. The most well-known New Zealander in China is Rewi Alley (1897-1987). Came to China in 1926. Well-respected by the communists. Along with Edgar Snow he had in 1938 initiated the movement for industrial cooperatives. I have met him several times, but do not know him well.

The temperature is in the seventies and the weather is lovely, but overcast. I went to see the agriculture exhibition but it was closed. The Chinese shut their exhibitions once a week but not on a Sunday.

Had an interesting talk on journalists and their work with Locaine, the AFP man. He declared that China was losing friends through their magazines. *China Reconstructs* and *People's China*, both unimaginative. What it needed was a Chinese version of the *New Statesman* and *Nation*. My own view was that both needed improvement, but Locaine had a point.

9 April

Rain, snow and sleet. Temperature fell to thirty-two degrees Fahrenheit. What a day. Spring has been put back for at least a week and the blossoms killed. Snowed the whole day, wind and cold coming from the Gobi desert.

16 April

Since early morning the streets have been lined up by people to welcome Marshal Voroshilov[22] of the USSR. Flags have gone up. The usual welcoming machinery got going in earnest. Papers full of his visit.

The twelve-mile route was lined with people all the way. The military airport was crammed with people. Premier Chou En-lai as usual made it a point to shake hands with all the diplomats. Then came Chairman Mao. Loud applause. I got some very close shots of him. The entire hierarchy was present: Chu Teh, Liu Shao Chi, Chou En-lai, Ho Lung, Peng Te Huai, Deng Xiaoping[23], Chen Yun, Chen Yi. The Wai Chiao Pu staff was in action asking us to join the diplomatic ranks and not loiter about taking pictures.

I had my first live look at a jet plane. It was an enormous machine and the absence of propellers was a novelty. Voroshilov made Mao & Co. wait for a few minutes before alighting. The Soviet leader is a short and stocky man. He is seventy-six. He was wearing a long coat but he took it off when he began his speech. Mao delivered a short speech of which I followed nothing. His pronunciation was all his own in Hunanese. Both stood on a platform. His speech was written in about one inch big letters. I wonder why most famous people do not like to wear glasses in public.

The Russian leader gave a long speech and at the end of it surprised everybody (most of all Mao) by embracing and kissing Mao. I hope my pictures come out well. I could not have been closer to them.

The drive back was a long drawn affair. Mao and Voroshilov drove in an open car (Nehru was the first to do this here in China and Russia in 1954 and 1955 respectively). Unlike Soekarno's visit there were no portraits at the city gates. The coming of Voroshilov was like the coming of the Mountain to Mohammed. The Chinese have come to stay as the leading communists in the world. There was nobody like Mao and few like Chou in Russia or in any other communist country.

Buddhism is now history in China. But the Buddhist temples were still standing strong. Few go to worship at these temples. Religious persecution was not in evidence. Peking has a sizeable Muslim population. They do not wear beards or Islamic dress. All in blue clothes.

7 May

I'm not writing about the 1 May parade. It was eye-catching and it did not rain as it did on 1 October 1956. Opening night of Chinese version of Kalidas's *Shakuntala*. Translated from Sanskrit by well-known indologist Prof Chi Hsien-Lin of Peking University. The Art theatre was full. I could only follow some of it. The choreography was impressive. So were the hero and the heroine. One handsome, the other beautiful and sexy.

The Chinese Culture Department was out in full force. Mei Lan Fang very much in evidence. Also Culture Minister Mao Tun and Kuo Mo Jo. I had few words with renowned philosopher Fang Yu Lan.[24] He is rewriting his *History of Chinese Philosophy* with a Marxist slant.

19 May

Meera Malik arrived. Full of enthusiasm and good intentions. She is a year junior to me. Her brother was at St. Stephen's with me. She is also here to learn Chinese.

26 May

Yet another airport ceremony. To see off the Soviet president. Such a waste of time.

Gradually the top brass turned up by 8:30. Mao had his famous cap on, but his suit was not ironed (not that it matters). In contrast the others, Chu The, Liu Shao Chi and Chou En-lai, looked like bridegrooms. Mao made a brief speech. The Russian president a longer one, and to the utter surprise of the interpreter added a sentence or two off the cuff. The speeches were the usual type. At the end, Mao made sure that the Russian did not kiss him.

I do not mind the austere existence we lead here, but the dreariness and drabness are not pleasing at all. One learns to be tolerant and put up with arid party propaganda. China is stable and secure but there is something missing.

30 June

About things in China I'm having second thoughts. The earlier enthusiasm was natural and to a point understandable. But I allowed other people to make judgments for me. I am intellectually left, traditionally right and professionally in a kind of no-opinion land. Hungary upset me as did Suez. The denial of human freedom enrages me as does the misuse of it, we have too much of one and the Chinese too little of the other.

I have been living in the Hsin Chiao hotel for over eleven months. On the thirteenth, I shifted into this, little one bedroom house on Tung Sung Po Hutung. It's nice having a place of one's own. It has a small courtyard – actually a lawn. My bedroom has a *kang** to keep me warm. The bathroom has a tub but no shower. The drawing room is large with a wooden floor. Painted red. Small, but adequate dinning room. Three servant quarters and three servants. Lao Wong is number one. The cook is a fat Muslim and the *ayah* is a genius. She washes and irons my clothes with amazing speed. All three in residence, are also plants of the government.

---

*Heating stove in the bedroom.

Not made a single Chinese friend in twelve months. Not possible to do so. We were never asked to go to any Chinese home, couldn't speak to anyone on the telephone. No telephone directory. Couldn't call anyone for a drink, or lunch or dinner. No informal social contact whatsoever. One needs inner resources to be on mental even-keel.

The Rectification campaign distressed me. I'm sympathetic to the Chinese experiment (not that they seem to care one way or the other) but the recantations, the reporting of private conversations, the duplicity, etc. I find these so disagreeable. So much has been done but the road of their progress was paved with charred bones and patches of blood, with purges and liquidations.

1 July

A sharp but heavy shower of rain, then humid heat and no electricity to help. The electricity cuts were not infrequent.

I discovered a scorpion in my bath tub, probably came in through the bath window. The problems of running a household can only be compared with the comforts it offers. I hate reptiles, scorpions, and insects. Not many dogs to be seen. The grim story was that they have all been eaten.

I have no contact with my neighbours. They have none with me. They would get into serious trouble if they contacted me.

I went to the NPC in the evening. I had been to that assembly hall before. The NPC session itself was dull. Bo Yibo[25] was mumbling away and the others, a thousand-odd were fanning their boredom away. The standing committee was on the dais, with Chu Teh, Liu Shao Chi, Chou En-lai in bush shirts. Soong Ching-ling was there too. The NPC is important in its own way. The heavyweights are all present. On the opening day Mao Tse Tung came and sat in the back row on the dais. I had to go to the NPC a second time to get the text of the speeches.

Dinner at the embassy for Soviet Ambassador Pissarev to Mongolia. He spoke no English. The dinner was a bit of a farce. The Vietnamese ambassador, who at the best of times looked as if he just escaped a fatal accident, turned up without his wife and never bothered to let us know. Then the Russian minister did not come, but he had a good reason; Chou En-lai had shown up at their embassy. The Albanian ambassador did not show up because he had not returned from his walk. The Bulgarian ambassador said he was having 'women problem' and could not come. Dinner lacked conversational sparkle. The films we showed were very good – *Kashmir* and *Darjeeling*.

4 July

Panikkar[26] of the commerce ministry arrived for our trade exhibition. The bus made in India too arrived. This morning we took a ride and succeeded in persuading the ambassador to join us. Reluctantly he agreed. He got down soon but Mrs Nehru stayed on. We all ended up at Pai's house. I walked back home. Mao came to the exhibition. Sat in the bus. I lighted his cigarette. Panu Guha said, 'Preserve the match stick.'

5 July

The Hundred Flowers are wilting. The dawn was turning into darkness. The recantations and confessions continued and the whole thing stank and seemed to be taking a very sinister turn. Private conversations of two decades ago were brought to light and discussed. Sons were denouncing parents. Shades of Orwell's *1984*. The intellectuals and other Rightist were being rounded up. Mela Chang too disappeared. My Chinese teacher, Dean Chang was downcast but said nothing.

In the Soviet Union, the old guard has been eliminated for not following the instructions of the twentieth party congress. The last of the Stalinists gone. A gesture due after Hungary. V.M. Molotov[27], G.M. Malenkov[28] and Lazer Kaganovich[29], all three sacked. Not likely to be shot. Molotov has been sent as ambassador to Mongolia.

Visited Prof Mahanalobis[30] of the Planning Commission. He was here as a guest of the government with his wife. A forthright and interesting man. Pessimistic about the implementation of our Five Year Plan. Said that the Chinese were ahead of us. Their implementation was first-rate. I asked him what we were doing about birth control in India. He said nothing except putting up posters in English in the large cities and advertisements in *The Statesman*. He said if things did not improve then a hundred Nehrus could not save us. He said that the plan was being sabotaged at each step. He also said that the Chinese statistics were not always reliable. He pointed out the great weakness of the IFS was on the economic side. No economic research, no economic reporting. 'Any fool can write a political report.' I liked that. Mahanalobis is a Cambridge man. I did not inflict Forster on him.

I am liking this comfortable house. If only one did not have to deal with fused bulbs, the wrong kind of electric iron, the buying of stores and the checking of accounts, it would have been a bliss. Is marriage the answer? The other day Han Suyin was here for several hours.

Yesterday we showed the film, *Gautam Buddha*, to some of the Buddhist diplomats and to our staff. I thought it was a great piece of work. Pictures made out of stills and yet so animated. But the commentary was of poor quality. How many of us realise that Buddhism was the religion of China for centuries? Only last week I visited a sight not too far from Beijing, where I saw huge Buddha statues carved out in the hills. A magnified Mahabalipuram.

No rain in Peking. Shanghai has had a downpour. Meera and I are to accompany the ambassador to Mongolia to attend the National Day Celebrations.

6 July

Accompanied the ambassador to the airport to receive President Ho Chi Minh.[31] He was in transit. Although we have no diplomatic relations with North Vietnam, we do have something to do with them. There was a fair gathering at the airport. Lots of flags. Many Vietnamese were present.

Ho Chi Minh was received by Chu Teh, Liu Shao Chi, Chou En-lai and others. Ho is a dear old man with a very pleasant and smiling face and a thinning beard. Short, small eyes, and spoke English. Was simply dressed, bush coat and uncreased trousers and chappals. Greeted all with folded hands. It is said he was a pro-Soviet. Perhaps.

Mr Yudin, the Russian ambassador also came out of the plane. Yudin got out quietly and walked to his car, which was parked by the side of the plane. He had apparently gone to Hanoi to convey to Ho the decisions of the Soviet government on the sacking of Molotov, Malenkov and Kagonovich.

7 July

Our departure to Mongolia was not definite. Yesterday at the airport I committed a diplomatic faux pas. Told a Korean diplomat that we were visiting his country. Thought he was a Mongolian. The North Korean was at once surprised and pleased. But I corrected the mistake immediately.

Another aspect of the Rectification campaign has unfolded. The anti-waste and anti-conservatives movement. The culmination is in the endless stream of old newspapers hanging like washed linen in all institutions. Even the roads are not been spared. This is probably the best possible use of old newspapers, they are being used as notice boards. I wonder if this is productive labour. Imagine the amount of hours wasted in producing these wall papers. What do they contain? The usual clap-trap about self-criticism, confessions. It's the Boy Scout and MRA mentality. In a more extreme form, but far superior in organisation. Cities are sending thousands to work in the countryside. All government offices too are sending their men. My friend Tsung from the Foreign Office is now at the Ming Tomb reservoir. Diplomats are to go to this reservoir to see it being constructed but at the last minute Chou put his foot down. This is combining theory with practice. In some ways New China is remarkably new. No one talked of losing face. Yesterday at the Russia-China football match, Sia Yen, the vice-minister came and sat down in the public stand, without any fuss and nobody even noticed him.

Met Madam Tan at lunch. Surprisingly I have not met her before. At seventy-five she retained her old world poise and grace with remarkable ease. Poor woman, fate could not have been more unkind to her. It was a far cry from the the Manchu days to Mao's China. Gen Tan, her husband died without getting a bed in the Peking University Medical College. They had shared their lives for the past fifty years and now it is all over. How utterly lonely must the Manchu princess feel. She has nothing to do with politics. She was paying for her noble birth. In a country, which was trying to abolish nostalgia, she reminded one of the past. She now gave lessons in French. Most western embassies kept her going. Spoke excellent English.

Ulan Bator
11:20 pm
9 July

Mongolia. Ulan Bator. The world of Chengis and Kubla. A vast land mass, juxtaposed between Russia and China. One million people live in an area equal to the UK, Germany, France and Spain combined.

I'm excited. The first Rajasthani to visit this remote country. Meera Malik and I left Beijing early in the morning. Flying after one year. Missed seeing the Great Wall. Flight bumpy. Gobi desert below us. Forbidding, treeless. Paths like phantoms, start at a point, get lost in the parched earth; red and bleak. Surprising to see patches of water.

After nearly two hours the clouds parted, the mist disappeared and out popped Ulan Bator, the capital of Mongolia. Green and beautiful, like the meadows of England. No runway. The airfield was full of cattle – grazing cattle. The pilot brought the plane down very low to scare away the cattle. A novel experience. Landed on the second attempt. Bumpy, cold and windy. We got out in our overcoats. Received by a gentleman who later turned out to be the Czech ambassador. Poor man. First Afghanistan and now Mongolia. The airport building consisted of two pre-fab rooms. An aimless and rather unending wait at the airport. More people trickled in to receive us and the Chinese ambassador to Mongolia. He had been to Beijing for consultations.

Later the Mongolian chief of protocol arrived. Meera and I, the Vietnamese ambassador, all put in one car. It reminded me of our Ambassador cars. The road to town was narrow. Our driver drove at break-neck speed. Suddenly there was a sharp noise like a gun shot. The driver opened his window and looked down at the tyre, one hand on the steering wheel and one foot on the accelerator. I shouted, 'There is a car coming from the other side.' He paid no heed. The car from the opposite direction was coming nearer. I closed my eyes. Our man at the last moment managed to avoid a collision. There was a tyre burst. Our man kept on driving. He finally stopped. We got into the car behind us and reached the guest house.

Lunch problems – due to linguistic hurdle. Kumis – fermented milk of a mare offered. We declined. I had a nice view from my room of Ulan Bator. A stream flows in front of the guest house. Lots of Yurts visible. We visited the Ulan Bator museum in the afternoon. Disappointing. The city was clean. A sort of miniature version of Moscow, especially the main square. Portraits of Lenin, Stalin all round the small Red Square. Equestrian statue of Mongol hero, Sukhe Bator in the middle.

Ulan Bator is a combination of Ruritania, Shangri-la, Communism, latent Buddhism and Lamaism. It is like a place you have never seen. Mongolia, first Socialist state in Asia. Lenin just took over Mongolia in 1921. The Soviets have done a lot, but the city had only one main road. An unreal world; a peculiar mixture of nomads and machines. Pace of life, very slow. Nothing happens unless one pushes.

After dinner we asked for coffee with milk. Three large glasses of Kumis produced. But they were doing their best to look after us. Cold enough for central heating, which has been put on for our benefit. For Mongolians this was summer. In the evening concert by Russian ensemble. The theatre was small. Mongolian audience in uninhibited rapture.

Our driver is a genius. We would, I hoped, outlive his driving.

10 July

Another cloudy and windy day. The little trickle of water has become a stream due to heavy rain. The bridge was cute but rickety. I climbed upto the Heros monument behind the Guest House. Panoramic view of Ulan Bator and beyond. The horizon seemed so very far away.

Totally cut off from everywhere. Not possible to get news. Heard a faint BBC announcer that Aga Khan[32] was dead. Then the static hit. No more BBC.

Ambassador expected at 10:00 am. The Foreign Office man was definite. The laundry came back pressed but not washed. A visit to the bank, cashed drafts. Manager in Mongolian dress. Very friendly. The Foreign Office man was rather strange. When I asked the manager if I could take his picture under that of Prime Minister Tsedenbal,[33] he said no, it was 'too political'.

On our return from the bank we were told to proceed to the airport. Ambassador was arriving. Our maniac driver was in a great hurry. We were allotted a small Skoda. When we got to the airport we were this time told that the ambassador was not coming. We later learnt that he had not even left Peking. No way we could telephone Peking. Just waited.

I ran into a British communist writer, Ivor Montegue. He has written a book on Mongolia, *The Land of the Blue Sky*. He was also an authority on table tennis. Visited the most well-known Buddhist monastery. Many sutras from India were preserved. Not too many people visited the monastery. Four or five Mongolian priests chanted in Pali. The chief abbot took us to his yurt. Luxurious. Thick carpets. Heating gadgets. He offered us kumis. Nothing would make me drink this horrible liquid.

Buddhism came to Mongolia on horseback. The extreme cold preserves tankhas and sutras written on small bits of wood and palm leaf. I know so little about Buddhism. Life in these monasteries must be very dull and lonely. The extreme cold lasts nine months. One sees horses all over the place. On them the Mongols conquered half the existing world. They built an empire but neglected to build a nation.

Ambassador arrived in the afternoon. Not amused at the non-VIP reception. It was for me so cold that even with my overcoat on, I was shivering. The ambassador thought this undignified. How does one look dignified when one is shivering? Ambassador has been given a young Mongolian interpreter, translates Mongolian into Hindi. She learnt her Hindi in Moscow! She knew Russian well. All Mongolians did infact.

Reception by the foreign minister at the Foreign Office. Big room with heavy furniture. Obviously brought from Moscow. The foreign minister spoke French and Russian. Few Mongolians speak Chinese.

Rumour spread that Molotov was in town. I talked to the second secretary of the Soviet Embassy. Here one gets a pleasant feeling of unreality, everything reminds one of something else, somewhere else. The fifteenth century rubs shoulders with the twentieth, as it does in India. The Mongolians were so friendly and wanted us to be friendly. But in which language?

We all went to the theatre in the evening in the Red Square. Marshal Budyonny[34] was the guest of honour. Handle bar moustache. Lots of medals. The show was ordinary. Lots of speeches. Lots of uninhibited Mongolian clapping. Budyonny was representing Soviet Union for National Day on 11 July 1957.

Had a look at Mongolian president – old and distinguished-looking but a figure head. Meera and I too were seated in the VIP box. Felt quite important. The cultural programme was unexciting.

11 July (National Day)

We all arrived at the Red Square early. Leaders laid wreaths at the statue of Sukhe Bator. Then the parade followed. Red Square looked very festive and full of people, some standing, some sitting. The Mongolian interpreter was getting on the ambassador's nerves. She kept talking to him about *striling* and *puling*![35]

In the afternoon we went to see Mongolian wrestling. All VIP guests, including Mongolian leaders and Russians were present. Marshal Budyonny, of course, was very much there. The Mongolians are great wrestlers, well-built, looked slightly sinister when they went for each other. The *akhara* looked the same as the Indian ones. I noticed the wrestlers wearing a strange vest, which only covered the back and left the chest and stomach bare. I asked the Foreign Officer for an explanation. Many centuries ago, there was a national wrestling competition. All wrestlers wore vests, which covered their bodies above the waist. The winner turned out to be a woman. That was too much for the men. To ensure that such an insulting thing never happened again, a new vest was designed to eliminate women participation in any national wrestling events.

The last function was a reception by Shamsrangin Sambu, chairman (president) of the Presidium of the Great Peoples Hural, Parliament. A Russian came up to me, shook hands and said, 'Raj Kapoor Kharashaw.'[36] Meera and I returned to Peking by train. We had to change trains at Mongol – China border as the gauges of Russian and Chinese trains are not the same.

I very much appreciate the ambassador giving me this opportunity to see Mongolia. An unforgettable experience. Letters from Manjit[37], Panchi Samode, Sagarie, Mandy.[38] Most welcome.

20 July

Rectification in full swing. Confessions, self-criticism became more frequent and sinister. Not an agreeable experience at all.

17 September

The venerable, nonagenarian, versatile painter of birds and shrimps and much more died yesterday aged ninety-seven. I'm so glad that I met him. The funeral committee with Chou En-lai and Kuo Mo Jo and Mei Lan Fang has been announced. No one actually knew how old Master Chih was, but it was generally accepted that he certainly was well over ninety. I was indeed fortunate to have met him once.

Vice-President Dr S. Radhakrishnan is to arrive this evening. He could not take off from Saigon. I have been deputed to discuss some bits of his programme with Wai Chiao Pu and Chung Nan Hai at Dream Palace where Chairman Mao and his colleagues lived. We now know that the vice-president will arrive the next day via Hong Kong, by special Air India plane. He will be staying as Mao's guest at Chung Nan Hai. His son S. Gopal and Jagat Mehta[39], the deputy secretary in the ministry dealing with China will accompany him.

18 September

The vice-president arrived in a special Air India aircraft from Hong Kong. He was received at the airport by Marshal Chu Teh, Liu Shao Chi, Chou En-lai, Soong Ching-ling, Chen Yi, Peng Chen, Ho Lung. Big crowd with welcome colourful banners. Chu Teh and our vice-president stood on the platform to make speeches. From another platform Pai translated. In his short speech, the vice-president asked his hosts to remember lessons of the past, practise moderation and seek virtue and righteousness.

From the airport he drove to Chung Nan Hai. I was attached to his delegation. The vice-president's right hand finger was heavily bandaged. It was crushed by a car door in Cambodia. All speculation about Mao Tse Tung not being in Peking to receive him, died down. The chairman returned to Peking last evening. I too am staying in Chung Nan Hai.

The vice-president has abandoned his turban. He had a black, round beret-on, wearing a black *achkan* and trousers. Looked impressive. At the banquet given by Mao, the chairman paid him the highest culinary compliment. With the chopsticks he was eating with, he picked up a morsel and put it in Dr Radhakrishnan's plate. The vice-president was a strict vegetarian. He managed to deal with the situation without making Mao feel uncomfortable. Also present on the table were Liu Shao Chi, Chou En-lai, Deng Xiaoping, Chu Teh, Kuo Mo Jo, Soong Ching-ling. The vice-president spent a few minutes talking to Soong Ching-ling. They had met in New Delhi in late 1955. The decorations on the main table were eye-catching. Superb food. Fifteen courses. Incidentally Han Suyin, who was back in Peking, was also invited to the Mao banquet.

Speeches in China are given at the beginning of the meal. The vice-president as usual spoke without notes. He praised Mao and his dynamic faith in non-dogmatic Marxism and added, 'Under your leadership socialism will become democratic and humanistic.' Hope springs eternal. He also spoke to the National Peoples' Congress. The turnout was modest. The tone was philosophical and a little didactic. He spoke about democracy and its impact on socio-economic and international affairs. He preached humanism and gentleness of conduct. He also praised Chinese discipline. The vice-president's speeches were not fully covered in the press. The *People's Daily* carried his photos with Mao and others on the front page, but speeches were drastically edited. Gopal gave me copies of the full text to, 'pass on to the Reuters' man'. I managed to give them to David Chipp.

The meeting with Mao was held in the chairman's study. I too smuggled myself in. Not quite. The Chinese knew I was attached to the delegation and staying at Chung Nan Hai. But I did commit an outrage. I took my camera in and took pictures. Here, I think I crossed the line. The talks with Mao included reference to Taiwan, Indo-China, Korea and Vietnam. Dr Radhakrishnan said if China and India worked together, the world would take note. Mao replied that this was true but that some countries did not like that. He said he was not worried about Korea or Vietnam, but Japan was another matter and saw Japanese militarism rising with the help of the USA. The vice-president asked Chairman Mao his views on coexistence to which Mao replied that he believed in it. The vice-president then came up with a complicated analysis of coexistence. Mao appeared perplexed. The vice-president said that the Taiwan problem would be solved peacefully. Time was on the side of China. Chairman Mao said he was willing to wait one hundred years.

Dr Radhakrishnan was received in the courtyard of Mao's house. After shaking hands, the vice-president patted Mao Tse Tung on the cheek. The chairman was taken aback. No one in China patted him anywhere. The vice-president was quick to put the chairman at ease by saying, 'Mr Chairman, don't be alarmed. I did the same thing to Stalin and the Pope.'

The visit was important. It could not have gone better. The philosopher carried himself well. His meetings with the top leaders were marked by respect for him. Kuo Mo Jo was quiet effusive. For me it was an interesting week. To be present at such meetings at the topmost level is no ordinary occasion. I like being at the centre of things, even though I just sat and took notes!

4 October

Great excitement The Russians have launched a space gadget called Sputnik. Ashok Bhadkamkar took some of us outside the city, with binoculars to spot the Sputnik, but it was cloudy and we saw nothing. The Chinese press, full of this Russian achievement. I'm a dud when it comes to science. But man-made flying objects in space is something to celebrate. No doubt the Americans must have been spending sleepless nights.

6 October

Drove to Ming tombs. Here in ancient days, Chinese emperors were buried. I was the only person at the sight. The road leading to the tombs was lined on both sides with huge statues of sitting elephants.

8 October

Went to Pei Hai park with Han Suyin. Climbed the Coal hill. Splendid view of the city. Most of the time she spoke about Vincent Ratnaswamy and her book on Nepal, which she was writing. I did not know what she did most of the time. She said that she travelled a lot. I took that with a pinch of salt.

1-8 November

Chairman Mao left for Moscow to attend the fortieth anniversary of the 1917 Russian Revolution. I was also present at the military airport. He was wearing a khakhi sola hat – reminiscent of his Yennan days. He shook hands with all the diplomats who came to see him off. The entire diplomatic corps were not invited, except the Socialists and Bandung countries. Chairman Mao's delegation included Marshal Peng Te Huai and the party's General Secretary Teng Hsiao Ping (Deng Xiaoping).

Peking is in a celebratory mood. Posters, pictures and slogans. Pei Ta is going overboard. Papers full of chairman Mao's Moscow stay and his programme here. He is outshining the Soviet leadership.

7 December

We have had a most interesting lesson to do this morning at the Peking University. It was in many ways symptomatic of what went on in the mind of a communist and how an awareness of national reconstruction was inculcated in virgin and uncritical minds. The lesson we did was about the bridge over the Yellow River.

The bridge spoke in the first person and described the neglect and pilferage it underwent under the KMT[40] (I don't doubt that for a moment) and how wonderful things were today (little doubts as far as the looking after of the bridge goes) but the Americans brought in the shape of moneymaking exploiters. To us the whole thing sounded and appeared absurd in the extreme, but I could well imagine a young Chinese boy reacting to it.

We have now been going to the Peita[41] for the past three months. I confess, I did not very much enjoy the first two months as they were given with the teachings of grammar, which was largely invented by the Peita itself for the benefit (should I not say the torture) of the foreign students. I never really got the hang of it and never did well in any of the weekly tests, but I feel none the worse for it. Now we are on solid ground and doing proper Chinese, and I'm no longer at sea.

We saw very little or nothing of the Chinese students at the Peita, which was such a pity. And yet, I would never have believed that such total compartmentalisation between the Chinese and the foreign students could be possible, but it was. Even the foreign students who resided in the university saw almost nothing of their Chinese colleagues, except for the teachers and the Fu Tao Yuan, invariably all the Youth Leagues or the party members. We had an Italian in our class, son of a prominent Italian communist who provided distraction by his linguistic antics.

In our department, there were as many teachers as there were students. The teachers were all young and took themselves terribly seriously. But our latest two were quite remarkable. The lady for the humour she aroused, and the man for the respect he evoked, with his gentle manners and soft voice. They all led Spartan lives and got paid a pittance. Yet they put their heart and soul in their work. It's all for the party, all for building a New China. None of our teachers spoke English. Some of them knew Russian, but that was of no help to us. My Chinese has vastly improved.

Just as we joined the university, the Cheng Feng Yun Dung was on its last spectacular and visual lap. The movement started in Peita with a condemnation of the Communist Party and the system, and ended by a monumental and sinister criticism of the Rightists and the critics of the system. Suddenly Mao changed track. Hundred Flowers withered. So did the Hundred schools. All opposition died down, most recanted, some did not and suffered daily public humiliation and criticism, one or two attempted suicide. The wall papers told their own tales and seemed to me a novel and strange way of carrying on a campaign of such importance.

I remember asking one of the young teachers if writing out all these huge posters, and then pasting them on the walls and then replying to them, was in any way remotely connected with the teachings of Marx or Lenin. Did she, as an intelligent person, consider this as a productive and worthy pastime for grown-up people: most of whom were teachers, they could surely meet in a room and thrash out their difficulties.

She did not, at first, understand what I was driving at. Later she hinted that my thinking was all wrong. The posters were of great value and afforded an opportunity to let off steam. It then dawned on me that it was almost impossible to put one's finger on what was going on in China, unless one thought as a communist did. I didn't. In so many ways the New China is new, in fact and deed. Not only in name.

The hangover from the past was there but there had been a fundamental change in so many aspects. The family was broken up, superstition gone, exploitation gone. Replaced by social justice and an equality of the kind never known and accepted here. It has been achieved in record time. A lot of people have been killed mercilessly. Like Stalin, Mao held the view that revolution is not an invitation for dinner. The price tag is blood, broken bones and much worse.

The Peita campus is beautiful, weeping willows all over. Had been a seat of learning and scholarship. Today both seem to suffer. It seemed more interested in producing ardent communists and red patriots rather than true scholars and academicians. Education was completely controlled and the students were subjected to the discipline of a primary school and lived very hard lives: To get up at 6:30 am, meagre breakfast. Classes began at 7:45 am. Meera, Bhutani and I too reached there at that hour. My Volkswagen was a great blessing. The central heating only started on 1 December 1956. For us, they had it on by 10 November.

The Chinese students had all their meals standing, as there were no chairs (agreed, that the Chinese way of taking food is such that it does not really matter whether one eats sitting or standing). They had their afternoon meal at 12 noon. Again in the afternoon more classes. Some sort of exercise in the late afternoon, no bath in winters and to cap it all, political meetings after dinner. Lights out at 10. How many of us in India can put up with this rigorous life for long?

Most of the students were government scholarship holders and got very little money to spend on luxuries. But they passed out hardened and dedicated men and not as softies.

In the evening we went to the station. The ashes of the late Dr M. Atal[42] were leaving for India. We had been decidedly aloof on this occasion. The least I would have expected, was to send the ashes by air. But the ambassador probably had good reasons for not doing so.

There was no doubt that the passing away of Dr Atal has been used by the Chinese for political ends. Chou En-lai turned up at his cremation. They tried their best for us to fall for their bait. I'm prepared to give them credit for taking care of an old friend. Many of them had genuine fondness for Dr Atal. He could not have died in a better place. He was the one, who at Yunnan, fixed Chou's broken right arm. In India, he was a forgotten man. The PM's condolence telegram saved a lot of face on our side.

10 December

I'm still in the hospital. I have been here by a week today. Came here on the third, with a nasty throat infection. As usual I let my imagination run amok. Imagined all the most dangerous throat diseases that existed. It turned out to be an inflammation of the fourth tonsil. Only children catch this infection. So there you have it. The first four days were pretty bad, I was really ill, and after every four hours the pretty nurses came and poured penicillin into my hips, twenty injections in total. I was very well looked after. Too well and too often fed. They feed you by Russian standards. I had stayed on to have a thorough check-up. It led to the most humiliating indignities being practiced on me. But it was worth it. I shed my amoeba and there was nothing wrong with me, except my conjunctivitis.

The language difficulty created the most unexpected (well, not so unexpected) situations. Hsio Pien and Ta Pien was just one of them. Then the urologist and his prostrate test just about got my goat. I tried to object in my not-so-broken-Chinese. He responded in English!

I have read considerably, Harold Nicholson's *Good Behaviour*, Compton Mackenzie's *Thin Ice*, Robert Payne's *Mao Tse Tung*, Somerset Maugham's *Cakes and Ale*.

Mela traced me to the hospital. Speaking Chinese and Russian fluently, she talked her way in. She is the most ravishingly beautiful woman I have ever seen. Great to have shared intimate moments with her.

I felt lonely and for the first time realised the value of people who donate, to build hospitals and others who work in the hospitals. The other great realisation has been the wonderful and courageous way my mother has suffered all these years. I salute her. Those unending years of pain, suffering and loneliness. What monumental courage and patience. Never again shall I be impatient with her; never again will I talk of her being removed to a hospital just for the sake of peace and comfort for herself. How could I ever be so selfish and base? We are all that she has, everything else she has given up for the four of us.

Diary—1958

20-26 January 1958

The ambassador and Smt Rajan Nehru have departed. Many farewell parties. He was being received by Chairman Mao in Canton.

A very special day for me. I'm acting as an interpreter at the reception at the Peking Hotel. It is Republic Day. We held a reception at the Peking Hotel. Premier Chou En-lai was the chief guest. I spent the better part of last night mugging up the chargé d'affaires speech. He would speak in English. I translated sentence by sentence in Chinese. I was both excited and tensed, slightly nervous. Not stage shy. Mercifully I did not let the side down. Many came to congratulate me, including the Chinese leaders. Pai was such a good Chinese interpreter and such a scholar. Following him was not an easy act. I could not equal him, not in a dozen years. Nevertheless, I passed the debut test. I was relieved; so are my generous colleagues who helped me.

1 February

Early morning to Peita. At 1:15 pm, accompanied CDA to see Prime Minister Chou En-lai. I took down notes. Meeting lasted for nearly forty-five minutes. Chou understood English well. He also spoke it once in a while. The more I stay here the more I realise that the future of Asia is going to be decided here and India shall have the closest relations with China. We need each other far too much and little differences should not come in the way of our friendship. I'm, for one, quite convinced that the Chinese have no territorial ambitions in our part of the world*. We have no large overseas Chinese population to bother about. The offshoot of this was that, I must know my Chinese language thoroughly.

The Americans have at last succeeded in launching a Sputnik, 30 lb, 6 ft in diameter, 19 thousand per hour. It would do them some good but it was likely to turn their heads and we would again hear that silly phrase of parleying from strength.

The three Rightist ministers Chang Po Chun, Chang Nai Chi and Lo Lung have got the sack finally. The *Peoples' Daily* and other papers carried the news. I wonder what these chaps will do! But they got away with their heads and here, hats off to the Chinese genius: communists they may be but they have not repeated a 1936-39 Russia purges. Stalin killed so many of his comrades. They have a better sense of history than the Russians.

I have had an unexpected raise last month. I see that as time goes by, the flesh gets weaker and weaker and the capacity to deny oneself any comfort or cash gets numbed by and by. I hope I shall be able to prevent this decay. Extraordinary how the environment effects one. I work in a set up where the material things count for most and I live in a country where people live Spartan and stoic lives, and really sweat for their bread.

23 February

Morse cast brought news of the death of Maulana Azad.[1]

31 March

Telegram from Han Suyin – 'Father deceased.' She would be arriving in Beijing on 10 April. Please contact me. C/O Tradinvest Hong Kong.

---

* How wrong I was; 1962 was only four years away.

10 April

I received Han Suyin at the airport and took her to the hotel. We spoke about her father. It was a sad reunion.

I passed my Chinese examination, both oral and written. I really worked hard. I have not done brilliantly, but well enough.

15 April – 1 May

I'm getting ready for my final departure from Beijing. On transfer to Delhi. Busy packing. Saying farewells, attending parties. Have disposed off my radio and record player. Also my car.

Much talk of the Great Leap Forward. I shall not see it implemented. Saw Lao Sheh, author of the famous novel, *The Rickshaw Boy*. Lived in great comfort.*

2 May

The goodbyes have been said. The departure time has arrived. I'm sad to leave. I liked Peking, with all its drawbacks. Saw history on a big scale being made by big men. Glad, because I shall see my parents after nearly two years. In some ways I have grown up. Left Peking for Hong Kong by train in the afternoon.

4 May

Had lunch with Suyin at the Peninsula Hotel. Took a ride in a train to go up to Victoria Peak in Hong Kong. Beautiful day. We were almost alone. A heavenly view of the harbour. I made a rather unoriginal remark – 'Here we get the peace that passeth all understanding.' Suyin made a vital addition – '... the peace that passeth all misunderstanding.'

---

* Committed suicide during the Cultural Revolution.

Part Two

*Premier Chou En-lai's
Visit to India
20-26 April 1960*

Prefatory Note

On my return from China in May 1958, I was allotted a nondescript administrative post in the ministry as under secretary. There I stayed for almost two years. My job had nothing even remotely to do with China.

In March 1959, I escorted the new batch of IFS probationers to meet the prime minister in his South Block office. Half way through the meeting, S. Dutt[1], the foreign secretary came in and whispered in the PM's ear. His expression changed ever so slightly. He announced that something urgent had come up in the Parliament and he got up to leave. The probationers were naturally disappointed. Later we learnt that His Holiness The Dalai Lama had crossed into India.

The Chinese government took a very hostile view of our giving His Holiness asylum. It was impossible for a communist regime to either appreciate, or try to understand, our traditional values. How could any Government of India refuse asylum to the most well-known and respected Buddhist in the world?

Jawaharlal Nehru made a most persuasive and statesman-like speech in the Lok Sabha on 27 April 1959. Quite rightly so. He had been greatly distressed by the 'tone and charges made against India by responsible people in China. They have used the language of the cold war regardless of truth and propriety. This is peculiarly distressing in a great nation with thousands of years of culture behind it, noted for its restrain and polite behaviour. The charges made against India are so fantastic that I find it difficult to deal with them.'

The speeches made in the National People's Congress in Peking were command performances and did little credit to those responsible for them. India and the Dalai Lama were attacked with unseemly verbal excesses.

Nehru clearly laid down the broad outlines of his China-Tibet policy: (1) Preservation of the security and integrity of India; (2) Desire to maintain friendly relations with China; (3) Deep sympathy for the people of Tibet.

> 'That policy we shall continue to follow because we think it is a correct policy not only for the present but even more so for the future... The Five Principles (Panchsheel) have laid down inter alia, mutual respect for each other...'

In the same speech he referred to his talks with Prime Minister Chou En-lai in 1956-57.

> '... He was good enough to discuss Tibet with me at considerable length. He told me that while Tibet had long been a part of the Chinese state, they did not consider Tibet as a province of China. The people were different, from the people of China proper, just as in other autonomous regions of the Chinese state the people were different, even though they formed part of that state. Therefore, they consider Tibet an autonomous region, which would enjoy autonomy. He told me further that it was absurd for anyone to imagine that China was going to force communism in Tibet...'

From the day the Dalai Lama walked into India in late March 1959, the character and content of Sino-Indian relations altered drastically. By the time Chou En-lai came to India in April 1960, the point of no-return had almost been reached.

I had followed the discussions in parliament throughout 1959 with professional interest and some disquiet. The situation in Ladakh took a serious turn, Chinese incursion in NEFA (now Arunachal Pradesh) caused alarm and by September 1959, the Sino-Indian border was no longer tranquil; Jawaharlal Nehru was entering unknown diplomatic territory and menacing foreign policy thickets.

As the only Chinese-speaking IFS official in the ministry, I was appointed liaison officer to Prime Minister Chou En-lai. During the next five days I saw Indian history taking a wrong turn.

20 April 1960

Prime Minister Chou En-lai landed at Palam airport. He flew in from Rangoon, accompanied by Marshal Chen Yi, vice-premier and foreign minister and Deputy Foreign Minister Chang Han Fu.

Prime Minister Nehru had brought several of his Cabinet colleagues to Palam, M/s G.L. Nanda,[2] Morarji Desai,[3] Krishna Menon,[4] Swaran Singh,[5] Jagjivan Ram,[6] Hafiz Mohd. Ibrahim.[7] Some Members of Parliament, left-leaning members were also at the airport. Some diplomats from countries that recognised China were present. There were also several dozen Chinese diplomats and nationals.

Prime Minister Jawaharlal Nehru too was a disillusioned man. He had invested so much, laboured so long to convince the people of India that his vision of amicable and cordial relations with China was the right one and an enduring one. Within six years the Panchsheel euphoria suffered a near lethal blow. His confidence was shaken. Hope was receding. Parliament was becoming involved in an aggressive way.

The welcome was subdued, if not chilly. No 'Hindi-Chini bhai bhai' slogans. Tension was almost visible. Pandit Nehru shook Premier Chou En-lai's hand with distant amiability. Both were high-voltage politicians. Both were charismatic, handsome, self-assured. Both were trying to be cordial but the circumstances were hostile to cordiality.

In his brief speech, Pandit Nehru said that relations between the two countries had been imperilled, confidence was shaken. It would be a difficult task to recover feeling of good faith and friendship. He invoked the Bandung spirit and Panchsheel. He hoped that, 'Our effort will be directed towards undoing much that had happened and thus recover the climate of peace and friendship . . .'

The Chinese prime minister began his response with, 'Your Excellency, Respected and Dear Prime Minister Nehru'. Premier Chou En-lai's speech was translated into Hindi. He saw no reason why problems could not be settled reasonably through friendly consultations in accordance with the Five Principles of Panchsheel. He sounded more optimistic and talked of thousands of years of friendship between, 'our people'. He said that China had always advocated a reasonable settlement of the boundary question and other issues. He had come with a sincere desire to settle all problems.

At the banquet in Rashtrapati Bhawan, there was an air of dejection. Pandit Nehru made a moving speech. The Chinese PM was more practical but no less keen on a reasonable and amicable settlement. For the first time in fourteen years our prime minister was confronted with the darker side of diplomacy.

Meeting with Vice-president Dr S. Radhakrishnan

21 April 1960

After laying a wreath at Gandhiji's Samadhi at Rajghat, PM Chou En-lai accompanied by Marshal Chen Yi, Vice-Minister Chang Han-Fu[1] called on the vice-president at 9:30 am. The meeting lasted till 11:15 am.

The opening remarks of the vice-president were spoken in 'sorrow than in anger'. He first said he was unable to accept the invitation of the Chinese government to visit China last October, because of serious clashes which occurred between the Indian police squad and the Chinese Frontier Guards near Kong La Pass.

The vice-president recalled that in a spirit of friendship India had not taken the Tibet issue to the UN in 1950. The same spirit was reflected in 1954 when the two countries signed the Panchsheel Agreement. The same goodwill was present at Bandung in 1955. A year later the Dalai Lama was persuaded to return to Lhasa by Prime Minister Nehru.

India had been pressing for China's admission to the UN. Even the news of Chinese incursions into Indian territory were not made known to the Parliament or the country. 'All this showed our genuine desire for friendship.' However, when border incidents took place, people of India were indignant. Prime Minister Nehru had advised restraint. In a democracy it was not easy to contain public reactions beyond a point.

The vice-president emphasised that friendship between the two countries was more important than some 'bits of territory'. The very spirit of the Buddha and Gandhi was being injured by recent regrettable border clashes. New territory is being claimed. Old Chinese maps have yet to be revised. This assurance had been given to 'our prime minister'. Dr Radhakrishnan added, 'Nehru is India's greatest leader and China's best friend. Minor problems and unjust claims should not come in the way of friendship.'

Chou En-lai in response said, the fact that he had come all the way from China was ample proof of their desire for friendship. People of both countries desired friendship. He referred to 'so many Indians' visiting the Chinese pavillion at the World Agriculture Fair as proof of the friendly feelings of the Indian people for the Chinese people.

The premier continued that there were historical reasons for the present problems. These were legacies of imperialism. The clash at Kong La Pass was unexpected, otherwise how could China have invited the vice-president only two days earlier. China had stopped sending patrols along the Sino-Indian border.

The vice-president said China had occupied Tibet in 1950. It reached Sinkiang in 1892. Thus there could have been no Chinese presence there, administrative or military. Ladakh was undoubtedly a part of the state of Jammu & Kashmir. Even the British recognised that fact. He went on to suggest that the problem should be solved in the lifetime of Nehru. After him it would become more difficult. There was great resentment in the country, only Nehru could restrain it. 'We do not wish you to return empty-handed. Please try to come to some settlement, in keeping with the self-respect of both countries.'

Premier Chou En-lai stated that China had exercised jurisdiction over Tibet for thirteen hundred years. Tibet became a part of China seven or eight hundred years ago. Sinkiang too has been a part of China. Dr Radhakrishnan said he was not a historian and did not wish to delve into details. Among friends it should not matter if it was necessary to give up some territory here and there. What are a few thousand square miles compared to the friendship of four hundred million Indians? The important thing was for the two people to be close to each other.

Marshal Chen Yi intervened. He held the vice-president in great esteem and therefore listened to him with keen interest. His response was, 'What are few thousand square miles of territory compared to the friendship of six hundred million Chinese?' He was forthright.

He proceeded to say that China, unlike India, had been bullied by a number of imperialist powers. Today's China could not be bullied by the imperialist powers. But when our Indian friends want to bully us, we don't know what to do. He then said China too had individuals like J.P. Narayan, but 'Chinese democracy controlled them'. We invited the vice-president to China to solve this unfortunate issue. This was Premier Chou's fourth visit to India. 'We have come looking for a solution.'

The Americans, he said, had a base in Okinawa, their Seventh Fleet was in Chinese waters. There were threats to China's security. Hence, China desired peace on the Sino-Indian border. 'We do not want to hurt India. We don't want to create two fronts, one against the West and another against India.'

The vice-president said India always opposed imperialism everywhere. In this regard, we had common attitudes. It could be possible to agree upon a solution on the basis of what the prime minister had said the previous night, quoting the Buddha – a victory for all and defeat for none.

Marshal Chen Yi had no doubt that Prime Minister Nehru wanted to settle this problem. The vice-president agreed. The marshal invited him to China. Dr Radhakrishnan accepted in principle.

He then referred to a newspaper report that Premier Chou En-lai looked grave after his discussion with Mr Nehru. 'Ours was a free press and some papers wrote things which were not accurate,' Dr Radhakrishnan added. To this Chou En-lai replied that China did not believe in such freedoms. If he smiled, Indian papers said it was a false smile. If he did not, then he was grave. Marshal Chen Yi drew attention to the Indian papers reporting of their meeting with Krishna Menon. It was not a secret. 'The Indian defence minister's meeting was arranged by the Indian government.' Premier Chou En-lai intervened in mild irritation – China, for the past ten years was busy with internal development. They had not aroused any anti-Indian feelings during this period.

The Chinese PM then went back to what the vice-president had said about China occupying Tibet and Sinkiang. That was not correct. Both were parts of China for centuries. He rather ominously added that if China was accused of occupying Tibet and Sinkiang, then they could say India had occupied Kashmir. The vice-president said this was not correct at all. Kashmir had always been a part of India from the dawn of history. There could be no comparison of Kashmir with Sinkiang and Tibet, which had been acquired recently. He concluded that all problems could be resolved in a spirit of mutual accommodation and friendship. Chou En-lai again said China had no claims on the south of the McMahon Line. Premier Chou asserted that China could not give up territory without any reason or justification. On the eastern sector, no government of China had recognised the 'so-called McMahon Line'. India had got control of the area after Independence. China has not violated the McMahon Line, even though it did not recognise it. China was for maintaining status quo. China has no territorial claims on the south of the McMahon Line. The meeting ended amicably.

On the drive back to Rashtrapati Bhawan, Chou said to me, 'Why am I being lectured on the boundary issue? I was discussing this with your prime minister. I only came to the vice-president for a courtesy call.' I passed this on to G. Parathasarthi.[2]

The temperature, 90.9 degree Fahrenheit. The political temperature, 101 degrees Fahrenheit. Our newspapers, particularly, *The Indian Express*, annoyed the Chinese guests. The cartoons too were verging on the lampooning side. Frank Moraes in today's *The Indian Express* has gone to extreme lengths. On the front page was an eight column headline 'Menon Invited to Intervene in Talks.' Next line, 'Nehru's Disquieting Acquiescence in Chou's Demand'. Chen Yi had specifically mentioned this to the vice-president.

I think the Chinese leaders are making a bit too much of the adverse coverage in the press. It is certainly not flattering, but they should have taken this one-sided reporting in their stride. In China, of course, they do not encounter this democratic hazard.

N.B.

Krishna Menon met Chou En-lai at Rashtrapati Bhawan after lunch. The meeting lasted nearly two hours. No one accompanied Menon. He had to muscle his way in. Pantji had managed to keep him out of the talks. He has inducted Sardar Swaran Singh, who was having discussions with Marshal Chen Yi. Sardar Sahib was not known for his expertise in foreign affairs or diplomacy.

In the evening the Chinese ambassador held a reception at the embassy, Jind House, Lytton Road. Nearly five hundred people had been invited, including the vice-president and the prime minister, senior Cabinet ministers, Indian friends of China, led by Pandit Sundar Lal,[3] diplomats, MPs and journalists and nondescript Leftists.

Meeting with Pandit G.B. Pant

21 April 1960

When we entered the residence of the home minister, there was a large number of people loitering in the extensive compound. The Chinese prime minister asked me if we had come to the wrong house. I assured him we had not. Even in the room where the meeting was held a few strangers were present. I sat in the farthest corner and could not clearly hear what was being said. Subimal Dutt, the Foreign secretary was present. So was Jagat Mehta.

This was what I could catch: The home minister said he was sorry for not being at the airport to receive the prime minister. The two countries had age-old ties and had lived peacefully. The recent events had come as a shock to the government and the people of India. He spoke in anguish. India never expected any problems from China. India had shown solidarity with China's national struggle even before Independence. The Congress party had sent a medical mission to China many years before Independence. India had regularly spearheaded at the UN the case for China being admitted. The prime ministers of India and China together initiated the Five Principles of Panchsheel. These were not being followed.

He assured Premier Chou En-lai that it was wrong to suggest that India had a hand in the revolt in Tibet. The people of India had been disturbed by events in Tibet. India had given asylum to the Dalai Lama because he was held in high esteem. It was also a humanitarian gesture. It should not be misunderstood.

Pantji brought up the Chinese map issue. India had brought up this matter in 1954. We were told those were old maps. They would be revised. But this did not happen. Confidence had been shaken. This had to be restored. Goodwill and friendship need to be restored for mutual benefit. Pantji continued that India had the impression that China had accepted the McMahon Line in 1954. India was not an expansionist nation. We do not covet territory of other nations. We wished China to be prosperous and the well-being of its people. We continued to desire cordial relations with China inspite of the recent unfortunate events on the border.

Premier Chou En-lai was obviously impressed by Pantji's personality and statesman-like presentation. Chou En-lai said China had never recognised the McMahon Line. He wanted the border problem to be settled by negotiations. China had not violated McMahon Line. The premier said China did not accept the Shimla Convention. The fact cannot be denied that India, after Independence moved into areas which were under the jurisdiction of Tibet. China made no claims south of the McMahon Line. China too had sentiments about the Himalayas. The northern parts belonged to China. They constituted a common border. On the western sector he suggested a joint survey. China had just concluded a boundary agreement with Burma after joint surveys. Premier said that he and the vice-premier, Chen Yi had come with sincerity to settle the border problem. They wanted differences to be narrowed and not widened. The feelings of the Chinese people should also be appreciated. He suggested that tension could be reduced if two sides disengaged to avoid further border incidents. Tibet, he said, had been a part of China for more than thirteen hundred years. The Tibetan Revolt was a creation of a few reactionaries who wanted to preserve serfdom.

China did not object to India granting asylum to the Dalai Lama but they objected to his carrying out anti-China activities. He referred to Kalimpong being centre of anti-China activities. Pantji, politely but firmly, disagreed with what Chou En-lai said about Kalimpong. Chou En-lai again said no central government of China had signed or ratified the Shimla Convention of 1913. Both agreed that relations between the two countries be strengthened and good-will restored.

President's lunch for Premier Chou En-lai at Rashtrapati Bhawan – I shall treasure the invitation card.[1]

P.S.: Pantji's return call could not have gone better. He saw Premier Chou En-lai in his suite in Rashtrapati Bhawan and charmed the Chinese leaders by not talking shop. Premier Chou En-lai lauded Pantji's role in the freedom movement. To this the home minister's response was, 'My role in the freedom movement has been exaggerated by generous friends.'

In the lift Pantji said to me, *'Theek tha ki nahin?'* (Was it okay or not?) I humbly agreed. I too was very much impressed by the old man's diplomatic elegance.

Front Row – Premier Chou En-lai, Marshal Chu Teh, Dr. Radhakrishnan, Chairman Mao Tse Tung, Ambassador R.K. Nehru, President Liu Shao Chi.

Second Row – Second from right V.V. Paranjpe, K. Natwar Singh, J.S. Mehta, I.J. Bahadur Singh – September 1957.

The Summer Palace, Peking

Dr Radhakrishnan with Chairman Mao Tse Tung
(photo by the author)

My house in Tung Sung Pu Huntung, Peking.
(now demolished)

Prime Minister Nehru, Premier Chou En-lai, Marshal Chen Yi, Sardar Swaran Singh, New Delhi, 1960.

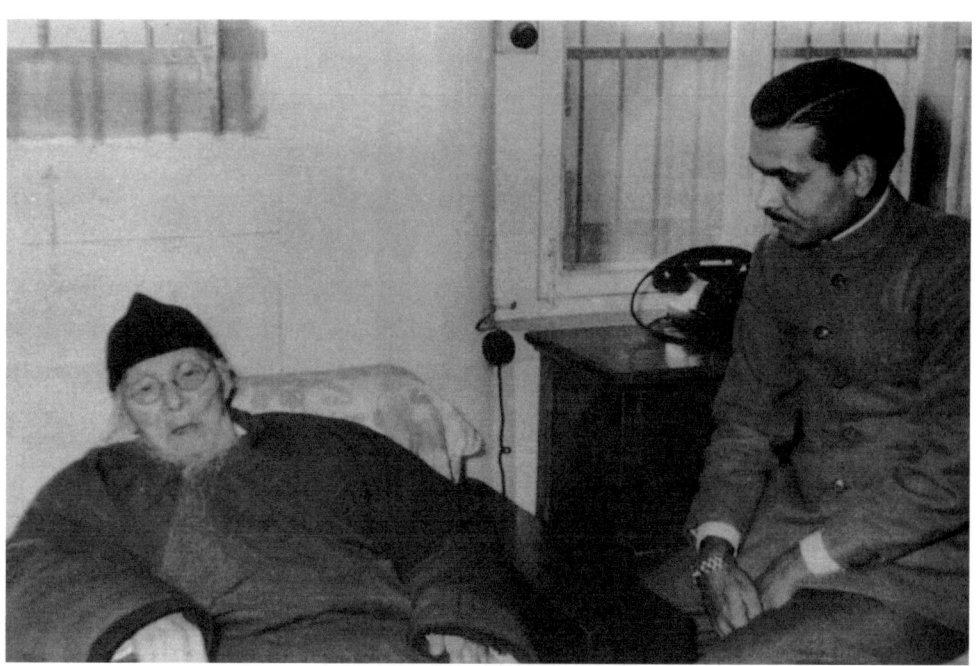

Ninety-six year old Chih Pai Shih and the author, Peking, 1956.

Prime Minister Jawaharlal Nehru speaking at his banquet for Premier Chou En-lai, sitting in a grim mood, next to Indira Gandhi 20 April 1960.

Author with Madam Soong Ching-ling also known as Madam Sun Yat-sen, in New Delhi, December 1955.

Deng Xiaoping with the author while Mr P.V. Narasimha Rao and Dinesh Singh look on.

In honour of His Excellency
Mr. Chou En-Lai,
Prime Minister of the
People's Republic of China.

Shri Natwar Singh

The Prime Minister

requests the pleasure of your company

at a Banquet

at Rashtrapati Bhavan

at 8-30 p.m. on Wednesday, the 20th April, 1960.

An answer is requested
to the Invitation Branch,
Rashtrapati Bhavan,
New Delhi.

为欢迎印度共和国副总统萨·拉达克里希南博士访华订于1957年9月19日（星期四）下午6时在北京饭店宴会厅举行酒会敬请

光 临

周 恩 來

Surprisingly this survived.
Invitation from Premier Chou En-Lai, 19 September 1957.

Chairman Mao welcoming President Voroshilov of the USSR, Peking, 1957.
(photo by the author)

Han Suyin, Peking, 1956
(photo by the author)

Mela Chang, Peking, 1957.

K. Natwar Singh, Prime Minister Rajiv Gandhi, Mrs Sonia Gandhi and Mr P.V. Narasimha Rao in fur-cap, Peking, 1988.

Chairman Mao Tse Tung
(photo by the author)

R.K. Nehru's Meeting with Premier Chou En-lai

21 April 1960

After an early dinner, I was reading Han Suyin's novel, '... *And the Rain My Drink*' when my telephone rang. I was to present myself at Rashtrapati Bhawan at 10:15 pm. Shri and Smt R.K. Nehru were calling on Prime Minister Chou En-lai at 10:30 pm.

The meeting between them ended at 1:00 am. I was by then deadbeat. I was the sole note-taker at this nocturnal meeting. At other meetings there was Jagat Mehta and one or two others. During the meeting with Vice-President, Pantji and Morarji Desai, I resorted to my own longish short-hand. For the R.K. Nehru meeting, I took down fairly extensive notes. The first forty-five minutes were spent on developments in Africa and West Asia.

Both Chou En-lai and Chen Yi were impressively well-informed about the latest events in both the countries. R.K. Nehru had his say. He too was up-to-date on Egypt and West Asia. He asked Prime Minister Chou En-lai to give his views on the upsurge in Africa. Chou En-lai said both nations had been steeled through experience to become free. In the next forty years of the twentieth century, imperialism would totally disappear although colonialists would try to hold out. But they are bound to fail particularly in the context of world politics and the development of science and technology, which would help nationalism.

The ambassador said that bearing this in mind, India, China and other countries must remain friends and nothing should be done to undermine this friendship. To this Prime Minister Chou En-lai replied, 'In the past year unfortunate events, some differences and misunderstandings had occurred between India and China. We must exert our joint efforts to dispel this dark cloud and it was now the great moment to do so. You have not been in China at this time and it is unfortunate that all this should have occurred when the new ambassador took over. We maintain that all that has happened is not what we expected. But it was a logical outcome of the revolt in Tibet and the coming of the Dalai Lama to India.'

Ambassador Nehru said that he was out of touch with events in China and Tibet but since his return to India, he had become aware of the deep shock which the people of India had experienced. The vast majority of the people wanted friendship with China, but friendship was only possible if each country respected the vital interests, rights and the national dignity of the other. The shock of Indian opinion was natural and Prime Minister Nehru had expressed it in moderate terms. Ambassador Nehru said he did not wish to go into details, but he was expressing the general feelings of people of India.

Chou En-lai said, 'In China, the Chinese have received just as much shock as the Indian people. But the Chinese government and the Communist Party have always restrained their resentment. The Chinese people have true friendship for India and our solidarity is very vital, not only for ourselves but for the world. The revolt in Tibet was a very serious affair. The Dalai Lama's revolt gave a great jolt to our people. Because of his religious belief we had respected the Dalai Lama and therefore we had postponed the reforms in Tibet. He had mentioned this to Prime Minister Nehru in 1957. But that same year some Tibetans in India, particularly in Kalimpong, put pressure on the Dalai Lama and carried out anti-Chinese propaganda and this assistance and encouragement from outside, emboldened the Dalai Lama to oppose the reforms and instigated the revolt. He wanted to do away with the nationalist people's liberation army and also to throw out the Han people. All this happened before the actual revolt.'

Ambassador Nehru, Chou En-lai added, would recollect that Chairman Mao Tse Tung himself told him that the Chinese government had postponed reforms in Tibet and reduced the size of their army from fifty thousand to twenty thousand and had also withdrawn some of the cadres.

Chou continued that in January 1957 he had spoken to the Dalai Lama about this when he was in India. In spite of all this, the revolt was started in Tibet. 'We had the power to arrest and imprison the Dalai Lama but the three letters that he wrote to us deceived us and he succeeded in escaping to India. We have no objection to the Indian government granting political asylum to the Dalai Lama. All countries have a right to do so. But the Dalai Lama is today carrying out anti-Chinese activities and encouraging the movement for an independent Tibet. This is beyond the definition of political asylum. Very recently, Tibetans in India celebrated the first anniversary of the revolt in Tibet at Kalimpong. This was naturally not liked by our people. Some people in India—responsible people—say that we are suppressing the Tibetans. But we are liberating them, by changing their lives by removing serfdom. But certain people in the upper strata of public opinion in India, although few, say that we are suppressing the Tibetans. We are shocked by this attitude. The developments in Tibet have a direct bearing on the border problem.'

Ambassador Nehru said that every country had its own way of functioning and in a democratic set up like ours, it was only natural that people should give vent to their resentment publicly and there was no way by which a democratic government could prevent them from doing so. But that should not undermine our friendship.

Premier Chou En-lai said that for a long time last year, violent anti-Chinese propaganda was carried out in India on the Tibet question. It was continued from January to June 1959 but this anti-Chinese propaganda had started several months before the reforms in Tibet and carried out not by few but by responsible political parties, Members of the Parliament and other responsible people in India. But all that is over now. Still, the Dalai Lama and his group continued to carry out anti-Chinese activities and, 'Let me assure you that his activities are not going to have any affect on Tibetans. Although we are distressed at the attitude of the Indian government towards the Dalai Lama, we did not mention this for a long time, though our people were shocked and pained.

'On this question, there were other reasons on our side and Marshal Chen Yi mentioned these to Sardar Swaran Singh and I too mentioned to Krishna Menon. It was beyond our comprehension as to how a country like India could support the tyrannical serf-holders of Tibet.'

Ambassador Nehru asked if the revolt in Tibet had any direct bearing on the border question. To this Prime Minister Chou En-lai replied, 'Yes. We are aware of the fact that there exists a dispute between our two countries around the eastern border. I have told Prime Minister Nehru that this question could be solved by peaceful means. We are, of course, not willing to recognise the McMahon Line but we assure you that we will not cross McMahon Line and enter Indian territory. This has been our understanding all along but at the time of the Tibet revolt, India mentioned the Shimla Convention and asked us to accept the McMahon Line and also the 1842 Treaty. We are not willing to accept either of them and we resent this new development. The Shimla Convention of 1913 was imposed on Tibet by the Imperialists, and the Central Government of China did not recognise it. Both of us are new countries and we can solve the border question in the same way as we have solved the dispute with Nepal but in no circumstances will China accept or recognise the secret convention signed by the Imperialists. Even Chiang Kai-shek did not accept the Shimla Convention. How can independent India and independent China be a party to this convention? For China, it is absolutely impossible to do so. But some responsible people in India want to impose this upon us. I want to again repeat that both these treaties were mentioned for the first time to us at the time of the Tibet revolt.'

He continued, 'As for the western sector, what you call Ladakh and what we call Aksai Chin, has always been ours and certainly for the last two hundred years. All our old maps show this. Of course, there are certain minor discrepancies in some of our maps but there is no doubt that the Central Government of China for the last two hundred years has exercised jurisdiction in that area. In 1950, we sent troops to Tibet from this territory and also to Sinkiang. Then we built a road there. We get supplies from this area. To all this India has never objected. It was only in 1958 that an Indian patrol party was sent to this area and this party we disarmed and sent back to India. In 1959, India raised a point that the border question in the west should follow the 1842 treaty. We have seen this treaty and are convinced that there is nothing in the treaty, which says that this region belongs to India. To us, this Indian demand is both new and shocking and has irritated our people very much. I have given all these details and backgrounds of this in my letter of 26 December 1958 to Mr Nehru. But, in spite of that letter we are willing to consider settling the eastern border, accept the Indian jurisdiction upto McMahon Line and assure you that we will not cross it.

'So, in the east a settlement can be found. We have never made any territorial claims but India says we have. Our people resent this and this has made this problem very difficult. But the responsibility is not ours. What has happened is very much unexpected from our friends. I'm placing before you the actual position. Our aim is still to explore ways of a settlement. As I have told you, we do not stress in public but I want to tell you all the facts. Only in the past two years things have become very complicated and we know that non-settlement of this problem will harm us both. That is why we have come to Delhi to try and reach some sort of a settlement and not to emphasise our differences. Whether we succeed or not, is to be seen. But our friendship is the most important thing. If we cannot settle now, we can find other and gradual ways and means to solve this problem. You, Mr Ambassador are deeply interested in India-China friendship and you know the background of our Tibet policy. Chairman Mao Tse Tung had himself told you about this policy several times. You can recollect that Chairman Mao Tse Tung told you about this when you were leaving China and when he saw you at Canton. So, whenever there are any differences, we think of you and that is why we invited you again because you understand our position. Because we are friends, that is why I have told you all this.'

The ambassador said that he agreed with the prime minister that friendship was essential between India and China not only in the interest of the two countries, but of Asia and the world. However, he would repeat that a friendly settlement was only possible if the vital interests, national dignity and rights of both the countries were respected. 'We all hope that step by step, these difficulties will be solved and friendship will be restored. I'm grateful to you for your invitation to come to China and I hope some time or other I will be able to come again.'

Marshal Chen Yi then said that he hoped that a settlement could be reached on the basis of mutual respect and accommodation. 'Our friendship is the greatest thing, the border question is subsidiary.' To this Ambassador Nehru replied that for India the border question was not a subsidiary matter. It was of vital importance. He drew the attention of the vice-premier to the fact that the border from Beijing was three thousand miles away, but from Delhi it was only a few hundred miles and that made a tremendous difference and affected our security.

Chou En-lai said in regard to security, 'We treat our southern boundary as boundary of peace. Chairman Mao Tse Tung has said that our enemy lies in the east and will come from the sea. We take India as a friendly country and we cannot turn our southern border into a national front. Mr Ambassador, you have mentioned security, dignity and friendship. Between us, there can be no other way and it is impossible for us to show weapons to each other and even to mention them.'

Marshal Chen Yi again emphasised that war between India and China was inconceivable. Prime Minister Nehru had said so in the Parliament. We must solve this problem in a friendly way. Ambassador Nehru said that war between two countries like India and China could not be a small affair. It would involve the whole world.

Chou En-lai said that war between the two 'was out of question and when we refer to friendly settlement of the border question, we do so in all sincerity, and we are not thinking of taking any action against each other but our endeavour shall be to put each other at ease, especially India. You know how high the plateau of Tibet is, but we cannot help placing our troops there and as I have said earlier, we have reduced our army there from fifty thousand to twenty thousand. But events in Tibet, last year, upset this.'

Ambassador Nehru said that apart from the border question, there were reports of a great concentration of troops on the Indian borders. Naturally, this had a strong reaction in India. 'Why have these troops been sent there? We also have reports of building of airfields.'

Chou En-lai replied that there were more aerodromes on the Indian side than on the Chinese side of the border. There was only one aerodrome in Tibet.

Ambassador Nehru said that the Himalayas were vital for India and we have to defend them. In so many other ways, they are part of India's history, culture and religion. 'We want our border to be peaceful and not a military one. Your Excellency will recollect that I suggested when I was in China, that we should have free and peaceful intercourse between India and the Tibetan region. We should have a peaceful and model border. I also suggested that there should be an air service between Lhasa and India so that people can move freely between the two countries. I earnestly hope that your talks will succeed, but I cannot minimise the deep concern of our people about recent events. Even those elements in India who are extremely friendly to China, have been upset by Chinese activities on the border.'

Chou En-lai said that the Himalayas meant much to them also. 'We have the same sentiments for them as you have. However, the endeavour should be to settle this question peacefully and as quickly as possible and this is why we are here.' He repeated that as a result of his visit, some solution would be found which would help to 'bring about step by step settlement'.

At about 1:00 am the ambassador said that he had taken too much of Chinese prime minister's time and he thanked him for receiving him.

Finance Minister Morarji Desai's Meeting with Premier Chou En-lai

22 April 1960

The vice-president hosted a private lunch at his residence for Premier Chou En-lai and Marshal Chen Yi. At 3:30 pm, I escorted Chou En-lai to the finance minister's house located in the president's estate. Marshal Chen Yi and Deputy Foreign Minister Chang Han-Fu accompanied him. Ambassador G. Parathasarthi, Jagat Mehta, Vasant Paranjpe and myself were the Indian representatives.

The first few minutes were taken up by inconsequential chatter. References to common colonial past, etc., were made. The finance minister said that India had lost out to the Muslims and then to the British due to our disunity. Premier Chou agreed.

Discordance started at the very beginning. Chou En-lai said the boundary problem was a legacy of history and would be solved. Morarji bhai disagreed saying history could not be blamed for the dispute. Trouble started only in the last three or four years. India had not told the people or parliament about the border troubles, hoping differences would be resolved in a spirit of good neighbourliness. This had not happened. Now, the parliament and people were angry. Chou En-lai said old maps were not accurate and had not demarcated the border properly. Both sides, however, agreed that current troubles began after revolt in Tibet. Morarji bhai said that India allowed China to become dominant in Tibet. In 1950 and 1954, India surrendered all privileges inherited from the British.

Chou En-lai made a lengthy response, blaming the Dalai Lama, his feudal and reactionary advisers. 'China respected the Dalai Lama as a religious leader that is why he was not arrested.' He pointedly said that the centre of anti-Chinese activities was in Kalimpong. The Dalai Lama was against reforms in Tibet. Serfdom existed in Tibet till China stopped it. The Dalai Lama was abusing the conditions of political asylum and was politically active. 'We object to this.'

On the boundary issue, he said China did not recognise the McMahon Line or the Shimla convention of 1913. Now since 1959, India wanted us to recognise both. This was not acceptable to us. We could not negotiate a settlement on this basis. He mentioned the Five Principles of Peaceful Coexistence.

In his response, the finance minister told that negotiations could only be held on the basis of agreement on facts; otherwise not. He emphatically denied any Indian role in the revolt in Tibet. He did not accept what the prime minister had said about Kalimpong.

According to Morarji bhai, it was the Chinese elements in Kalimpong who were creating trouble for India. Prime Minister Nehru in 1957 persuaded the Dalai Lama to return to Lhasa. He is highly respected in India. People of India have friendly sentiments about Tibet. 'You imposed your system in Tibet by violent means. We are not going back on the agreements we signed in 1950 and 1954.'

The FM mentioned the name of Dr K.I. Singh,[1] who went to China to carry out political activities. 'India had not objected. India had a democratic system. We have accepted people's verdict in Kerala where the communists are in power. India had no territorial ambitions, yet we are called Imperialists.' Chou En-lai said K.I. Singh was not permitted any political activity in China. As the PM of Nepal he actually criticised China.

Morarji bhai then rubbed in the point of India, that every year, at the UN, India supported China's case for membership. 'We did so because it is the right thing to do. Panchsheel has now become one-sided. We cannot for the sake of friendship give up territory, which is ours. The boundary problem can be settled not through war but through negotiations. But we must first agree on facts.'

Premier Chou agreed that matter must be settled through mutual agreement. War was ruled out.

The finance minister asserted that China must withdraw troops and then talks could begin. If this did not happen, then there could be no discussion. Premier Chou En-lai categorically stated that China would in no circumstances accept the McMahon Line. He was willing to accept Indian jurisdiction south of the line, where China had no territorial claims. He held forth on Kalimpong, which was full of spies. The Dalai Lama's relatives were active in Kalimpong. Desai responded that China too had spies in Kalimpong. [Chou En-lai went red in the face.] Chou En-lai asked how the Indian government allowed Tibetans in Kalimpong to hold an anti-Chinese convention. Desai said the convention was not sponsored by the government. All kinds of conventions are held in India, some, even against the government. He mentioned Lenin working in London. No one restricted his movements. We did not want anyone to conspire against China but we cannot prevent free speech. This is fundamental in a democracy. The Municipal Hall in Kalimpong was not a government building. Municipalities in India are autonomous bodies. They can let out their halls to anyone.

The Chinese premier again said that the Dalai Lama was engaged in political activities. Prime Minister Nehru had told him that the Dalai Lama would not be allowed to indulge in political work. But he was doing so. Desai said, not so gently, that Chou En-lai was being unjust. The Dalai Lama was not preparing to march into Tibet. All he said was that he would like to go back to Tibet. How could we prevent him from saying so?

Chou En-lai said there was no campaign against India in China. Desai asserted that the responsible people in China had 'called us a reactionary government'. Chou En-lai's response was quick and curt. 'The portraits of Chairman Mao and the prime minister of China were burnt in India.' Desai retorted that his effigy was burnt recently, adding that even Gandhiji's effigies had been burnt. Premier Chou En-lai, getting a bit worked up, said Indians had the freedom to abuse China but China had no freedom to criticise India. Desai in a waspish tone said he was being frank and tried to explain India's viewpoint. Chou En-lai retorted that the finance minister had said enough. Desai shot back, 'The Chinese prime minister said more than enough.'

He added that all he was trying to say was that he condemned his people for abusing China. If that was not so, then India would not have sponsored the case of China at the UN even after the Tibet revolt. Premier Chou En-lai, calming down, thanked the finance minister for helping on the UN front. He then spoke about the western sector saying it was under China for two hundred years not four or five years. China had every right to build roads there. Desai firmly replied that he did not agree with this.

Acrimony continued. Premier Chou En-lai said that China sent troops to Tibet in 1950. Desai countered that this did not mean China could make claims on territory which belonged to India. The Chinese premier made a conciliatory reply. There was no need to quarrel. The matter could be resolved by mutual agreement and accommodation. This was not good enough for Desai who said there was no question of India giving up any of its territory. However, he was confident that a satisfactory agreement would be found.

The meeting finished at 5:40 pm. It had not been a pleasant encounter.

In the car, I sat next to the Chinese prime minister. I could feel and see how annoyed he was. Perhaps, the astutest diplomat in the world, he obviously did not feel comfortable dealing with second category Indian leaders.

Why our prime minister has inflicted Morarji Desai on Chou En-lai beats me. I suppose he has his compulsions. Morarji belonged to the ultra right wing of the Congress.[2]

25 April

At the end of the morning session of talks at Teen Murti House, Pandit Nehru saw me and said, '*Phakey ho rahe hain?*' (Are you starving?)

Ambassador Parathasarthi and I had been sitting in the ground floor drawing room. It was evident the talks had not gone well.

In the evening at the home minister's reception at Rashtrapati Bhawan, in honour of Chou En-lai. Dinner at the Chinese Embassy. On the way back from the embassy our car broke down on Rajpath, half-way between the India Gate and the Rashtrapati Bhawan. Chou En-lai was not perturbed but his security people in the follow car were agitated. R.N. Kao[3] and I were most embarrassed. We finally reached Rashtrapati Bhawan a little before the press conference being held by the Chinese PM.

During the day it had become apparent that the Nehru-Chou talks had failed. The much awaited joint-communiqué had been issued. I got a copy with some difficulty and read it hurriedly sitting in a waiting room. One gaping hole is the absence of any reference to Panchsheel or the Five Principles of Peaceful Coexistence. Officials of two sides were to meet between June and September in New Delhi and Peking. They were to submit their report by September.

As there was no joint-conference the Chinese premier acted quickly. He held a press conference at 10:30 pm in the Rashtrapati Bhawan. I sat in a corner and observed the chaotic scene before Premier Chou En-lai and Chen Yi arrived. Very large number of Indian and foreign correspondents present. Lots of cameras and movie cameras. Bulbs flashing. Noise and more noise. We Indians are immune to noise. A hush and silence as M/s Chou and Chen Yi arrived.

He read out a lengthy statement, saying all the right things. From the very first question Chou En-lai dominated the press conference. He answered questions without appearing to be overawed but tense he certainly was. One young lady correspondent asked how he looked so fit and elegant at his age of sixty-two. The premier replied, 'Thank you. I lead the life of a disciplined oriental.' Tension eased.

He next read out the six points on which there was, according to him, common ground:

1. There exist disputes with regard to the boundary between the two sides.

2. There exists between the two countries a Line of Actual Control upto which each side exercises administrative jurisdiction.
3. In determining the boundary between the two countries, certain geographical principles such as watersheds, river valleys and mountain passes, should be equally applicable to all sectors of the boundary.
4. A settlement of the boundary question between the two countries should take into account the national feelings of the people towards the Himalayas and the Karakoram mountain.
5. Pending a settlement of the boundary question between the two countries through discussion, both sides should keep to the Line of Actual Control and should not put forward territorial claims as pre-conditions, but individual adjustment may be made.
6. In order to ensure tranquility on the border so as to facilitate the discussions, both sides should continue to refrain from patrolling along all sectors of the boundary.

He answered questions about the McMahon Line, the eastern and the western sectors. Cleverly, he brought in the Five Principles of Peaceful Coexistence. The Dalai Lama was mentioned and his 'betrayal' commented on.

The final intervention was by *The London Times* correspondent, Neville Maxwell. To the relief of the Chinese prime minister he said that all correspondents had to meet their deadline, etc. Soon the press conference ended. It was past 1:00 am.

26 April

Prime Minister Nehru saw him off at Palam. During the drive to the airport I requested Chou En-lai to autograph a photo of his which I had taken on the day of his arrival. He graciously obliged.

Morarji Desai took me aside and asked me to send him a copy of the record of his meeting with Chou En-lai. I said I would do so. Pandit

Nehru held a mini-press conference after Chou En-lai's departure. He put his hand round me and smiled. That was rewarding enough.

Prime Minister Chou En-lai arrived at a moment of grave crisis facing Sino-Indian relations. He came looking for a settlement. But he returned a disappointed man.

Part Three

*Prime Minister Rajiv Gandhi's
Visit to China
19-23 December 1988*

Prefatory Note

If I were asked to name one achievement in my fifty years' involvement in foreign affairs and diplomacy, I would, with pride, point to the breakthrough in Sino-Indian relations in December 1988. Prime Minister Rajiv Gandhi's visit was a landmark event, with wide ramifications.

Rajiv Gandhi appointed me as Minister of State for External Affairs in October 1986. In the past twenty months he had changed two ministers of state, Messers Khurshid Alam Khan[1] and K.R. Narayanan.[2] Cabinet ministers, B.R. Bhagat[3] and Shiv Shankar[4] met the same fate.

Within three weeks of taking over, I arrived at certain conclusions. Indian diplomats had an unenviable task, in conducting and implementing our diplomacy and foreign policy. They went about their task with one hand tied behind their back.

Relations with the USA, China and Pakistan were highly unsatisfactory for a number of years. Our diplomats were not responsible for this. The political masters were. The prime minister, in a light-hearted manner, generally spoke derisively about, 'you IFS chaps'. This I told him was not fair. Each one had come through one of the most demanding competitive examinations in the world. With some exceptions, the IFS were as good as the best anywhere.

The prime minister from time to time asked me to accompany him on some of his foreign trips. The first time was in March 1985 for the funeral in Moscow of Konstatin Chernenko,[5] the Soviet general secretary. Later in the year he invited me to be with him at the Commonwealth

Summit in the Bahamas. In August 1986 he took me to the Non-aligned Summit in Harare, Zimbabwe.

I can't pretend, I did not relish these jaunts. But there was a less pleasant aspect, which was inevitable in the circumstances. There was no unrestrained joy at my inclusion in these delegations. The incumbent Minister of State did not take kindly to this arbitrary encroachment by the Minister of Steel/Fertiliser on his turf. Neither did it make the Cabinet minister comfortable. Anyway, I did my best not to tread too often on sensitive toes of my ministerial colleagues. Sometimes I did. It could not be avoided. The fact was that I knew the foreign policy, diplomacy game better than any of them. Why I was not given a Ministry of External Affairs job initially in 1984 is another story. It's not a pretty one.

Soon after taking over in 1986, I had a long discussion with the prime minister. I put it candidly to him, 'What is your foreign policy vision? What are your priorities?' He countered, 'What are yours, Natwar?' This gave me the opening I was looking for. 'I have one paramount priority – to improve relations with China.' I told him that I began my diplomatic career in China. I was the first IFS officer to opt for Chinese as my language. I had been the liaison officer to Chou En-lai when he came for his final discussions with his grandfather in April 1960. We had then, missed a great opportunity to resolve the border problem. We now have three options: (1) Not to disturb the status quo; (2) War; (3) Negotiations. Status quo suited China. War was not a realistic option. Negotiation was the only practical policy. And negotiations had to be held at the highest level. Even in November 1962, Nehru had told the parliament that ultimately the dispute had to be resolved through negotiations.

Prime Minister Rajiv Gandhi was an impatient listener. He asked me what I had in mind. I said the time had now come for him to seriously think of paying an official visit to the People's Republic. His grandfather had made his passage to China in October 1954. For all practical purposes our relations with China had been in the diplomatic deep-freeze for over two decades. One of the reasons was the existence of an influential anti-China lobby in New Delhi. These heavyweights included M/s P.V. Narasimha Rao,[6] G. Parathasarthi[7] and S. Gopal[8].

All three had the 1962 hang-up. One of them kept saying, 'Chou En-lai killed Panditji.' No great country should allow sentimentality to take precedence over objectivity. These well-meaning pundits had immobilised Indira Gandhi's foreign policy.

Mao Tse Tung's gesture to Brajesh Mishra in 1970 was unfortunately, not taken seriously. Times, I said, had changed. But we had not. Our inactivity had been exploited by Pakistan. President Nixon[9] and Henry Kissinger[10] had used Islamabad as their link to China. That was a great feather in their diplomatic cap.

By this time the prime minister was both, restless and interested. I told him I would take only a few minutes more, 'You have 413 Congress MPs in the Lok Sabha. You are Jawaharlal Nehru's grandson and Indira Gandhi's son. No one can ever accuse you of any foreign policy sell-out. A prime ministerial visit to Beijing was overdue.' I remember his exact response, 'I have no 1962 hang-up. You start thinking about a possible trip.'

Almost immediately thereafter the Sumdorong Chu mini-crises intensified. In early December, Arunachal Pradesh was given full statehood. The Chinese protested. But eventually the excitement and tension died down. In the meanwhile, we had actually moved forward in the area. The chief of the army staff was General K.S. Sundarji.[11] He had a rather exaggerated opinion of his military worth. I remember a meeting in Room No. 9 of the Parliament House in November 1986, of the Political Affairs Committee. The prime minister presided. All the civil and defence top brass were present. The Army chief made his presentation on Sumdorong Chu and also the western sector. He announced rather nonchalantly that India could take on both China in the east and Pakistan in the west. I could scarcely believe my ears. K.P.S. Menon,[12] our ambassador in China intervened, to point out that this was *deja vu*, 1962 in another guise. The Army chief was dismissive of the seniormost IFS officer.

A.P. Venkateswaran,[13] the Foreign secretary met the same fate. None of the political heavyweights raised any objection. P.V. Narasimha Rao, N.D. Tiwari,[14] K.C. Pant,[15] Buta Singh[16] were all looking at the prime minister. Present also was the inexperienced Arun Singh, Minister of State for Defence, who thought Sundarji was the cat's whiskers on military matters. I asked to speak. I said that I was surprised to hear the observations of the Army chief. A military reverse in the east would bring the government down in spite of its huge majority. I then looked Sundarji in the eye and asked him, 'General, in 1962 we had Krishna Menon to sacrifice. In 1986, whom do we sacrifice, you or the prime minister?' End of the meeting, if I remember it right.

Prime Minister Rajiv Gandhi was endowed with an uncluttered, practical, not an introspective mind. Action, not reflection was his forté. He did not spend time contemplating problems; he was looking for answers and solutions. He could be impetuous and infuriating. He could equally charm you by his disarming candour. Like his grandfather, he had not an iota of the poison of malice or pettiness in his character.

He was only forty years of age when fate thrust the prime ministership on him. The circumstances could not have been more painful. He rose to the occasion, like a modern day Caesar. His stunning good looks, his style, his panache, his sang-froid, his capacity to switch off, his natural wit, his immense self-confidence made him an enormously large figure. He always looked fresh and buoyant. Some of that freshness rubbed on us. Like John F. Kennedy,[17] Rajiv Gandhi had a gamesman's sense of politics. I don't want to carry this comparison too far, because Kennedy had an acute sense of history that Rajiv Gandhi lacked.

Unlike his grandfather, his mother and Kennedy, Rajiv Gandhi did not read books. This was a serious shortcoming. Michael Foot[18] wrote, 'Men of power have no time to read, yet the men who do not read are unfit for power.' This is an extreme view, but there is much to be said for it. Rajiv Gandhi made no claims to being an intellectual. But he was receptive to ideas. Rajiv Gandhi enjoyed being prime minister; sometimes excessively.

On China, he excelled himself. This would be his enduring foreign policy achievement. For decades we had, for all practical purposes, no realistic China policy. Rajiv Gandhi changed that. While he spent some time on acquainting himself with the essential nitty-gritty of the Sino-Indian relationship, he looked at the larger picture. That is an essential quality of leadership. Most importantly he was not intimidated by any of the Chinese leaders, whose experience compared to his, was vast.

He embarked on his visit to China well-prepared in more ways than one. Over the past one year we had worked hard to get a national consensus supporting his visit to China. This was of vital importance. He preached nuclear non-proliferation on the one hand, and on the other, he went ahead with the nuclear weapons programme. The Chinese were fully aware of this.

Regrettably, 1987 was a dry year for Sino-Indian relations. First, the Brasstacks fiasco took place and we came near a military conflict with Pakistan. Then came Bofors. Bolt from the blue. It nearly derailed the Rajiv Gandhi government. The rest of the year, the prime minister got embroiled in the Sri Lanka ethnic conflict.

I was also involved in the muddy and bloody Vietnam-Cambodian crisis. It was a highly combustible situation. The stakes were high for the USSR, China, the ASEAN countries and the US. We were a player, but not a heavyweight one. On a visit to Hanoi in January 1987, the Vietnamese foreign minister, Co Thach[19] took me into confidence about his country's decision to withdraw their troops from Cambodia by 1989. He asked me to convey this important decision to the ASEAN countries. I asked Co Thach why he could not do so himself. He said, 'You have much more credibility than Vietnam on this.'

In the next six months, I paid several visits to the ASEAN countries to 'sell' the Vietnamese decision. Initially, there were no takers. But gradually they began shedding their doubts. Two years of hard work culminated in the International Conference on Cambodia, held in Paris in July-August 1989.

This was then the background in which Prime Minister Rajiv Gandhi undertook his historic visit to Peking in 1988. Expert in playing the power game, Deng Xiaoping was aware that the India of 1988 was not the India of 1962.

For Rajiv Gandhi too, it was the high point of his prime ministership. He displayed boldness, visionary and inspiring leadership. He was both audacious and prudent. The grandson of Jawaharlal Nehru did not let the pressure of the past to derail the present. His personality reflected the spirit of the age. His weltanschauung resonated with that of the great Deng Xiaoping. It is exhilarating for me to have had a modest share in the making of history.

18 December 1988

No meeting of Council of Ministers or Congress Working Committee (CWC) on the China visit. There should have been one. I thought I had almost got Rajiv Gandhi to agree. Thirty-six Congress MPs were on standby for the past forty-eight hours for a briefing.

The Hindi TV programme with V.N. Gadgil,[20] Jitender Prasad and Vinod Mishra, the journalist, has been widely seen and much acclaimed. I got across what I wanted to, not pitching it too high or underplaying excessively the significance of the visit. I worked hard and persuasively to change the political mood in the parliament and the country on this all important Rajiv Gandhi's visit to China.

He worked on his speeches most of the day. He was good at cutting out the fat. Not a conceptual thinker, but a practical one. He had no time for pointless hair splitting.

Read Henry Kissinger on Mao and China. Brilliant, fascinating and self-serving. He, of course exaggerated his role, but the man was a conceptual operator. Having been in China in the mid-fifties and seen Mao, Chou and Deng at close quarters, I had to hand it to Kissinger for getting their characters, thinking and style on the spot. Unfortunately, Nehru took a somewhat romantic view of India-China relations. Deep down in his heart he did not believe in realpolitik. Mao and company did. Nehru totally misjudged Stalin and ignored the ruthlessness with which he practised realpolitik at home and abroad. As late as 1951 Nehru was praising Stalin. Stalin and Churchill were two world figures who did not condole Gandhi's assassination. When a statesman has absolutely no scruples, he acquires exceptional operational flexibility. Stalin had no scruples.

Left for the airport at 10:15 am. The establishment was out in full force – most ministers, service chiefs, Cabinet secretary, etc. Ran into Shiv Charan Mathur – we were both civil and avoided mentioning the unpleasant.

Took-off at 11:45 am. Air India special aircraft. Fifteen minutes late. P.V. Narasimha Rao, Dinesh,[21] Shankaranand[22] and I got into the plane. Around 11 am, before the plane took off met Simi Garewal.[23] She was travelling with us – doing a film on Rajiv Gandhi. Still, a beauty. Weather - not too cold. Dinesh and I put on our sleeping suits to the envy of all. Left of me was Suman Dubey. What an utterly unpretentious chap! Intimate with Rajiv and Sonia. Got up at 4:00 am and changed. Sunrise over China at 35,000 feet. My mind went back thirty-two years – travelled to Beijing by rail, it took thirty-six hours. Ferry crossing at Wu Han – July 1956.

Landed at Capital airport outside Peking – Rajiv Gandhi, Sonia Gandhi received by Minister of Metallurgy, Qi Yuanjim, his wife and Ambassador C.V. Ranganathan.[24] Temperature, -seven degree farenheit. Endless motorcade. All by myself in Car No. 6 – crisp, hazy morning. Time, 8 am. Frost. Trees looked like skeletons. Road in perfect condition. Lots of traffic – many more vehicles on road as compared to 1956 – it's another city, another epoch. The Hutungs were fast disappearing. Multi-storeyed buildings had come up in vast numbers. Most were hideous. Roads widened. Impressive avenues – tree-lined. More colourful and varied dress – both for men and women. Taxis! Yes, taxis. Whoever heard of a taxi in 1956 or even '58. The uniform, blue and blue, much less in evidence. Cycles less than 1984.

Drove past Peking Hotel, Tien An Men – magnificent and unique. Mao's huge portrait still in its old place on Tien An Men gate. His embalmed body lay at the other end. Orderliness was evident everywhere. No filth. No one in tatters. No one without warm clothes. No one without shoes.

Arrived at Diaoyutai State Guest House at 9:00 am. Villa No. 2 for me. I think Hem, Ritu and I stayed here in 1984. Rajiv Gandhi's suite across the lake, No. 18. Diaoyutai made internationally known by Nixon and Kissinger. Both stayed in this secluded retreat in the heart of Peking. Chung Nan Hai, the Elysian abode of Comrade Deng Xiaoping and the lesser party bosses were next door. Only two armed guards visible at huge, red-coloured gate leading to the residence of the mighty. Security arrangements in communist countries are less visible than in democracies.

Mao Tse Tung has been given short shrift by Deng Xiaoping. He was all-powerful but remained deliberately elusive. Audiences were rare and carefully-planned.

19 December 1988

10:00 am – Ceremonial welcome by Prime Minister Li Peng[25] at the Great Hall of the People. Prime minister looked spic and span. Inspected Guard of Honour. National anthems played. Ours a bit off-key. The PM introduced his delegation to Li Peng. Not an attractive man to look at. What a contrast from Chou En-lai.

10:15 am – delegation level talks began. Formal statements were made by the two prime ministers. The PM held three meetings with Prime Minister Li Peng. All aspects of Sino-Indian relations discussed at length and in detail. Li Peng told the PM that his visit marked a new direction in Sino-Indian relations. His government had decided to take concrete steps to resolve boundary issue. Both agreed to revitalise and restructure bilateral relations. Both emphasised the importance and relevance of the Panchsheel initiated by Chou En-lai and Jawaharlal Nehru. Neither avoided reference to serious differences in 1962. But that was the past. Necessary to look towards the future. Both agreed that long-term view should be taken. Together both countries should workout solution of the boundary dispute, keeping in mind the national honour.

Li Peng emphasised that both sides should adopt positive attitude. He linked his mantra of 'mutual understanding and mutual accommodation' with Panchsheel. The PM said he had some difficulty with 'mutual accommodation'. He suggested 'mutual acceptability', or 'mutual interest or mutual benefit'. 'Words are not important substance', said Li Peng. The PM said he too looked into the substance. In Li Peng's view, mutual accommodation did not imply conceding territory. Li Peng stated that the undeniable fact was that the Sino-Indian boundary had never been delimited. (This was the Chou En-lai line that Nehru rejected in 1960.) If the boundary had been delimited or demarked, no accommodation on territory could be possible. He elaborated what he meant by mutual understanding. It meant understanding each other's viewpoint.

Intense discussion followed, never ill-tempered but on realistic lines. In all, the two prime ministers spent over five hours to remove hurdles and chalk out future contours of Sino-Indian relations. No mean achievement. Li Peng accepted Rajiv Gandhi's proposal to establish three working groups. The first Joint Working Group would deal with boundary question. The next with economic relations and the third with trade, science and technology. The PM told me it was not smooth-sailing but he managed to get what he had set out to get.

One session was largely devoted to discussing international relations. Here too there was broad agreement. The most significant developments for China were: the end of the very serious Sino-USSR conflict and the end of the Vietnam War. Vietnam's decision to pull out their forces from Kampuchea was welcomed.

The PM gave Li Peng a gist of his discussions with Mikhail Gorbachev.[26] Li said Gorbachev would be visiting China early in 1989. Li Peng informed the PM that relations with the USA were good. The US was China's second largest trading partner after Japan and had abandoned 'Two-Chinas' policy.

While the prime ministers were busy with their discussions, the two foreign ministers had a side-show to camouflage their unemployment. Qian Qichen[27] and P.V. Narasimha Rao and their supporting casts met from 3-5 pm. On the Indian side were Dinesh Singh, Shankaranand, myself, K.P.S. Menon and C.V. Ranganathan. Nothing earthshaking transpired. The real interest was in the original, not in photocopies.

Drove to the Temple of Heaven. The old city wall was gone – so are most of the Hutungs. The charm of Beijing was already fading. Vast jungle of uniformly tall ungainly apartment blocks had replaced the curved bamboo roofed houses. It was neater but not elegant. Except for the Tien An Man Square and the Forbidden City, nothing of the old Beijing survived. It would look like any other large modern city – no individuality, no soul and after some years, no memories.

Far too many people with the PM's party – PM in leather jacket with fur collar. Sonia in sari – no gloves, no socks. The Temple was in good condition. Not an architectural wonder. I first came to the Temple with Han Suyin in July-August 1956.

The guide went on a bit. When we were at the round marble pavilion at the far end of the temple, he pointed to a spot and said, 'If you stand here and wish, your wish will come true. In times of famine the emperors came here to pray for rain.' I saw Sonia looking at me and saying with her eyes, 'Let's move.' I said to the guide, 'Before it starts raining let's move.' We did.

Prime Minister's Meeting with President Yang Shengkun

10:30 meeting with President Yang Shengkun (eighty-one) at the Great Hall of the People. This was constructed in 1959 to mark the tenth anniversary of 1949. A monstrously large, sprawling building, with endless reception rooms and wind-swept corridors – the Acropolis could fit into one wing – we met in a large square hall with chairs in C shape. The old boy spent thirteen years in detention during the Cultural Revolution, which he called a frightful disaster. Tibet on his mind. Welcomed our statement that we recognise Tibet as an autonomous part of China. I passed on to the PM a slip telling him to repeat our formulation without any mention of sovereignty. Also to add Sikkim for good measure. He used a tiny part – no mention of sovereignty but on Sikkim, he later asked me to speak at my level. While going out he said, 'They seem very worried about Tibet. *Ghabrai huwe legte hain.*'

Lunch at the Beijing Duck restaurant. Remembered eating here in September 1984 with Hem and Ritu. I preferred the 1956 version – better food, more authentic. You select the duck you wish to eat. This new avatar, too gaudy and touristy. Host Wu – I met him in September 1984. He touched the ticklish subject of our clearing the agreemo for the new Chinese ambassador. I told him that unless regret was expressed about the objectionable article he wrote in one of their papers regarding Indira Gandhi, agreement would not be given. Wu said they held Indian leaders in high esteem, etc. The regret followed.

In 1984 he was in a Mao suit, today in suit and tie. Sat next to the PM; spoke about his first visit to India in 1951. Recalled meeting Jawaharlal Nehru and Indira Gandhi. Endless toasts ending with *kampei* – bottoms up. No much serious talk.

K.P.S. episode: The Foreign secretary rightly felt deeply humiliated and wounded. To keep him out of talks with Li Peng was an error – it was compounded by including Gopi Arora[1] in the talks. Ambassador Ranganathan was also kept out while Chinese ambassador in Delhi was with his PM. These things matter in diplomacy. The PM was rather impatient with diplomatic rigmarole.

Shankar Menon, a mild-mannered gentleman, brought up in the long established diplomatic tradition, rightly felt outraged. He heaped his ire on Ronen Sen[2] at breakfast, in the presence of others. The Ministry of External Affairs had been insulted and humiliated. A bad showing all round.

Food passable. Narasimha Rao starved. Dinesh enjoyed himself. Also Shankaranand. I was still trying to fathom in what *Khushi* Shankaranand has been brought here. He was, if nothing, a single-minded character as far as his priorities were concerned. When I went to brief him on China on the 18th in Delhi, all he talked was about the wicked Brahmins who surrounded the PM. Later I learnt that M.L. Fotedar had suggested his name. Rajiv told me he had been rewarded for his help in the Bofors Joint Parliamentary Committee over which he had presided.

No speeches at lunch. We were all presented marble ducks resting on little wooden base. The Chinese ambassador sat next to me. His wife on my left. Both fluent in English. He was an odd man out in a tropical white suit with temperature, -2 degree Celcius!

Drove to the Great Wall with S.K. Mishra.[3] I should have taken Sarla Grewal[4] with me as she wanted to drive with me but did not (She was hurt and rightly so. I would try making up this evening). I told the PM that I first trod on the Great Wall in 1956. I was the only one on the wall that day. Now, swarms. Dirt road gone. Four-lane highway. At the Wall, Rajiv and Sonia mobbed by our media. Today it was not too cold. Dinesh and I had ourselves photographed with Simi Grewal.

Sonia got an attack of asthama. 'My inhaler is not working,' she said to me. I had left mine at the guest house. She had her own programme.

I was so fortunate to have been well-advised by Shri Jyoti Basu, elderly statesman and chief minister of Bengal, who was very supportive of this visit. I remember meeting him at his Delhi – Circular Road – residence on 28 June 1988. Surprisingly, he did not get to see Deng Xiaoping. McMahon line was the main barrier. I told Mr Basu, that in case of Burma, they had accepted McMahon Line.

Mr Basu told his Chinese hosts that India being a democracy, it was necessary for the government to take public opinion into confidence. There was parliament, opposition, elections. China was a socialist country. The party and the government were one. This was not so in India. It was therefore easier for China to take the initiative in resolving the border dispute. He also said that China harping on Arunachal Pradesh did not help. The whole of India felt strongly about this matter.

I mentioned Prime Minister Rajiv Gandhi's forthcoming visit to China. He welcomed it but said, 'It will have to be carefully prepared.' Chinese shared our view to keep the border tranquil. 'But why have they not recognised Sikkim as a part of India?' asked Basu. Chinese said this was a formality. I asked him if he reminded them of how correct we had been on Tibet. Never have the Chinese said that Kashmir is a part of India.

I asked Basu what his overall impression was. He said that the Chinese were in no hurry to solve the border problem but keen to improve relations in other fields. Mr Basu came impressed with the two Eco-Zones and Hong Kong. 'China will have many Hong Kongs.' He spoke of the PM's idea of an aerial survey of the border. According to him, Chinese were not too enthusiastic about the idea.

21 December 1988

Before the meeting with Deng Xiaoping we visited Forbidden City.

All its splendour, space and beauty make it an overwhelming experience. The guide mentioned Pu Yi,[5] a legendary figure. When I asked about the film, *The Last Emperor* his unexpected forthrightness came as a tonic: Pu Yi died in Beijing in 1967. The PM was interested to know something about the man. During the height of Japanese imperialism he was made the emperor of Manchuria. Spent many years in prison in post-1949 China. Our princes got away rather lightly.

Rajiv Gandhi and Sonia fascinated with the regal splendour of the Forbidden City. I pointed out Chung Nan Hai to Rajiv Gandhi who asked, 'Did Mao live in the Forbidden City?' I told him he did, in a fairly modest house in Chung Nan Hai, in the compound of the Forbidden City. Mao lived frugally. His study, where he received Radhakrishnan in 1957 was a small one, lined with books, some manuscripts tied with strings, scattered on the floor. He was a voracious reader, like Lenin, Stalin and Nehru.

The Climax: Meeting with Deng Xiaoping

On the political side, I was the only one familiar with the writings of Mao Tse Tung, Chinese history and some acquaintance with Chinese literature. As a young, junior diplomat I had observed that Mao's China was far more accomplished in diplomacy than we were. Conceptual thinking went hand-in-hand with strategy and tactics. Chinese statecraft was subtle, nuanced and hard-headed. Ultimately, it worked in the realm of power. Their leaders, broadly speaking were well-versed in the history of the seventeen dynasties which had ruled China. Confucianism had been rejected by Mao. Most senior Chinese leaders were Long Marchers. Something like our top-level freedom fighters.

To make sure that China indeed was keen to welcome Rajiv Gandhi, the prime minister sent P.N. Haksar[1] to Beijing in May 1987. He had extensive talks with top Chinese leaders (not Deng Xiaoping). On his return he told Rajiv Gandhi that there was genuine interest among the Chinese leadership for the prime minister visiting China.

External Affairs Minister N.D. Tiwari too stopped in Beijing on his way back from North Korea in 1988.

Much excitement in the Indian delegation. Meeting with Deng Xiaoping fixed at 10:30 am at the Great Hall of the People. Deng appeared wearing a grey Mao suit. His opening words were, 'I welcome you, my young friend. This is your first journey to China.'

PM: 'Yes.'

The Deng-Rajiv handshake lasted quite a while. It signalled that Deng wanted the Indian prime minister's visit to succeed. Symbols send messages in China, more than in any other country. Had the handshake been a perfunctory one, the visit would have collapsed then and there. 'I met your grandfather and your mother when they visited China in 1954. I was then the general secretary of our party.'

The world and Indian media present were all hanging on every word and noticing every gesture. Each word Deng uttered was premeditated, carefully delivered. The handshake produced an electrifying effect. So public a gesture was indispensable for the success of the Indian prime minister's visit. Decades of sterile unfriendliness seemed to melt away. For those present it was a moment of history. So far Chinese media has been correct but restrained. This would now change dramatically and it did.

Deng said relations at that time were very good between our countries. The PM responded that relations then were indeed very good. Then followed some unpleasantness (this, he put delicately). We should try to get over our differences and look to the future. Deng said that was his wish too. Yes, we should look to the future. There was so much the two countries could do together.

Rajiv Gandhi introduced P.V. Narasimha Rao, Dinesh, Shankaranand and me to the diminutive Deng. The two leaders then withdrew. So did we – but in different directions. Narasimha Rao was visibly upset and peeved that the PM had not asked him to accompany him for his talks with Deng. But PV was a great peever.

Late at night I saw Rajiv and asked how the talks with Deng had gone. He seemed pleased and relaxed. 'We have moved forward. 1962 is now behind us.' This was indeed good news. Since he loved lighter moments, he told me this gem: 'Deng had said he was now old. That was why he had called me "young friend"', adding that his age was about double Rajiv's. 'Not quite,' Rajiv said. Deng said he was forty years older than Rajiv. This time he agreed. Then, wit took over. He told Deng of the recent visit of a minister from the Democratic People's Republic of Korea who presented him with ginseng, adding it would make him forty years younger. He told the North Korean that would land him into deep trouble. This amused the old man. The PM thought Deng was hard of hearing. I informed him that he was.

Without being patronising, Deng advised him to befriend the younger people who were now running China, Zhao Ziyang[2] and Li Peng. In future, if he wished to discuss business he should contact them. Shades of Mao Tse Tung who, in 1971 said more or less the same thing to Nixon, 'Business? Discuss with the premier. Here we discuss philosophical matters.'

Deng's tour d' horizon was of immense significance. As was his vision. He emphasised that both the countries should take advantage of the improved international environment to go ahead with economic development of China and India. He considered this in common interest of both. Global equilibrium could be helped by China and India coming closer. Deng laid great emphasis on the economic development of China and India, for the next few decades. To talk of the twenty-first century being the Asian century is unrealistic. He wanted development not only for China and India, but for humankind as a whole – first China and India have to eliminate backwardness and poverty. Deng summed up his country's foreign policy thus – oppose hegemonism, maintain world peace.

With the USSR, main differences were on Vietnam's invasion of Kampuchea. Also on their misadventure in Afghanistan. Thirdly, China wanted withdrawal of one million USSR troops from the Sino-Russian border. On China's insistence and after Gorbachev took over, these matters were being dealt with more sensibly. There was good progress on all three issues. This was positive element in their relations with Russia. Deng spoke of his conversation with Reagan,[3] whom he asked to abandon policy of 'four unsinkable submarines' – Taiwan, South Korea, South Africa and Israel. There has been change in varying degrees in US policy on all four. Relations now normal with the USA.

Deng also recalled the message he had sent to Indira Gandhi in 1977, while on a visit to Nepal through the then Indian foreign minister. Deng saw no reason, why China and India could not improve their relations. Both countries have common interests. He added that a genuine beginning of improvement in relations was Rajiv Gandhi's current visit. He thanked him for coming to Beijing. The PM said Deng

Xiaoping had taken many initiatives which had resulted in his visit. It was Deng's personal initiative, which started the process.

On Israel, Deng Xiaoping had said to the American leaders that their support for three million Israelis had incurred enmity of many millions of Arabs. America wanted to be the policeman of the world. That was hegemonism, it would not work and we would not accept it as well.

Neither Deng Xiaoping nor Rajiv Gandhi wasted time on details. Neither of them mentioned the boundary dispute at their meeting. This, the PM was to discuss with Li Peng and to the lesser extent with Party Secretary Zhao Ziyang whom he had met in New York in 1988.

In Deng's view, human kind was facing two vital questions – peace and development. There was some hope for peace as there was improvement in the Sino-US relations. East-West relations were also producing satisfactory results. The development scene was less promising. A large portion of the globe is covered by developing and underdeveloped countries. The North-South dialogue has not shown progress. One-fifth of the world is doing very well, but not willing to share wealth with other nations.

He was at his best talking about the twenty-first century being the Asian century or the Asia-Pacific century. He had reservations about this premature conclusion. In the Asia-Pacific region, Japan mattered, so did the four emerging economies. To these should be added Australia and New Zealand. Of course the US too was a very important Pacific power. (I had earlier told Rajiv Gandhi what Deng had, some years ago, said to a western newsman about China dominating the twenty-first century. Deng said before talking about twenty-first century, he first wanted China to arrive at the twentieth century.) In the judgment of the Chinese statesman, the Asia-Pacific century would not become a reality without development of China and India. Both countries must work hard to end poverty and backwardness. No quick fixes or magic formula for dealing with weighty problems. He also made acute observations on South America. Without the development of Brazil, there could not be a South American century.

He said China would, for the next fifty to sixty years concentrate on all-round economic development. He went on to say that China had undertaken in earnest reforms in opening up to the outside world.

When China becomes developed, then she would fulfil her obligations towards humanity and the Asian continent. China would work diligently to improve relations and cooperation with the developing world, particularly with India.

The PM rose to the occasion. He said the more he spoke to Deng Xiaoping, the more he saw similarity of views. There was a common assessment and added that the pasts of both nations were similar. Both India and China struggled against colonialism and imperialism. In the case of China, Japanese imperialism was also a factor. Both wanted development, social justice and peace. Both have achieved political independence. Now both must ensure their economic independence. He said Deng symbolised the Chinese revolution and spearheaded the modernisation revolution. He agreed with Deng that political tensions were being eroded and the USSR and the US were on more cordial terms. The new international atmosphere was less tense. That was a good and welcoming situation.

Deng Xiaoping next came to the subject that went to the heart of Sino-Indian relations. After giving the matter mature consideration and after exchange of views with several world statesmen, he said he had come to the conclusion that Panchsheel – the Five Principles of Peaceful Coexistence approved by Chou En-lai and Nehru could be the basis for taking forward the international dialogue. Deng said that since both nations did not live up to these principles, Sino-Indian relations suffered a setback. In other words, both countries did not adhere to the Five Principles. He preferred the Five Principles, to the Ten Principles agreed at Bandung in 1955. The Five Principles were explicit and transparent. They shunned bloc politics and hegemonism. These principles should be the norms for conducting international relations, between states and between neighbours according to Deng. He confided that the Soviet Union was in favour of the Five Principles.

He next came to the hardcore of his exposé. Deng stated that India and China must themselves put these Five Principles into practice. Guided by these principles, China and India could make adjustments in their respective policies. He put this for the Indian prime minister's consideration. (Age bowing to youth.) We needed to benefit from wisdom embedded in these principles. A certain strategic boldness was required to implement what he had proposed. He also expressed a desire to include reference to the Five Principles in the Joint Press Communiqué. The PM said he was attracted by the idea. Deng was quick and direct. He asked the prime minister, 'That means we have reached an agreement!' The PM agreed, adding that more had to be done. This was only the start. Deng stressed the point. 'Does this mean we will together state the Five Principles, which we have jointly initiated in our joint press statement?' While agreeing, the PM said the world was still stuck with outmoded thinking – hegemony and bloc politics.

In the Chinese leader's view the world was changing and the thinking of people would also change. He then made a startling observation. China made mistakes and wasted twenty years. Since the fall of the Gang of Four in 1976, China has changed. China had substituted class struggle with the pursuit of modernisation. China was opening up to the world. There were changes in every field and the PM would see that for himself when he travelled outside the capital.

In conclusion, the PM said that in India we were doing much the same thing. Old barriers, roadblocks were being knocked down; opening way to modernisation. This reflected itself in the performance of our economy. In the last four years there have been tremendous changes which reflected the growth of the economy.

Deng Xiaoping wished the PM success. Both China and India needed development, he added. For this, both needed to change. Deng then stated that on that day, 'We had talked on every extended topics.' He added that on bilateral relations, Rajiv Gandhi would have further talks with Li Peng and with Zhao Ziyang. Deng asked the prime minister if the meeting could be concluded on this note.

PM thanked Deng, but suggested New Global Economic Order should be mentioned in joint communiqué. The present economic order was exploitative and biased against developing countries. In the future, as the political order stabilises, and hegemonism and bloc politics subside, the pressure would increase much more on the economic side. Perhaps we could also work together in this area.

Deng Xiaoping readily welcomed the idea. The two orders were parallel, the New International Political Order and the New International Economic Order. He believed that they have to be worked on in parallel lines. He added that in 1974 he had devoted time to this aspect in his UN speech.

The PM suggested that this could be worked into the Joint Press Communiqué. Deng agreed, adding that for real development, they would have to rely on their own efforts. Deng said that this did not mean that they close themselves up. He said China would have to look for friends from all directions and accept all assistance that conforms to their conditions. 'You have done so,' Deng told Rajiv Gandhi. The PM said closing doors does not help. He realised that. Deng said China had suffered for that, for closing doors. The PM invited Deng Xiaoping to India. He accepted.

Going over the momentous events of the day the thought occurred to me, what a privilege to be a part of this new beginning in Sino-Indian relations. Full marks to Rajiv Gandhi for this breakthrough. He took a calculated risk. It payed off. Boldness is a major weapon in the quivers of big leaders.

In the afternoon the PM spoke at the Qinghua University. He had worked assiduously on this speech, the only major one on this trip. It had a personal flavour, 'I represent a new generation in India. I was but a boy in the heyday of Sino-Indian friendship.' It had a historical dimension laced with a pinch of philosophy. It ended on a high note:

'We are summoned by our past to the tasks which the future holds. We have a mutual obligation to a common humanity.'

In the evening the meeting with indologists was lively. Good atmosphere. Friendly and warm views expressed by all. Met a friend of P.N. Haksar whose name I did not catch. Several former Chinese ambassadors to India also present.

Ambassador's reception for the PM to meet the Indian community. Dull. After reception the PM asked me to wait. When we met he said, 'I goofed. I should have taken the Foreign secretary with me.' The PM asked what could be done to assuage his feelings. I suggested he should send for KPS and tell him the lapse was regrettable and that he would be invited to all his subsequent meetings with Chinese leaders. Mercifully the media has not got scent of this faux pas. Shades of Kissinger, who had kept Secretary of State Rogers out of talks with Mao in 1972.

I mentioned to the PM that we might attempt a new resolution in the Parliament. The 1960 Resolution cannot be undone but a fresh one would take precedence over the 1962 resolution. It was adopted when emotions and passions ran unrealistically high. Today we have 413 Congress MPs. Not so in 1962. 'This is a very good idea, Natwar. We have two months. You take charge of it.'

I asked about the composition of the SAARC delegation for the Islamabad summit next week. Rajiv Gandhi said MEA had not sent my name. 'How can Natwar be left out?' he asked the MEA. He instructed me to go to Islamabad a day or two earlier than himself. I said I knew the Bhuttos well. I had been to SAARC Summits in Bangalore and Kathmandu. Rajiv Gandhi said he knew that.

Dinner in suite. I had changed and got into bed when a call came for a meeting with the PM at No. 18 at 9:00 pm. Hellishly cold. The PM, Dinesh and I talked for sometime about forthcoming press conference. The PM was not complimentary about PV. Not pulling his weight. Negative, indecisive and uncommunicative. Lacking condour. PV had a powerful horoscope.

In passing, I mentioned to the PM that Nixon had called on Mao twice. Mao had not returned either call. On both occasions, Nixon had been summoned at short notice, when Nixon tried to draw Mao out on specifics. Mao taking the high ground and speaking as a modern day emperor conveyed to Nixon to discuss these with Chou En-lai. 'Really?' the PM exclaimed. The PM surprised us by telling us that Deng had several people with him during their meeting. 'I could have taken you all with me.' For such a vital meeting he should have selected the delegation himself.

The crucial meeting could not have gone better. That was the crowning moment of the visit. I slept late but soundly.

22 December 1988

I'm writing this in the five-star Sian Hotel. Four years ago, Hem, Ritu and I stayed here. I was then a civil servant. Our suite was a more modest one. This one is twice as big. Rajiv and Sonia have a huge one. The Chinese sense of aesthetics is subtle and sensitive. Sian is the place to experience it.

We left Beijing three hours late. Sian airport was fog-bound. Before departure three agreements were signed on civil aviation, science and technology and culture. The two prime ministers were present. A group photograph was taken. Champagne toasts. We were hard put to stick to our phoney tea-totalism.

As we had time on our hands we all moved to the large room from which one could see the frozen lake in the middle of the Diaoyutai State Guest House. The two prime ministers and their wives were in one group. We, the lesser homosapiens in another. I sat with my opposite number. Asked him about his assessment of visit. He repeated what Deng Xiaoping had said. I too said we were more than satisfied. A new beginning had indeed been made. Both sides had worked hard and in a friendly ambience to reach this welcome stage.

PV joined us. My counterpart moved to another table. A little later, one of the Indian pressmen joined us. He asked PV, 'Rao sahib, are you satisfied with the outcome?' 'Yes. But do not quote me in your report. You can attribute this to Natwar!' I said I had no objection. By this time Li Peng had left with his entourage. We still had nearly two hours on our hands. Dinesh, Shankaranand, I and Montek[4] took a short walk. Montek said China would maintain seven per cent growth till end of the twentieth century against ours of five per cent. In twenty years China will be far ahead of us unless we act quickly.

Took off at mid-day for Sian. At Sian, large numbers greeted the PM in spite of the cold and fog. Did the round of the Great Wild Goose Pagoda and the Museum. Buddhist past much in evidence at both the places. Then to that wonder of wonders, the Terracotta Warriors and Horses. Weather wet. Sonia most excited. The little bronze carriage takes one's breath away. Two thousand years ago China had such skills, a sliding window with a 'jali' was manufactured. This treasure was accidentally discovered by a farmer digging a well, only a dozen years ago. Much has been done to make the place a tourist destination. Four years ago it was still somewhat primitive.

Governor's banquet at 6:30. I sat next to a man who had worked with Dr Kotnis. On my suggestion the PM invited him to India. The man was so overcome that he went up to the PM to drink to his health. The PM made a moving speech. I left early to do my TV programme with M.J. Akbar for Doordarshan via satellite for 9:50 IST. Went off well. I used some material given by Gopi.

The PM sent for me late at night. Very relaxed. Busy with his computer. Had all data on China with him. Explained to me how the computer works. I was impressed but none the wiser. I am, when it comes to computers, decidedly underdeveloped. I asked, 'Have you anything on Sian? The PM replied in the negative. I gave him thumbnail history of China's ancient capital, from where began the silk route. Also about the 1936 Sian incident when Chiang Kai-shek was arrested by his own generals. Chou En-lai, was sent from Yenan by Mao to get his most bitter enemy released. Chou succeeded.

The PM asked about PV. 'Can I speak frankly?' I asked. 'Yes,' said the prime minister. I suggested Narasimha should be made a governor. Also that the PM should take over MEA with two ministers of state. K.K.[5] was shaping well. Panditji was EAM for seventeen years. The PM said he wanted to restructure MEA. Did not brush off my suggestion. I might have planted a seed. I said if we had to go ahead with New China Policy, PV should be instructed to get actively involved, more committed. He is erudite, has a cultivated mind but lacks a well-defined, rooted point of view on grave matters of foreign policy.

Told him that I was leaving for Islamabad on the 27th. We drank Coca-Cola. He said the Coke people wanted to get back to India. I said China had allowed both Pepsi and Coke to be set up there. They were neither squeamish nor did they have any commercial inhibitions.

'I could not bring Shiv Shankar on this trip because he had quarrelled with the Chinese finance minister at New York.' The same Chinese foreign minister, I said was his host at the Beijing duck lunch. He smiled. While talking he kept himself busy with his computer. Our brains are capable of making us do a multiplicity of activities simultaneously.

Before leaving, he showed me PV's compact tool kit and his inflatable pillow. Made me put it on round my neck. Very comfortable and practical.

I congratulated him on the success of the tour. He made pleasing remarks about my role. He showed me the gift the Chinese gave him on the plane, 'Travel by Chinese Airways and good luck.' I wondered if Chinese had developed a sense of black humour. The PM was very amused. These few days I noticed how, not so subtle sartorial changes had overtaken Chinese leadership. Except Deng, all wore ties. In the 1950s, no Chinese wore a tie, only diplomats. Not me. I wore bandgala. I put in a good word about Gopi. I remarked that I would have been eaten alive if the visit had failed. 'Me too,' said the PM. Gopi also instrumental in Haksar's secret visit to Beijing early in the year.

The PM, at times, had weird notions about diplomacy. Some weeks ago, when I was discussing this trip with the Chinese ambassador to Delhi, he somewhat hesitatingly said, 'Mr Minister, we are sometimes confused at the manner in which your government functions.' I was a bit put out and said, 'What precisely do you mean?' 'We do not know who is in charge of this important visit. Gopi Arora, Ronen Sen, K.P.S Menon or Bhandari?' I told him to relax and keep dealings with Gopi Arora and Ronen Sen only.

The PM asked me to speak to Mani Shankar Aiyar.[6] Some media 'blokes' had complained against him. His uncontrolled talkativeness gets him into trouble all the time. During the 7th NAM Summit in Delhi in March 1983, Indira Gandhi asked me to get rid of him. I saved his neck. I rather like him. He did a superb job as consul general in Karachi.

23 December

Emplane for Shanghai at 8:00 am in Chinese aircraft. On the flight to Shanghai, the PM came over to me twice to share a joke. Also asked me to look at his Shanghai speech. In Shanghai we transacted no business. I was last in Shanghai in 1957. The city was drab and depressing. Not now. It's being transformed at a fantastic pace. The countryside has not changed much. We visited a farm and one industrial township. The latter obviously spruced up for the PM's visit.

Rajiv and Sonia have been put up in the villa where Mao Tse Tung used to stay, whenever he came to Shanghai, which was not often though. His favourite holiday spot was Hangchow. Lunch given by the famous mayor of Shanghai, Comrade Zhu Rongji.[7] I have now had enough of Chinese food. Left for New Delhi by a special Air India plane at 3:00 pm Shanghai time.

24 December

Rajiv Gandhi telephoned twice in the evening. I called back twice. Gopi, Parathasarthi and I have to discuss follow-up action plan. The PM heard adverse reports of the Saturday Club meeting at IIC, where A.P. Venkateswaran and some others were critical of the China visit and its outcome. Called it propaganda exercise and little else.

The three of us met in my study and gave eleven-point plan. I read it out to the PM. He asked me to send him a note. I also informed him of PV's and K.C. Pant's observations on the visit and joint press communiqué. PV said that he was not in favour of the visit but we should now make best of the situation. We have got a year's reprieve. Raja Pant, normally sound, made incomprehensible remarks about some sentences in communiqué not having been broken into two. 'The Chinese have got what they wanted. What have we got?' I said what he had expected were not wonders. In diplomacy even a modest progress is worthy of respect. The PM had put an end to thirty-four years of diplomatic drought.

PV came out with his swan song of 'We need not have gone', 'I was not in favour', etc. I said rather firmly and formally, 'Rao Sahib, I do not know about you, but I have been in favour of the visit hundred per cent. Let there be no mistake about it.' He was taken aback. I was not impolite but I was forcefully candid. Sometimes he was philosophical, at others avidly didactic. What a coruscating mind he had.

Raja Pant belligerent about Ministry of Defence and his generals. 'If the choice is between believing what the Chinese say and what my officers' say, I shall always believe our people. I cannot function otherwise.' I did not know what to make of this pronouncement. He said this to no one in particular. But said he did. It was recorded.

Thus, we had two senior ministers, who had reservations about the PM's China policy. PV and GP had, all but, sabotaged the fifth round of talks which I had with the Chinese in Beijing in 1984. Raja Pant was tied to his great father's legacy. Pantji and company had cornered Prime Minister Nehru in 1960, at the time of Chou En-lai's visit to Delhi. Now, I understand what Shankaranand meant by 'these Brahmins surrounding Rajivji'.

PV said, 'The visit has given us one year's reprieve.' Gopi said that we had entered the period of socio-economic-political crises and we had to have some realism in our policies. It was vitally important to take advantage of the changing world situation. The visit to China had produced positive results.

Most of such meetings were inconclusive. I found them mentally exhausting and functionally useless. The vaporous platitudes and the proliferating clichés got me. For PV, platitudes were a cause, and not just a linguistic slight of hand.

In next few days we would be contacting all opinion makers and China experts to take them into confidence about the PM's China breakthrough.

26 December

Meeting on Nepal in the PM's room. He and I opted for tough line with the king. Heat to be put on, his not so Majestic Majesty. I asked if I could be excused attending the noon meeting. Rajiv Gandhi said I should be present. What a grind!

At the meeting on Pakistan, Ronen Sen briefed us on his meeting with Benazir Bhutto in Karachi. I had no idea that he had been asked to meet Benazir Bhutto; neither did PV. She was most anxious to sign no first attack and other agreements with us. Pakistan foreign office was in favour. Nor I, till I heard Aftab Seth and Ronen. If we could have breakthrough with Pakistan also, Rajiv Gandhi would end 1988 with a high diplomatic flag flying over him.

I asked the PM if I was needed for the Cabinet briefing. He said, 'Yes.' George telephoned around 11:00 am. The PM wanted Fotedar,[8] Shiela,[9] Gopi and me to organise Cabinet ministers to speak in favour of the China trip.

I spoke several times to M.L.F. – he had doubts about Raja Pant. Said he would meet him. Then changed his mind, 'Let us watch him.' Bhagat,[10] Sathe,[11] Bhajan Lal[12] would launch discussion. PV would open this diplomatic innings in the Cabinet.

Meeting at 5:00 pm. PV made an undramatic but careful presentation. Rajiv Gandhi has made spectacular progress on the Sino-India front. The country has more than welcomed the outcome of Rajiv Gandhi's trail-blazing passage to the modern middle kingdom.

Appendices

Appendix I

Dr S. Radhakrishnan's Speech on Leaving Peking, 27 September 1957

I have spent a few happy and delightful days in this beautiful city and on the eve of my departure from here, I would like to express my gratitude to Chairman Mao Tse Tung, the government and people of China for their very warm hospitality to us during our stay. We have had a memorable experience.

By your sufferings and sacrifice, efforts and exertions you have wiped away the pain, the bruised pride, the humiliation and the insults which you endured for generations. From what little I have seen, your people have a lively vision, a buoyant outlook, an eagerness for action and a capacity for hard work. Disciplined enthusiasm has become a part of your national ethos. I have learnt a great deal and I am impressed by the drive of the government and the determination of the people to work for their economic, social and cultural betterment.

We, in our country, are facing problems of social and economic reconstruction which you are tackling. The submerged people of the world are asking for a tolerable life not merely for the few but for all. They do not accept the evils of famines and floods, drought and disease, ignorance and superstition as inevitable. The feeling of resignation has given place to hope and expectation. If we overcome poverty, raise standard of living, we add an entirely new dimension to human life.

Both our countries believe in democracy. The binding principle of democratic societies is spontaneous conformity, not enforced obedience. The peoples' will should prevail. We cannot crush their wishes, cannot trample on their dreams. Through mutual education, the government and the people come nearer to each other, till the interests of the rulers and the ruled coincide as in Ram-rajya or the ideal state of the Indian conception. As I walked round the Physics Wing of the Chinese Academy the other day, I saw wallpapers freely discussing political problems of fundamental importance. One discerns in the peoples' thought a strongly anti-bureaucratic accent, greater freedom of expression, an insistence on fallibility of governments. These features are in the best traditions of democracy. Democracy is governed by moral standards and your civilisation for centuries has been a moral one.

A nation which is cut off from its roots cannot last long. You have always accepted whatever was valuable in the past and rejected what was injurious. Life is a transformation. It is the adaptation of the old to the new challenges. You are even today accepting whatever is helpful to you from other cultures and discarding what is unhelpful. It is true of your country that the more it changes the more it remains the same.

That the soul should soar and mingle with its own infinitude is the spirit of Taoism. To Confucius, humanity is God and the harmony of social life is the goal of man. Infinite compassion is the spirit of Buddhism. The supreme canon of life is the subordination of the individual to the good of the community. Your great teachers insist on social consciousness and development. Your Constitution grants freedom of religious belief. Study and research in religions are encouraged and the result is likely to be a rejection of obscurantist superstitious beliefs and the acceptance of a reasonable and ethical account of the supreme ends of fife.

There is a popular view which treats the whole being of man as social, a function of his methods of economic production and the social relations they produce. There are different sides to the human being; there is the biological man, there is the social or socialised man, the member or component of the political group, nation and the economic man. There is also another dimension to the human being, where he is alone, where he has the chance to change himself and become a member of the new society. It is only in freedom that a man can discover what he really is. It is the individual who feels pain and joy, who bears responsibility, does good or evil. If we overlook this side of human nature, we turn the subject into an object. The objectification is at once the necessary condition of freedom and a perpetual threat to it. Man must limit the objectification to what is essential for his freedom. As his fellowmen should be equally free, each individual has to submit to certain limitations.

This submission is not servitude, as it is accepted in the freedom of the spirit. A good society should lead to self-enhancement and not self-obliteration.

It is possible, for a modern state to use all its energies and resources for promoting the life and health of its citizens, which would have seemed incredible a few years ago. But this very scientific and technological revolution is capable of producing instruments which will destroy all human life whatsoever. Man is now poised in uncertainty and agony between the death of an old order and the birth of a new one. Conflict and tension are in the air. After the two World Wars and the rise of new regimes, we have become hardened, dulled, numbed. Too many dreadful things which once seemed incredible have happened. These are not aberrations peculiar to some people. They are the consequence of some deep-seated derangement in our minds and hearts. A tendency to objectification, a lapse into mindlessness are responsible for this situation. To despair of the future is an act of treason. We must win through.

The technological revolution has helped us to conceive the whole of mankind as one being. If we look at the areas in the world where there are tensions and conflicts, Germany, West Asia, South-East Asia, we sometimes feel that mankind has forgotten its vision of humanity as one and is in the grip of an insanity which is generally the prelude to self-destruction. If our passions get out of control, the world will be plunged into a dark age. It has happened before in the chequered history of mankind. We must make the choice which will ensure the survival and progress of mankind. We are at one of the crossroads of history. We cannot reduce man to nature, history to a natural process. It is a moral drama in which individuals participate.

Thinking-men all over the world are profoundly alarmed lest man should now, in the lust for material power, lose touch with the spiritual forces which could transform human life into better social forms.... Only these forces can save man in this hour of need and set his soul towards higher ranges of being.

You are now busy building your new economic order, which will tax all your strength and resources for many years to come and you can do so, only if there is peace in the world. I have no doubt that you will soon be able to make valuable contributions to the endeavour of civilisation to build a happy human home on earth.

A great American president as long ago as 1856 stated clearly America's policy on the whole question of recognition of other nations. He said, 'It is the established policy of the United States to recognise all governments without a question of their source or their organisation, or of the means by the governing persons attain their power, provided there be a government *de facto* accepted by the people of the country.' The United Nations Organisation admits into its membership all peace-loving states which accept the obligations contained in the UN Charter, and in its judgement are able and willing to carry out its obligations. There are some in the United Nations who have not carried out their obligations. There is an increasing world opinion in favour of the admission of the People's Republic of China into the UNO. It is our hope and wish that the People's Republic of China will soon find her due place in the United Nations Organization.

The UN Charter requires us to turn away from the military road and set to work to reconcile our differences in a peaceful way. We must eschew every trace of pride, learn that all men are brothers. He who hurts others hurts himself. The interdependence of mankind is increasingly forced on our attention by political, economic and even military happenings. Given a period of peaceful coexistence, every social system, every political structure will shake off its weaknesses and develop on lines which are suited to its conditions. In the not-so-distant-future, we will find ourselves together as members in a peaceful family of nations.

Before I conclude, I may say that our two countries have had centuries of cultural exchange untroubled by any unhappy incidents, political or military. We have grown richer by each other's offerings. The foundations of our relationship were laid by our ancestors, Chinese and Indian, with infinite patience and sacrifice nearly two thousand years ago. The road built by them across the barriers of race and language in the pursuit of truth, love and cooperation should be an inspiration for our future comradeship. I wish to convey to the people of China our best wishes in their great enterprise of building a new China – liberal, democratic and socialistic.

APPENDIX II

Prime Minister Nehru's Speech at the Banquet Held in Honour of Chou En-lai, 20 April 1960

We are meeting here today, to do honour to the prime minister of China who is our respected guest not only in his individual capacity, but also as the representative of a great nation. We have had the privilege and pleasure of welcoming him on several occasions previously to our country. It was a matter of deep satisfaction for us that the two great countries of Asia – India and China, were forging bonds of friendship in the present age, even as they had lived in friendship through ages past. This friendship and cooperation appeared to us as a guarantee of peace in Asia. Thus, this friendship with this great neighbour of ours became one of the cornerstones of India's policy.

We meet today, however, under different circumstances – serious disagreements have unfortunately arisen between us. This is a misfortune for all of us and, I think, for the whole world. It is a double misfortune for us in India because, we have been conditioned for long years past to believe in peace and in peaceful methods and to consider war a thing of horror, unbecoming to civilised nations. We have opposed not only war but also what is called the cold war because this represented the approach of hatred and violence. We have endeavoured to follow, in our limited and imperfect way, the teachings of two great sons of India – the Buddha and Gandhi.

It is strange and a matter of great sorrow for us that events should have so shaped themselves as to challenge that very basis of our thinking that caused our people to apprehend danger on our peaceful frontiers along the great Himalayan mountains; which we have loved for thousands of years and which have stood as sentinels guarding and inspiring our people.

You, Sir, have been here at this critical moment and we welcome your visit. Much has happened which has pained our people, much has been done which we think should have been undone, much has been said which had better been left unsaid. We have to try to the best of our abilities to find a right and peaceful solution to the problems that have arisen. That solution must be in consonance with the dignity and self-respect of each country as well as in keeping with the larger cause of peace in Asia and the world.

We have raised the banner of peace before other countries and we and the world at large can least afford, to let this slip from our hands.

We meet here, at a difficult and crucial moment in the world's history and in our own relations. Thousands of years of two great and ancient civilisations stand witness to our meeting, and the hopes of millions of citizens for a happier future are tied up in our endeavours. Let us pray for our success so that we may be true to this part of ours as well as the future that beckons us. For our part, I can assure you, Mr Prime Minister, that we shall strive to do our utmost so that our efforts may lead to success and to the maintenance of peace with dignity and self-respect of both our great nations. As the Buddha said, 'the real victory is the victory of all which involves no defeat.'

I feel that you have the same urge for peace and cooperation and that, with our joint endeavours, we shall not only halt the unhappy process of deterioration in our countries' relations, but also take a step towards their betterment.

Appendix III

Talks between Prime Minister Nehru and Premier Chou En-lai, 25 April 1960

PM: 'Yesterday our officials held a meeting. Since the time is limited, we may perhaps discuss the question of a draft communiqué. We have made a draft of the joint statement which Your Excellency may like to see.'
(PM handed over the Indian draft communiqué to Premier Chou En-lai).

Premier Chou: 'We too have drafted a communiqué on the basis of the talks of the last five days and I would like you to have a look at it. The contents, however, differ to some extent.'
(Premier Chou handed over the Chinese draft to the PM)

PM: 'There is a good deal of difference between our draft and Your Excellency's draft. You have mentioned certain matters on which we do not agree. You have mentioned that we hold unanimous views on the six points. We do not agree to most of them and in a statement of this kind one must avoid controversial matters, otherwise it would be argumentative. It should represent both viewpoints without entering into any arguments. I would therefore suggest, that we should take our draft as a basis for discussion.'

Premier Chou : 'As to these six points mentioned in the draft, they have been mentioned several times, and yesterday Your Excellency said, that you did not have much to say about them but that you only wanted some clarification on Point No. 4 and I gave that clarification. Therefore, I thought that in principle, these points were acceptable to Your Excellency.

'As regards Point No. 1, we have said that our boundaries are "not formally delimited". This wording is taken from one of the letters of Your Excellency. As regards the point regarding territorial claims, I have already made explanations. As regards stopping of patrolling, there was some difficulty in accepting Your Excellency's suggestion on the western sector and I promised to give an answer. Therefore, I feel that mention of these points in this draft is not without basis but if Your Excellency objects then we will not press it. My impression, however, has been that Your Excellency did not raise any objection to them when they were put forwarded to.'

PM: 'I'm afraid it is not quite correct. I had expressed my view on these matters earlier and I think it was not necessary to say it again. You said that there was a dispute on the boundary. Yes that is so, and that there are areas under actual control of either side, and I said, that it is probably so. But that was not in this context. On Point No. 4, I had pointed out that if we accepted this, it would mean that practically we have settled our disputes. I did not say anything because, I thought we had made our position sufficiently clear; and it is certainly not correct to say that I agree to these points. For example, when you said that the dispute existed, it was not a matter for agreement or disagreement on my part, since you were making an assertion about the existence of a dispute. Our claim all along has been that, although the boundary is not marked on the ground, it has all along been well-defined through various ways. There may, of course, be difference of opinion on this but our position is clear.'

Premier Chou: 'It is, of course, good that Your Excellency has further clarified your point of view. It proves that there are still differences of opinion, as you have said. Our views, we have already stated in our draft, but I would now like to say something about your draft.

'From Your Excellency's draft, one gets the general impression that after the last six days of talks, we only agreed on procedural matters, but that there was no progress whatsoever. But that is not my appraisal. I think some progress has been made. I cannot say, that there has been no difference at all, or that as if no exchange has been made, that we did not review the historical background or that there has been no difference as compared to the days when we had not met. Some progress has been made, and this is a fact. To give an impression disappointing to our people, and to the world who are interested in these talks, would not be desirable, because this matter does not concern not only our people, but the entire world. Therefore, I think that the main spirit of the draft, should be positive. Particularly, it would be better if Para. 3 in your draft is revised.

(i) Para. 3 could be revised to some such effect: "both parties explained their stands, viewpoints, ideas and about the solution of the question the talks enabled both sides to further understand each other. Although both parties did not reach a further agreement, they reached an agreement on procedure..." Such a thing will be more positive, in conformity with the facts, and is not embarrassing to the Government of India.

'I further feel, that something should also be said about the prospects after report of officials on both sides has been submitted, viz: there should be some mention that the two prime ministers will meet again. This will give hope to our people. We feel, that no matter how great the difficulties may be, they must be overcome. We came with great hope and we want that hope to persist.

(ii) As regards the last sentence in Para. 5, it is still our view that while our officials are examining factual material, we should stop patrolling all along the border in order to avoid any clashes. The idea of stopping patrolling was put forward by Your Excellency yourself. Your Excellency said yesterday that, in the eastern sector it is all right, that there is no patrolling by Indian troops, and that near Kinzamane, only a few Tibetan refugees came in. I also had made inquiries on this point and found that it was not a group of Tibetan refugees, but according to our information, the original post set up by the Indian army at Kinzamane had been moved to a place one kilometer northwest of the original post. The new post is at Dama where a company of Indian soldiers is now stationed. This place has only six families with twenty-nine inhabitants, all Tibetans. Perhaps Indian troops might have done this. But it shows that Indian forces have not only stopped patrolling, but have even pushed their post forward. This brings them nearer to our post at Lotsun and the difference between our post and this new post is only four kilometers. So, such a situation does exist in the eastern sector. I received this information just before I came here. We have given strict orders not to open fire under any circumstances and also strictly ordered our forces not to do any patrolling along the line.

'Regarding the eastern sector, we have given assurance that, our forces will not exceed India's line of actual control. As far as we can see, Kinzamane exceeds this line. But in the western sector, Indian government has not given us a similar assurance and, therefore, the problem arises. It is a vast area, and most places are without inhabitants. So, if in some places where we have no posts, the Indian side establishes posts, then the posts on both sides would be in a very zigzag position. That would make problems very complicated. Therefore, we have suggested stopping of patrolling all along the border. This would give some kind of a guarantee, and it seems to us that during further examination of material, we should at least have some such kind of a guarantee.

'I have a few suggestions regarding Para. 6:

(i) We might add, in addition to the reference to the Paris Conference in the draft, our support to prohibition of nuclear weapons.

(ii) We may also extend our support to the just struggle of the African, Asian and Latin American people against imperialism, racial discrimination and in defence of their independence. If it is possible, we may specifically condemn the government of the Union of South Africa for taking repressive measures against the African people. If that is not possible, we might put it in a general way.

(iii) We may also reiterate, that Geneva Agreement should be respected by all parties concerned. This is particularly because, India is the chairman of the Supervisory Commission.

'At the end, I suggest that one point should be added to your draft stating that, I have cordially invited Your Excellency to come to China, and that you would do so at your convenience.

'I also find that there is no mention of the Five Principles in the entire draft.

'Perhaps, according to Your Excellency, these principles have been shaken. But it is not so. We still feel that, these principles should govern our relations.

Some temporary or superficial phenomenon might be interpreted by some as our not conforming to the Five Principles. But, as Your Excellency has mentioned, there is no basic conflict of interest between our two countries, and so, we should continue to reaffirm our faith in the Five Principles. In Chinese we have a saying which says – "A good horse can be seen only from the distance that it covers and the heart of a person is seen only by events." Our friendship has stood the test of time in the past, and I am confident that it will continue to stand the test of time, for a thousand years to come. These are mainly my views. There are also some technical suggestions, but these I will not go into.'

PM: 'Your Excellency has referred to many matters. The initial difficulty for me is that, even your referring to all these matters shows a difference in the approach of the two sides. How to bring these differences close together in a statement of this type? Because, in a brief joint statement like this, we cannot have arguments. We cannot mention the difference in our approaches, viz., the Indian view and the Chinese view and so on. It would be out of place.

'You say that a more positive approach is desirable. Yes, provided it has a good basis. The position is definite. These long talks have not convinced each other of the rightness of the other's position. We can express it argumentatively, or in a brief manner, as we have tried to do in the draft.

'Your Excellency mentioned including something about "the prospects after receipt of the report". What can one say about this? If we say something, it will only be some pious sentiments and will not lead us anywhere. It will be airy and without much meaning.

'I agree, that we should approach with hope and try our best.

'Your Excellency referred to stopping of patrolling and more particularly, to Kinzemane. According to your information, our post has moved forward. I am not aware of this. We had an inquiry, and I was told that no patrolling was done. Normally speaking, we should have been informed if such a thing had happened. However, since you have mentioned it, I will make inquiries again.

'Broadly speaking, I am in favour of stopping patrolling activities which would lead to a clash, but, there are many areas of patrolling and they are not against anybody, particularly in a vast area like the western sector. I admit, that we should avoid patrolling, but does it mean that our patrols should stay in their post, without moving out between these vast areas? They have to have some communication and it is a normal thing which does not involve any conflict. Therefore, to stop all movements will not be practicable, but we should issue strict orders that they should refrain from activities which would lead to armed clashes.

'Your Excellency referred to Para. 6, that mentions about international affairs. You mentioned that we should include something about prohibition of nuclear weapons. We have been saying it all the time, and we support such prohibition, but the fact is that, this point is not before the Paris Conference but is being discussed as a separate issue. As regards struggle in Africa for independence and racial equality, we have also expressed our opinion frequently, clearly and in very strong terms.

'But the main question is, whether referring to these things in this kind of a statement would be appropriate. I am afraid that this may lead to many kinds of criticisms both from our people here and others.

'Frankly speaking, our people will say that you talk about other areas, but you do not talk about Tibet. I do not want to say anything about Tibet. But according to our information, statements have been made in Tibet, by important representatives of the Central Chinese Government, like Chang Ching-Wu and Chang Kuo-Hua that Bhutan and Sikkim are parts of Tibet, that Ladakh is a part of Tibet, that areas upto Teesta (near Siliguri) come under Tibet, and that the areas north of the Brahmaputra are also parts of Tibet. In addition, there are broadcasts of Lhasa Radio and speeches of the Youth League and Women's League meetings. I do not know whether these are responsible or irresponsible people, but such reports affect our peoples' mind and they will say you talk about distant places like Africa, but you do not say anything about surrounding territories like Bhutan and Sikkim, with whom we have intimate relations through treaties and practices.

'Your Excellency said in your letter, that borders between China and Bhutan and Sikkim do not fall in the scope of these discussions. As far as we are concerned, they fall within the scope of these discussions and we are responsible for their borders.

'I have also referred to the Bhutanese's enclaves in Tibet. There are some eight villages, especially near Kailash mountain, where the Bhutanese officials have been deprived of their belongings and the Bhutanese government has asked us to raise this matter with you. All these I am mentioning just to show how difficult it is to enter into a world survey, even in matters where there can be no disagreement. Your Excellency also referred to Indo-China and I believe that for the same reason, a reference to it in the present context would seem inappropriate.

'As regards Five Principles, we believe in them and even if they are not acted upon, they still remain good. But a reference to them in the present context would be immediately criticised. The people will say that these principles have been broken and still we are talking about them.

'As regards including Your Excellency's invitation to me in the communiqué, it is not normally our practice to refer to such invitations in joint statements. Mr Khrushchev came here and wanted us to put it in the statement. Mr Nasser referred to his invitation in a statement but he did it independently.

'The point is, we are taking steps. If these steps lead to it, certainly I shall be most happy to follow them up.

'As regards prohibition of nuclear weapons and general desire for peace, etc., which Your Excellency mentioned, just two days ago, I read an article in the *Red Flag*, the journal of the Central Committee of CCP. It contained an appeal of preparation for wars and the development of nuclear weapons to win wars. All these create reactions, and people feel that the Chinese government is not as anxious for peace as we thought it was, and that it wants to develop its nuclear weapons.'

Premier Chou: 'Does it mean that there would be no changes or amendments at all in the draft statement?'

PM: 'Of course there can be some minor amendments. If you insist on mentioning the prohibition of nuclear weapons, we can certainly include it. But the general structure should remain the same.'

Premier Chou: 'At the very beginning, I said that we will take your draft as the basis. Although I have talked a great deal, my suggestions are actually few. Since this will be a joint statement, I thought that possibility for the exchange of views should be allowed. Except for some technical matters regarding wording, etc., which can be left to our officials, I suggest that, if Your Excellency will agree, we may go through the draft para by para and exchange views.'

PM: 'Yes.'

Premier Chou: 'I would like to revert to Para. 3 again, particularly the first sentence, "these talks did not result in resolving difference that had arisen". This sentence puts things in a negative perspective. My suggestion is, that we should revise the sentence without saying anything in such specific terms. It may be something as follows, "Both parties explained their stands, viewpoints and ideas about the solution to the question and achieved further understanding although differences between the two sides remain."

'This is in conformity with facts because we do have a better understanding of each other than before. How does your Excellency like this idea?'

PM: 'We may perhaps add before the first sentence, another sentence to the effect that "both sides explained their respective viewpoints" or "respective viewpoints were understood better". But the first sentence is still correct.

'Incidentally, I may mention that, all along we have been talking about the border question. Actually, it is something more than the border question. It does not merely refer to a narrow sector but large areas around the border.'

Premier Chou: 'Yes, it is true, but then we will have to explain not only the western sector, but also the eastern sector in the same manner. The details of wording we can, however, leave to our officials.

'As regards the second line in Para. No. 4 on page 2, where the sentence ends as follows, "draw up a report for submission to the two governments", I would suggest, that we should add something like the following to show some hope, "In order to facilitate further talks of the two prime ministers". If Your Excellency does not agree to this wording, then we may add something like "in order to facilitate a reasonable settlement of the boundary question". I am suggesting this just to express a hope.'

PM: 'Well, perhaps we might say "in order to facilitate further consideration of this question".'

Premier Chou: 'I would suggest an alternative expression. These are actually the words taken from one of your Excellency's letters —"in order to facilitate further exploration of avenues for a settlement of the boundary question".'

PM: 'But officials can hardly do that, i.e. exploration of avenues. It has to be done at a higher level.'

Premier Chou: 'When I say "further consideration", it means consideration at a higher level.'

PM: 'Wordings we will consider further.'

Premier Chou: 'As regards the last sentence of Para. No. 5, I suggest that, we should provide for stopping of patrolling all along the border.

'When we say stopping of patrolling, it does not mean stopping of all movements, but that we should not send any patrols to the border, to avoid clashes. The question is that in the western sector, the Government of India does not accept that the other side has a line of actual control. It is precisely here where the danger lies. As Your Excellency has said in the Parliament, the border in this area is undelimited.'

PM: 'Our actual border is 150 miles away.'

Premier Chou: 'According to us, in this area [the western sector], our boundary has all along been like this. Our administrative jurisdiction has always reached this area and the area has been under Khotan and Rudok. Our revenue officers have also been going to these places wherever there has been any need. There is no time for making any surveys, but we can examine the documents. In the western sector, the Chinese do have a line of actual control but the Indian government does not accept it. Therefore, the situation is mobile. Although, we say we want to avoid clashes, the danger remains. I would therefore, still propose our choice of words, namely, "both sides should stop sending patrols to the border". This does not mean that all movements should be stopped. Does Your Excellency think that this would be appropriate?'

PM: 'On the western sector, as Your Excellency has said, it is a mobile border. But it is mobile only as far as occupation is concerned, not in theory. So it is difficult to call anything a precise border. Your Excellency said, that this area [western sector] has been for a long time under your control, and that you have been collecting revenue there. Our claim is that for many years it was not under occupation and there is no trace of occupation till recently. Other people have been there and, as I said earlier, I have myself been to places which are now reportedly under Chinese occupation.

'If you say "a border", then we have to acknowledge a border and therefore we should better say that we "should avoid any movement which may lead to a clash".'

Premier Chou: 'I do not say that the western border is mobile. We are definite as to where our border lies. As I have said earlier, our border lies along the Karakoram watershed and Kongka Pass in the middle sector. This has always been regarded as our border, and our jurisdiction has always reached the border. When I said "mobile", I meant that the administrative personnel could not be stationed there permanently because there are no people. But, it does not mean that the border is mobile. I find on the Indian maps that the borderline in this sector has changed four times, and two times there has been no borderline.

'Your Excellency says, that we should merely say "avoid movements". If there are movements only in areas under your control, it will not lead to clashes. But what we ask is that, your forces in the western sector, like our forces in the eastern sector, should stop patrolling.'

PM: 'Your Excellency has said that our maps have been changing. It is not so. You refer to maps which are ninety-eight years old. But a complete survey was done only ninety-six years ago and since then the Indian maps have not changed. In some there may be a colour shade, in some there are firm lines. This is because these are vast areas. You say, that your administrative personnel have been going there. We say the same. So there is a clash of factual statements. Therefore, I would still like to suggest the wording "avoid movement which may bring about clashes and frictions". Otherwise, it means for all practical purposes, we accept the border as claimed by China.'

Premier Chou: 'Alright, let's leave the wording to the officials. Now, we come to Para. No. 6. I had mentioned three international questions. Your Excellency said that, prohibition of nuclear weapons was not on the agenda of the Paris Conference, and therefore, there was no point in mentioning it. It makes no difference to us, whether it is mentioned in the communiqué or not.

'But we would like to make this clear, that China like India, has all along favoured prohibition of test and production of nuclear weapons. The Chinese government has made many statements on this. I also spoke at the People's Congress recently and suggested that all Asian nations should sign a pact for an atom-free zone.

'Your Excellency mentioned an article in *Red Flag*. It is permissible to give theoretical articles, giving two kinds of thinking like (1) which advocates immediate stopping of testing and production of nuclear weapons, and also destruction of the nuclear weapons already manufactured. This is, of course, a more thorough way of ending the nuclear threat, so that the atomic energy is used only for peaceful purposes. There is also, the other way of thinking (2) War-mongering groups are still using great piles of nuclear weapons to intimidate certain countries, and these countries are forced to seek a way out. As soon as these countries learn the technique and have atomic weapons in their possession, there will be a possibility of reaching an agreement on disuse of these weapons. The same thing happened in the First World War, in the case of chemical warfare. So, there are two things. One, is to take initiative to appeal for cessation of testing and production of nuclear weapons. We favour such an agreement. But war-mongering groups have a monopoly and we must endeavour to get such weapons. Therefore there are two ways of thinking, both maintaining abolition of nuclear weapons. This does not mean that we advocate a nuclear war. Your Excellency can understand quite well, which of the two countries is under greater threat, undoubtedly China.

'There are very large military bases in South Korea, Japan, Taiwan, the Philippines, Vietnam and even Pakistan. Many of these are armed with nuclear weapons. The warheads are controlled and can be used by the USA any time it chooses. China, in this regard is weak and if the USA pushes a button, we will suffer heavy loss. Our position is different from the position taken by India, of peace and neutrality. We praise it, but India should also understand the great threat to which China is subjected, and therefore, we must write articles to remind and educate the people of our country. We cannot watch with folded hands, destruction coming to our country. What we face, is the threat of powerful US imperialism and revived Japanese militarism. Besides, these are facing only us and no one else.

'In passing, I would like to take this occasion to mention the flights of unknown aircraft in the last two months, particularly in February and March. The Government of India, had mentioned that there were unknown aircrafts flying over Sino-Indian boundary. We have found that these aircrafts are American. I would like to inform Your Excellency, that they have flown over six times over this area. They start from Bangkok, sometimes go via Burma, sometimes through China to cross over the Sino-Indian boundary, in Tibet they go right up to Chinghai. They come for the purpose of subversion, dropping Chinese agents, trained in Bangkok, supplies weapons and wire sets. We have captured these agents, supplies, radios, etc., in each case. On their return journey these planes flew to Bangkok or to Karachi. We have confirmed all these flights. These six flights flew on the following dates: 10, 11, 12, 16, 17 February and 9 March. Only one flight, on 23 February, still remains untraced.

'I can assure Your Excellency, that we do not allow our aircraft in Tibet to cross the present actual line of control by the Indian side. Firstly, we have few aircrafts in Tibet, and it's difficult to fly over the high Himalayan ranges. We have also sent a note to Burma, and have told them that they have full right to shoot or bring down these planes when they come into their territory. These aircrafts mostly do right flights. I am mentioning this to show, that we are facing threat not only from the sea side, but also from the mainland and we will take appropriate measures in dealing with these aircrafts.

'Your Excellency mentioned about Tibet. I would like to say a few words about it. You spoke about the statements by the responsible people in Tibet, but I have not read them; so, I cannot say anything about it. But, I can say this much that from top to bottom, there is no one in the Chinese government, who has any intention of raising the history of Bhutan and Sikkim, in order to give rise to a new dispute. In the two documents, we have already said that we have no border disputes with Bhutan and Sikkim and that their border does not fall within the scope of this discussion on the three sectors. We have also stated, that we respect the relations between Bhutan and India and Sikkim with India, and our attitude remains the same.

'If Bhutan wants to raise the question of its tax collection activities in Tibet, it can be settled in an appropriate and friendly manner. As regards Tibet, we have settled the question in accordance with the interests of the serfs, who form the majority of the Tibetan population, and in the interest of the freedom of the Tibetan people. The rebels constitute a very small minority. Apart from those who fled away, those who still stay in Tibet can get land, if they wish to till it. The nobles can get compensation for land if they support the democratic reforms. I am sure, that the economy in Tibet will develop and the Tibetans will prosper.

'As regards those who fled to India, we have no objection to the Indian government giving asylum to them. We have also noticed that your government has allowed freedom to them only for religious activities rather than for political activities. But, we have also noticed that ever since the Dalai Lama came to India, till today he has carried on political activities in India and outside far exceeding the scope of freedom set for him by the Indian authorities. Kalimpong still continues to be the centre for conducting anti-China activities by them in India. We have made reservations regarding the Dalai Lama and his followers but their activities, which have exceeded the limits set by the Government of India, not only continue but at the same time they are also encouraged. This will only hinder their return to the fatherland. We can only deplore this.

'As regards the South African question, Your Excellency mentioned that, some people might link it up with the question of Tibet because of the general suppression in South Africa. But the question of Tibet is different. In South Africa, the people oppressed are the majority of the people, while in Tibet, the majority has been emancipated. Only a minority of serf-owners are denied the opportunity to exploit the serfs. I am glad to know, that Your Excellency also agrees that the Geneva Agreement should be respected. I would, however, like to bring to your notice that the Agreement is being repeatedly violated by the USA and the Laos government. This is causing great worry to the North Vietnam government. The "patriotic front" in Laos is suppressed. I do hope that India, as Chairman of the Supervisory Commission, will take effective measures to improve the situation.

'If Your Excellency thinks these [international] questions should not be mentioned in the joint statement, that is alright. If Your Excellency also feels that we should not mention anything about our government's invitation to Your Excellency to visit China, that is also alright.

'I however, feel that it is a matter of great regret that the Five Principles are not mentioned. We continue to firmly believe in them.

'I have stated all my views. I will take this draft back and tell my colleagues about the three points about which we have talked about. We are not very satisfied with this draft. Frankly speaking, I do not like this draft much. I feel that a better statement should be issued. But, since Your Excellency has put forward the draft and you insist on it, we will try to persuade our colleagues.

'If they agree, then at 4:30 pm, I will send one of our officials, Mr Chou Kuan Hua, to meet officials of your side [the Foreign Secretary]. They can meet and fix the wording. I may also have an opportunity to discuss the matter further at the tea party of the home minister, if need be. If, however, the officials meet with serious difficulties, then we can talk again at 6:30 or later on separately.'

PM: 'I would like to take the opportunity of mentioning something about the working of our mission in Tibet, particularly, the difficulties faced by them. As you are aware, our trade agency at Gyantse is having numerous difficulties regarding its buildings. The houses were washed off by floods and they have not been able to get land so far. Then, there is also the question of the Ladakhi Lamas and the citizenship question of the Kashmiri Muslims. But, I will present a note on these points.'

Premier Chou: 'I will welcome such a note. I can also assure Your Excellency that, now that the Tibetan rebellion has been put down, democratic reforms are being carried out and social order established our relations in Tibet will improve, our relations in the field of economy and culture, etc., will, I hope, improve and I also hope that mutual visits will be more frequent.'

Appendix IV

Prime Minister Rajiv Gandhi's Speech at Qinghua University, Beijing, 21 December 1988

I am delighted at this opportunity to visit this renowned university. It is a symbol of what modern China has achieved. A symbol of the Chinese pursuit of excellence.

Thirty-four years ago, my grandfather, Jawaharlal Nehru came to China as a messenger of peace and goodwill and found here a spirit of both. Between India and China that spirit is now being rekindled.

The coming together of India and China in the early fifties was a development of historical international importance. Not only did it presage friendship between the two most populous nations of the world, counting between them a third of all humankind, it represented what was for the time a unique example of two great nations, with two totally different economic and social systems, coming together to give a practical demonstration of peaceful coexistence among different systems. Placed in the context of the epochal change brought about in the world by the independence of India and the liberation of China, among the most important events of the mid-point of the twentieth century, the friendship which Jawaharlal Nehru sought with China was one that could fundamentally effect the destiny of humankind.

Apart from the immense potential for world peace and cooperation implicit in peace and cooperation between India and China, there was also the imperative of facing together the common problems with which both countries were confronted. We have both ancient civilisations, with memories going back into the deepest recesses of the distant past, who had both undergone a prolonged period of national trauma caused by the strangling of our freedoms, the parcelling out of our economies, the stultification of our social and moral progress. We both saw the liberation of our nations not so much as the culmination of a struggle, but as the beginning of an opportunity to serve our people, build our economies, transform our societies and take our countries forward.

Through the period of our struggle for freedom and your struggle for liberation, India and China viewed developments in each other's countries with deep sympathy and understanding. Our great national poet, Rabindranath Tagore, started a Chini Bhavan (the House of China) at his universal university, Visva-Bharati, at Santiniketan, of which I now have the honour to be the chancellor. Our involvement in your liberation struggle found expression in the immortal mission which Dr Kotnis led to China. Jawaharlal Nehru envisaged friendship between India and China as a major pillar of the post-colonial world order.

India and China worked together for peace in Asia and the world, when they first emerged from the thraldom of imperialism. Together we saw that the world order was vitiated by confrontation, by a lack of respect for the sovereign equality of nations, by intolerance of alternative national systems for the organisation of political, economic and social life. We saw that our newly won Independence would be secure only in a world which had liberated itself from the assumptions and prejudices of the past.

A striking example of the persistence of past prejudice was the refusal to recognise the People's Republic of China – the culmination of the Great Revolution which had swept China. India was among the first to recognise the great and welcome change that had burst upon your country. Those who refused to recognise that the China of the Opium Wars had been consigned to the pages of history, began menacing the New China from different directions and in different ways. Through this period of tribulation, India stood by China.

Another manifestation of the persistence of the old ways into the new era was the attempt which was made to restore the colonialisms that had crumbled during the Second World War. The attempt was doomed, but not before hundreds of thousands had perished in this dangerously reactionary endeavour. The agony was long drawn-out in Indo-China relationship. India and China, representing the resurgent voice of Asia, worked towards ending colonialism everywhere, taking the world from under the shadow of the past into the sunshine of the new era.

Together, India and China articulated a new philosophy summed up in the Panchsheel, the Five Principles of Peaceful Coexistence: respect for territorial integrity and sovereignty; non-aggression; non-interference; equality and mutual benefit; and peaceful coexistence.

There have been many momentous events in the three-and-a-half decades that have gone by since we jointly adopted these principles. We have had serious differences among ourselves, leading at one stage even to armed conflict. We have not always been of one view on international issues.

In contrast to the warmth of our friendship and a shared sense of purpose which marked our joint endeavours in the early years, the last thirty years or so have been a period of estrangement. Contacts between us have been sharply reduced. Information about each other has become the preserve of scholars, instead of being the knowledge of people. A sense of persisting differences prevailed over the earlier sense of common perceptions and common goals. Despite this, India and China held similar views on a number of matters of international importance and India continued to support China on such crucial issues as the restoration to China of its rightful place in the United Nations system.

We have seen vast progress in each of our countries. Where once there was a China of famines and shortages, now there is a China self-reliant in feeding its people. Where once there was a China with, but nascent industry, now there is a China looking with confidence and conviction towards becoming one of the world's major economic powers in the twenty-first century. At one time, China suffered from low levels of literacy, backward-looking social practices and rapid population growth. Now there is a China respected the world over for what it has achieved in giving education to its people, promoting social progress in different spheres of human endeavour, and making a remarkable effort at population planning.

India too has undergone a major structural transformation. We too have overcome our vulnerability to famines and food shortages and are now self-sufficient in food grains production. Our industry has developed from its earlier fledgling stage. Today, we have a broad industrial base with a highly diversified industrial structure. In education, we have steadily increased our literacy rates and we aim at universal elementary education by the beginning of the next decade. Social progress has been evident in such areas as the removal of untouchability, affirmative action in favour of the disadvantaged sections of society, education for girls and the integration of women into the mainstream of the nation's progress.

Both our countries have given high priority to the development of science and technology. Your achievements in space are truly remarkable and justly admired. You are doing important work in the frontier areas of superconductivity, medicine and biotechnology. We, in India, are also working in these areas. We are among the few countries which have developed remote-sensing satellite technology for the management of natural resources. We have made useful advances in many areas of industrial and defence electronics and material sciences. In telecommunications, we have developed our own digital switching system. Both of us have significant capabilities in the field of software development including work in the most sophisticated areas. There are possibilities of India and China undertaking joint research in critical areas of electronics.

While there is comparability and complementarity between what we have achieved, it is interesting that we have achieved what we have in ways that are remarkably different from one another. The three pillars of India's modern nationhood are parliamentary democracy, secularism and socialism.

We have a multiplicity of political parties and elected legislatures at the central and state levels, in addition to elected local bodies. Governments are formed by the party or combination of parties constituting a majority in the legislature and are in turn responsible to the legislature. At periodic intervals, normally of five years, electorate renews or changes its mandate. Our system allows for different parties to come to power at different levels at different times. It also allows for different parties to rule at the centre and in the state and in the local bodies at the same time. Equal rights are guaranteed by our constitution and assured by our democratic process to all minorities – religious, ethnic or linguistic. Our judiciary is independent of the executive, our press is free to report, comment and criticise. We believe that freedom of expression and the free exchange of views are not only intrinsically valuable, but have also promoted stability in our society by furnishing safety valves which forestall social and economic pressures before these trigger off an explosion. Democracy has enabled us to maintain a steady course through four decades of rapid change.

The second pillar of our state is secularism. It is a word with different connotations in different languages. We mean by secularism that the state in India does not interfere in the religious practices of its citizens, nor does it encourage the mixing of religion with politics. The state has no religion. At the same time, our state respects the religious sensibilities of our people, values the spiritual and cultural strength which religion imparts, and ensures full freedom of worship and propagation for all religions. Nearly twenty per cent of our population belongs to various religious minorities. The largest among them are the Muslims. All our religious groupings have a high and honoured place in our society, with the assurance that no section of our people will be discriminated on the grounds of religion. Special programmes have been put in place to assist minorities in need of special assistance.

Socialism in India is indigenous to our experience and our conditions. It is not a dogma. It is responsive to changing circumstances. It has had the resilience to develop with time. The focus of our socialism is the upliftment of the poor, succour to the weak, justice to the oppressed and balanced regional development. To attain these ends, we believe the state must control the commanding heights of the economy and that self-reliance should be the first principle of development. We stress that the pattern of progress must be so designed, as to give all parts of the country equitable opportunities of growth and all sections of our people an equitable share of the fruits of development. Our emphasis on balanced regional growth and our accent on the reduction of social disparities have meant stressing the imperatives of growth with considerations of equity. Our socialism sees the thrust of the development effort as growth with social justice.

Our development strategy is one of planning for a mixed economy. The state sector is predominant in core and heavy industry and also in much of infrastructure. But most of the light industry and all of agriculture is in the private sector. Our development objective is the modernisation and transformation of our economy with an overriding priority to the elimination of poverty. Planning on a democratic framework necessarily places great importance on evolving a consensus on goals and instruments. At times, this imposes constraints in the larger interest of democratic consensus and participation.

This strategy has served us well. We have succeeded in setting our economy on an accelerating growth path. Agricultural productivity and production have increased steadily, and the vulnerability of agriculture to the weather has been reduced. Industry is now growing rapidly. We hope to accelerate our growth further in the next decade. Food grains output will be doubled over the next ten to fifteen years. Our perspective plan envisages the eradication of poverty and unemployment by the end of the century.

But many problems remain. Our rate of growth of population remains too high. While impressive increases in food grains production have been recorded in many parts of our country, the task ahead is that of spreading this Green Revolution to new areas and to new crops. We have to diversify agriculture and promote greater value addition. We have to make our industry more efficient and competitive, with better products and higher quality. We believe that much sharper domestic competition is necessary to ensure this. It is also necessary, progressively, to open up our industry to the pressures of international competition.

To tackle these problems, we in India have taken, as you in China have done, new steps and new initiatives in economic policy, while remaining true to our basic principles. We have embarked on a process of planned liberalisation, giving much greater autonomy to our public sector enterprises and greater flexibility to our private sector to invest, expand and upgrade technology. Indian industry has reached a stage where it must increasingly integrate with the world economy in terms of technology, quality and cost competitiveness. We are encouraging foreign investment where it can help our efforts to modernise. We are also trying to decentralise planning and decision-making to secure better results. This is especially important for our strategies of rural development. A key element of this strategy is increasing peoples' participation in the planning process.

In this context, your own bold experiments in economic reform are of special interest to us. They have already produced rich dividends for China. We believe we have much to learn from your experience. Some of what we are doing in India may also be of interest to you. No two developing countries are more similarly placed than yours and ours. Despite differences in philosophies of planning and methods of management, India and China can give and take a great deal from each other. We believe, you share this view as well.

I represent a new generation in India. I was, but a boy, in the heyday of Sino-Indian friendship. I was still a young man when differences were convened into conflict. I have grown in a world which has not benefited but only been disadvantaged by estrangement between India and China. I have come to office with the firm conviction that, between ourselves, we must make a new beginning. I am heartened that the Chinese leadership is more than prepared to put behind us past rancour and past prejudices. I am heartened that we are both prepared not to be mired in the past. As we enter the last decade of this century, India and China are called upon to look forward, not behind, to reach out to new horizons, to seek new vistas of friendship and cooperation, to explore new paths of benefit to each other and of benefit to the world.

I do not believe our joint advocacy of peaceful coexistence was either a coincidence or an accident of history. It arose out of certain perceptions which had grown out of our historical experience. I would like to dwell a little on this.

The distinguishing characteristic of the civilisations of India and China is not so much their antiquity as their continuity. Nevertheless, specific interactions between our civilisations have not been continuous despite the thousands of years that our respective civilisations have run a parallel course of continuity. The exchanges were, perhaps, at their most intense during the period of the three kingdoms in China when there was much trade and travel between India and China, when Indian art influenced Chinese art, when the artefacts and products and technology of China came to India. For centuries, Indian ports were a regular point of call for Chinese ships. The prosperity of the Choia Empire in southern India was largely based on their trade with China. Till today, the fishing nets of Kerala, on the south-west coast of India, are called Chinese nets and designed on the Chinese pattern. This phase in our mutual exchanges was bracketed by the accounts left behind by two of the greatest Chinese travellers to India: Fa Xian in the fourth century AD, who visited our university at Nalanda, which housed a large Chinese community and Xuan Zang in the seventh century AD, who was a guest at the court of our last great Buddhist emperor, Harshavardhana.

It was the message of the Buddha that led to an awakening of awareness and an intensification of exchanges between our two great civilisations. It had given us insights into the human condition which are more profound and long-lasting than would be indicated by a mere cataloguing of when Bodhi Dharma sailed to Canton or Yi Qing came to India. Drawing on these insights, Jawaharlal Nehru declared here in Beijing thirty-four years ago:

'Fear and hatred and violence have darkened man's horizon for many years. Violence breeds violence. Hatred degrades and stultifies, and fear is a bad companion.'

It is perhaps such insights which enabled our two contemporary systems, so different from one another, to formulate common principles for the sustenance of the new world order which we sought together.

Another characteristic of our civilisations which perhaps led us towards the concept of peaceful coexistence was our millennial experience of synthesis. It helped us recognise that the modern world demanded understanding and respect for the diversity of political and economic systems the world over. While others sought to impose uniformity by persuasion or force, India and

China spoke up for coexistence among different social and economic systems. It was an affirmation made by two ancient civilisations, now turned into two modern states, but following very different social and economic systems.

I am conscious of the fact that, although India and China were the architects of the Five Principles of Peaceful Coexistence, our own relations have not always conformed to these principles. We have had differences of perception and differences of opinion. Yet, what must not be forgotten in a listing of differences, is a listing of commonalities in our world outlook. There has been significant parallelism in the views expressed by India and China on a wide range of issues relating to world security, the international political order, the new international economic order, global concerns.

In regard to environment and space, matters of momentous significance such as the Law of the Sea and the Antarctic Treaty, information and communication, culture and art, there are and there have been differences. But, considering the fact that India is a member of the Non-aligned Movement and China is not, that India is a member of the Group of 77 and China is not, that India is not a nuclear weapons power and China is, it is significant that there is such a wide area of commonality between our points of view and so much scope for further dialogue for the attainment of shared objectives.

Now, as the spirit of the mid-fifties is rekindled, the time has come to end our estrangement and make a new beginning. We must find an acceptable solution to the boundary question within a realistic time-frame. This can be achieved in an atmosphere of mutual understanding and mutual confidence. The border issue is a complex one, touching as it does upon the emotions and sentiments of our people. These aspects have salience in China too. We need patience, wisdom and statesmanship to resolve the issue for the mutual benefit of our peoples. The core of any solution that may emerge is mutual acceptability. We should jointly endeavour to find such a solution in order to put relations between India and China on a solid basis. We are determined to move in this direction. It is important that while we search for a solution, peace and tranquillity are maintained in the border areas. I have every hope that during this visit, we will, together with our Chinese friends, build a better political climate for the solution of the border issue.

Cooperation between India and China should be expanded significantly. Trade between us is far below the potential of our economies. Cooperation in science and technology is still to take off. I believe that economic, scientific, technological and cultural cooperation between the two countries will greatly contribute to better understanding between our people and our governments, and will indirectly help us in solving complex problems. We are at an important conjuncture in world affairs. There is a palpable relaxation of tensions and evidence of dialogue replacing confrontation.

The people of Namibia are at long last on the verge of securing their freedom; their struggle for Independence has been a saga of courage and dignity. However, in South Africa, the abomination of apartheid persists. We demand comprehensive, mandatory sanctions against Pretoria under Chapter VII of the United Nations Charter, failing which we apprehend an unprecedented blood-bath in the struggle to end this iniquity.

There has been a radical turn of events in West Asia. The Palestinian state has been proclaimed. It has been recognised by both China and India and other peace-loving countries the world over. We are glad that dialogue has begun between the United States and the Palestine Liberation Organisation. We extend our wholehearted support to the three-point Palestinian peace initiative put forward by our brother, Chairman Yasser Arafat. The spirit of tolerance which he has evoked, is in keeping with the traditions of Asia and the aspirations of our continent.

In Kampuchea, a solution appears to be emerging which could both end the conflict and forestall the resurgence of the forces of genocide. We would welcome cooperation among all concerned in fostering a just and equitable settlement in Kampuchea which will ensure the independence, sovereignty and non-aligned status of that country, free of outside interference and intervention.

In South Asia, a new dawn is breaking. South Asian regional cooperation has made a good beginning. Recent changes in Pakistan, with the emergence of a democratically elected government led by Prime Minister Benazir Bhutto, have opened up encouraging prospects for enduring friendship and goodwill between our countries, reflecting the natural affinities and affection which the people of India and Pakistan have for each other. In Sri Lanka, the Accord which I signed with President Jayewardene, guarantees the unity and territorial integrity of that country and has brought respect, recognition and a meaningful devolution of powers to the Tamil minority. In the Maldives, our immediate response to the call for assistance from a friendly neighbour in this hour of need, has ensured the triumph of the democratic will of the people of the Maldives against the forces of subversion and destabilisation. In Afghanistan, we are persuaded that strict respect for the Geneva Accords will lead to the emergence of a government based on national consensus, which can ensure the independence, integrity and non-aligned status of the country, provided there is a complete cessation of all outside interference and intervention in the affairs of that country.

At this crucial turning point in contemporary history, we must assess afresh the work that India and China can do, individually and together, in fashioning the new world order which is emerging from the chrysalis of the old.

The two major nuclear weapon powers have agreed in principle that a nuclear war cannot be won and must not be fought. Mahatma Gandhi and Jawaharlal Nehru recognised this in 1945, in the immediate aftermath of Hiroshima and Nagasaki. It augurs well for the future of our world that this perception has now gained wide currency. We are encouraged that this principle has received practical expression in the form of a dismantling of intermediate nuclear forces and the initiation of a process designed to secure strategic arms cuts.

The moot question before us is whether these first-ever steps of nuclear disarmament presage movement towards the elimination of all nuclear weapons, or do these steps merely presage a marginal adjustment in global strategic deployment, perhaps even the shifting of the nuclear arms race into new and ever more dangerous dimensions?

In answering these questions, the task before us is not just to wait upon events but to influence them. India and China can together do a great deal to ensure that the moves which have now been initiated proceed in the only direction which promises sustained peace and sustainable development. To this end, our first step must be to resuscitate and revitalise our decades-old commitment to the Five Principles of Peaceful Coexistence.

There are two basic arguments which sustain nuclear weapons. The first is that, as such weapons have been invented, they cannot now be disinvented. The second is the doctrine of deterrence which holds that, it is only your capacity to destroy your opponent which forestalls your opponent from destroying you.

The danger of universal destruction through the use of nuclear weapons arises not so much from the fact of their invention as from an international system which concedes their need and legitimises their possession and use. It is the old order which resulted in the invention of these terrible weapons. We cannot wish away these weapons but we can certainly alter the world order which has given them legitimacy and tolerated their continued existence.

As regards the doctrines of deterrence, they have not worked in the past because the balance of power is an inherently unstable balance, which all the parties concerned are all the time attempting to upset in their favour and to the disadvantage of others. For deterrence to be credible there must be commitment to the use of the instruments of deterrence. But in the era of nuclear weapons, the use of such weapons will only lead to global holocaust.

Therefore, nuclear disarmament requires not only the dismantling of nuclear weapons but, even more importantly, the dismantling of the mentalities which go with these weapons. We need to evolve generally accepted principles of international security to replace doctrines of deterrence. We need to evolve systems of conflict resolution which forestall the resort to arms. We need to promote thinking about the world order required, to sustain a world beyond nuclear weapons. Advance thinking on these matters is essential. Otherwise, even after nuclear weapons are eliminated, the danger will remain of the world slipping back into the nuclear arms race. That alternative process of thinking could best commence from the five principles of peaceful coexistence which India and China were the first to enunciate. The alternative process of thinking cannot limit itself to security and the international political order alone. It must embrace economies, the environment, space and our common heritage.

As developing countries, India and China share common concerns about the functioning of the international economic order. The world economy continues to be characterised by inadequacies and imbalances which hamper development in the developing countries. India and China have been hurt much less than many other developing countries but neither of us can afford to be complacent. Both in the area of international finance and in the area of trade, there are disturbing trends which weaken established multilateral institutions and mechanisms. The world pays lip-service to interdependence and cooperation but, commitment to these concepts in practice is less evident. These trends are dangerous for the North as well as the South. We must reconstruct a consensus on international economic cooperation. We believe that India and China can work together in international forums to bring about a new international economic order, based on the recognition of global interdependence. Without this, the new international political order would be of little comfort, difficult to attain and impossible to sustain.

In the last decade, political and economic changes have been leading to the emergence of a multi-polar world. The European Community seems to be firmly set on establishing an integral European economy by 1992. Though unresolved questions still remain, Japan has emerged as a major economic centre whose decisions influence the rest of the world. The inherent strength and vitality of the American economy and specially their advanced technology, remain crucial to the international economy. The Soviet Union is restructuring its economy with profound global implications. How these power centres will act and react on each other and how they will impact on the developing world are matters for serious analysis. The intertwining of economic power and military strength could create new security concerns. It is all the more important then that we actively work for a new international order where questions of peace and security are settled through non-violent means.

Another area of international action in which fruitful cooperation between India and China is indicated, could be in regard to the environment. We have both suffered the consequences of environmental degradation. We have both worked on programmes designed to make conservation an integral part of the development process. We have both recognised that the cost of preserving the environment is an essential component of the cost of development, because if these costs are not recognised and paid for, degradation will exact a much higher price than conservation. There is much work we can do together, many lessons we can learn from each other, and something we can add to the world's repository of knowledge by conscious cooperation in the interests of sustainable development.

We are both committed to the peaceful uses of outer space. We have both protested against attempts to misuse space for military applications. We both believe that nothing could be more dangerous than the shifting of the nuclear arms race into this new dimension. We are also both concerned at space being converted into a garbage dump for the technological experiments of the advanced economies. Like the seas and the sea-bed, space too is a common heritage of mankind. It is a heritage which all of us must work together to preserve.

Between us, we are the repositories of some of the most significant treasures of the human inheritance. We believe in international cooperation to preserve and promote the cultural heritage of humankind. When UNESCO came under siege, India and China were together on the same side in defending the organisation and asserting its vital role.

Now that the world is beginning to explore the possibility of coexistence in preference to deterrence, of cooperation in preference to rivalry, of interdependence in preference to beggaring the neighbour, of nuclear disarmament in preference to nuclear escalation, it behoves the original advocates of the Panchsheel – India and China – to set themselves up as an example to the world.

I see optimism in both India and China today; optimism about the progress our countries can make, optimism about realising our goals of development, optimism about the levels of cooperation we can reach, optimism about the work we can do together to restore our countries to their traditional position in the vanguard of human civilisation, optimism about the contribution we can make to rebuilding the world order nearer our hearts' desire.

We are summoned by our past to the tasks which the future holds. We have a mutual obligation to a common humanity. India and China can together give the world new perspectives on a new world order, which will ensure peace among nations and justice among peoples, equality for each and prosperity for all, freedom from want, a world where we live together in happiness and harmony.

APPENDIX V

India-China Joint Press Communique Issued on 23 December 1988

At the invitation of Premier Li Peng of the State Council of the People's Republic of China, Prime Minister Rajiv Gandhi of the Republic of India made an official goodwill visit to the People's Republic of China from 19-23 December 1988. Accompanying His Excellency Prime Minister Rajiv Gandhi on his visit to China were Mrs Sonia Gandhi, Mr Narasimha Rao, Minister of External Affairs of India, Mr Dinesh Singh, Minister of Commerce, Dr B. Shankaranand, Minister of Law and Justice and Water Resources, Mr K. Natwar Singh, Minister of State for External Affairs and other Indian officials.

Premier Li Peng and Prime Minister Rajiv Gandhi held talks in an atmosphere of friendship, candidness and mutual understanding. President Yang Shangkun of the People's Republic of China, General Secretary Zhao Ziyang of the Central Committee of the Communist Party of China (CPC) and Chairman Deng Xiaoping of the Military commission of the CPC Central Committee had separate meetings with Prime Minister Rajiv Gandhi. During his visit, the two governments signed an agreement on cooperation in the field of science and technology, civil air transport, and the Executive Programme for the years 1988, 1989 and 1990 under the Agreement for Cultural Cooperation. Both the premier and the prime minister were present at the signing ceremony. Prime Minister Rajiv Gandhi, Mrs Gandhi and their party also toured historical sites and scenic spots in Beijing, Xian and Shanghai.

During their talks and meetings, the leaders of the two countries had a wide exchange of views and ideas on bilateral relations and international issues of mutual interest. Both sides found such talks and meetings useful as they enhanced mutual understanding in the interest of further improvement and development of bilateral relations. The two sides made a positive appraisal of the cooperation and exchanges in recent years in trade, culture, science and technology, civil aviation and other fields, and expressed satisfaction with the relevant agreements reached between the two countries. They emphasised the vast scope that existed for learning from each other.

They stressed/highlighted that the Five Principles of mutual respect for sovereignty and territorial integrity, mutual non-aggression, non-interference in each other's internal affairs, equality and mutual benefit, and peaceful coexistence, which were jointly initiated by India and China, which have proved full of vitality through the test of history, constitute the basic guiding principles for good relation between the two states. These principles also constitute the basic guidelines for the establishment of a new international political order and the New International Economic Order. Both sides agreed that their common desire was to restore, improve and develop India-China neighbourly and friendly relations on the basis of these principles. This not only conforms to the fundamental interests of the two people, but will actively contribute to peace and stability in Asia and the world as a whole. The two sides reaffirmed that they would make efforts to further their friendly relations.

The leaders of the two countries held earnest, in-depth discussions on the India-China boundary question and agreed to settle this question through peaceful and friendly consultations. They also agreed to develop their relations actively in other fields and work hard to create a favourable climate and conditions for a fair and reasonable settlement of the boundary question while seeking a mutually acceptable solution to this question. In this context, concrete steps will be taken, such as establishing a joint-working group on the boundary question and a joint-group on economic relations and trade and science and technology.

The Chinese side expressed concern over anti-China activities by some Tibetan elements in India. The Indian side reiterated the long-standing and consistent policy of the Government of India that Tibet is an autonomous region of China and that anti-China political activities by Tibetan elements are not permitted on Indian soil.

With regard to the international situation, the two sides held that in the present-day world, confrontation was giving way to dialogue and tension to relaxation. This is a trend resulting from long years of unswerving struggle by the peace-loving countries and people of the world against power politics. It is conducive to world peace and to the settlement of regional problems. It also facilitates the efforts of all countries, the developing countries in particular, to develop their national economies. India and China will make their own contributions to the maintenance of world peace, promotion of complete disarmament and attainment of common progress.

His Excellency Prime Minister Rajiv Gandhi, Mrs Sonia Gandhi and their party expressed heartfelt thanks to the government and people of the People Republic of China for their warm and friendly hospitality accorded to them.

Prime Minister Rajiv Ganhi has invited Premier Li Peng to visit the Republic of India at his convenience. Premier Li Peng has accepted the invitation with pleasure. The date of the visit will be decided upon through diplomatic channels.

APPENDIX-VI

Concordance of Chinese Names and Places

Chiang Kai-shek	Jiang Jieshe
Chou En-lai	Zhou En lai
Chu Teh	Zhu De
Liu Shao Chi	Liu Shaoqi
Lin Piao	Lin Biao
Mao Tse Tung	Mao Tsedung
Peking	Beijing
Peng Te-huai	Peng Dehuai
Teng Hsiao-ping	Deng Xiaoping
Wai-chiao Pu	Wai Chiao Bu

Endnotes

Preface

1. Chou En-lai (1898-76), prime minister of China 1949-76; one of the great diplomats of the twentieth century; charismatic, astute, wise, cautious, daring and ruthless; came to India in 1954-56, 1957 and 1960.
2. Rajiv Gandhi (1944-91), prime minister of India, 1984-89.
3. Jawaharlal Nehru (1889-1964), prime minister of India, 1947-64.
4. Chiang Kai-shek (1887-75), supreme ruler of China 1927-49; escaped to Formosa; visited India in 1942; met Gandhiji and Jawaharlal Nehru.
5. Mao Tse Tung (1893-1976), founder of New China; revolutionary leader, got rid of his colleagues of the Long March during the Cultural Revolution, 1966-67; became semi-senile in old age and remained chairman of the party till death.
6. Edwina Cynthia Annette Mountbatten, Countess Mountbatten of Burma (1901-60), wife of Lord Louis Mountbatten and last vicereine of India.
7. *Selected Works of Jawaharlal Nehru* (Second Series), Vol. 27, pp. 66-70.
8. Chen Chen Tho – leader of the Chinese delegation who came to India in December 1954.
9. K. Kamaraj Nadar (1903-75), chief minister, Tamil Nadu (1954-63); Congress president (1963-69).
10. T.N. Kaul (1913-2000), counsellor, Indian Embassy, Peking 1950-52; minister, 1952-53; joint secretary, MEA, 1953-56; ambassador to several countries and then foreign secretary, 1968-71.

11. Soong Ching-ling (1893-1981), widow of Dr Sun Yat-sen; vice-president of People's Republic of China, 1968-72; friend of Jawaharlal Nehru; visited India in December 1955.
12. The Long March was a military withdrawal by the Red Armies of the Chinese Communist Party (CCP) to put off the quest of the Chinese Nationalist Party army.
13. Joseph Stalin (1879-1953), general secretary of the Communist Party of the Soviet Union's central committee, 1922-53; chairman of the council of ministers, 1946-53.

Part I

Diary—1956

1. Govind Singh ji.
2. Gossi Sotto – Mexican student at Miranda House, Delhi University, 1951-54.
3. Han Suyin (b.1916), has written extensively on China, including a biography of Chou En-lai, *Eldest Son;* her novel, *A Many Splendored Thing* was an international bestseller; the author and Han Suyin have been friends for fifty-two years.
4. Ashok Bhadkamkar (1921-76), served in the Royal Indian Navy, 1944-47; joined IFS, 1947; looked after me in Peking like a brother; died in Cairo, where he was the ambassador.
5. E.M. Forster (1879-1970), English novelist, author of *A Passage to India*.
6. Colonel Vincent Ratnaswamy, (d. 2003).
7. R.K. Nehru (1902-79), ICS, 1925; foreign secretary, 1952-55; secretary general, MEA, 1960-63.
8. N.A. Khrushchev (1894-1971), First Secretary of the Communist Party of the Soviet Union, 1953-64.
9. Bernard Shaw (1856-1950), Irish playwright; awarded Nobel Prize for Literature, 1925.
10. Ahmed Ali (1910-94), Pakistani novelist, diplomat and scholar; author of *Twilight in Delhi*; migrated to Pakistan, 1947; Pakistan government issued a commemorative stamp to honour his memory in 1995.

11. Souvanna Phouma (1901-84), prime minister of Laos, 1951-54.
12. V.V. Paranjpe (b.1928), greatest Chinese scholar India has produced; spent many years in China; was Nehru's interpreter when he met Mao Tse Tung and Chou En-lai.
13. Mela Chang, half-Russian, half-Chinese, good-looking and worked in a shop owned by an Indian.
14. Liu Shao Chi (1898-1969), president of China, 1960-65; disgraced during the Cultural Revolution; died painful death.
15. R.K. Patil, ICS, led a delegation to study the state of agriculture in China; he had been Minister for Food and Revenue in the Central Provinces and Berar.
16. D.K. Barua (1914-96), member, Assam Legislative Assembly; Member Lok Sabha and Rajya Sabha; Congress president in 1974; cabinet minister in Indira Gandhi's government; chief minister, Assam; broke with Indira Gandhi during Emergency.
17. Hutheesing (1907-67), younger sister of Jawaharlal Nehru; got to know her in my early teens; her sons, Harsha and Ajit were in Scindia school with me; wrote an autobiography, *With No Regrets* and *Dear to Behold*, biography of her niece, Indira Gandhi.
18. P.P. Sundarayya (1913-85), popularised concept of Vishalandhra; elected to the Rajya Sabha, 1955; resigned immediately to contest elections; member of Andhra Legislative Assembly, 1956-67.
19. E.M.S. Namboodiripad (b.1909), founder member of the Congress Socialist Party; secretary of Kerala Provincial Congress Committee, 1934 and 1938-40; joined CPI, 1941; general secretary, 1953-56, 1962-63 and 1967-68; chief minister, Kerala, 1957-59.
20. P.C. Joshi (b.1907), first general secretary CPI, 1935-47.
21. C.R. Mandy edited *The Illustrated Weekly of India* for almost two decades.
22. Tarlok Singh (d.2005), studied at LSE; ICS, 1937-62; private secretary to Jawaharlal Nehru; member of the Planning Commission, 1947-67.
23. Elias Bradsdorff (1912-2002), Danish academic whom I met in Cambridge.
24. Juan A. Parrochia (b.1930), Chilean architect and urban planner.
25. Chinese word for meeting.
26. Kuo Mo Jo (1892-1977), a major figure of Chinese literature; also an archaeologist; not a member of Communist Party; translated the works of Walt Whitman (1819-92) into Chinese; close to Chou En-lai.

27. Robert Ellis (b.1916), assistant, MEA 1941-48; superintendent, Indian Embassy, Peking; in charge of ciphers, 1955-57.
28. Tanka Prasad Acharya (1914-92), founder of the Praja Parishad, 1935; prime minister of Nepal, 1955-56.
29. Ahmed Soekarno (1901-70), first president of Indonesia, 1945-67.
30. J.N. Chaudhuri (1908-83), military governor, Hyderabad state, 1948-49; chief of the Army Staff, 1962-66.
31. Ananthasayyanam Ayyengar (1891-1978), freedom fighter; first deputy speaker, Lok Sabha, 1952-56; speaker, 1956-62.
32. G.V. Mavalankar (1888-1956), first speaker of Lok Sabha, 1952-56; died on 27 February 1956.
33. J.B. Kripalini (1888-1982), joined Gandhiji, 1919; general secretary of AICC, 1934-46; Congress president 1946-47; left Congress and formed his own party; lively parliamentarian; differed with Indira Gandhi's government.
34. Lakshmi Menon (b.1899), minister of state for external affairs in Indira Gandhi's government.
35. P.C. Lal (1917-84), Chief of Air Staff, 1969-73.
36. Peng te Huai (1902-74), one of the ten marshals; defence minister, 1949-59; dismissed and disgraced when he criticised Mao at the Lushan conference; tortured during the Cultural Revolution.
37. Subroto Mukerjee (1911-60), Chief of the Air Staff, 1954-60; choked to death in a Japanese restaurant.
38. Kalidas (AD 355-414), renowned classical Sanskrit poet and dramatist; author of *Meghaduta*, *Shakuntala* and *Kumarasambhava* among other well-known works.
39. Rabindranath Tagore (1861-1941), Bengali poet, visual artist, playwright, novelist and composer whose works re-shaped Bengali literature and music in the late nineteenth and early twentieth centuries; won the 1913 Nobel Prize in Literature.
40. David Marshall (1908-95), well-known lawyer; chief minister of Singapore, 1955-56.
41. Thakin Nu, (1907-95), prime minister of Burma, 1947-57, 1958 and 1960-62.
42. Chen Yi (1901-72), military commander and politician; vice-premier, 1954-72; foreign minister, 1958-72.
43. Mei Lan Fang (1894-1961), the greatest Peking Opera dancer, who always played feminine roles.

44. Uday Shankar (1900-77), world renowned classical dancer and choreographer.
45. Walter Ulbricht (1893-1973), first deputy premier of East Germany, 1949-71.
46. David Alfaro Siqueiros (1896-1974), well-known Mexican mural painter; member of Communist Party.
47. Gamal Abdel Nasser (1918-70), president of Egypt, 1956-70.
48. Satish Gujral (b. 1925), painter, sculptor, muralist, graphic designer and architect; awarded Padma Vibhushan, 1999.
49. Lathsahib – my elder brother, Bhagwat Singh; M.A (Cantab); worked for the UN in New York for thirty years; has lived in New York since 1963.
50. Ranbir Vohra – born in pre-partition Punjab; graduated from Government College, Lahore 1946; Beijing University, 1956-59.
51. Rajendra Prasad (1884-1963), freedom fighter and Congress president; president of India, 1950-62.
52. Husein Shaheed Suhrawardy (1893-1963), prime minister of Pakistan, 1956-57.
53. Lu Hsun (1880-1936), short story writer, editor, translator, critic, essayist and poet; considered to be the founder of modern Chinese literature
54. Premchand (1880-1936), foremost writer in both Hindi and Urdu during the early twentieth century.
55. I.J. Bahadur Singh (b. 1915), counsellor, Indian embassy, Peking.
56. Chaudhuri Hyder Hussain (1890-1966), member of Lok Sabha, 1952-57.
57. Edgar Snow (1905-72), his book *Red Star Over China*, published in 1937, was a worldwide bestseller and made Mao's name known in the West for the first time.
58. Radha Raman (1904-82), member of the Lok Sabha, 1952-62; president, Delhi Pradesh Congress Committee, 1948-51, chief executive councillor, Delhi, 1972-77.
59. Maxim Gorky (1868-1936), Soviet author.
60. Lady Feroz Khan Noon (1920-2000), Austrian who married Sir Feroz Khan Noon, 1945.
61. Shahryar Mohammad Khan (b.1934), retired as Pakistan's Foreign secretary; grandson of the Nawab of Bhopal; after retirement became president of Pakistan Cricket Board; was at Corpus Christi College, Cambridge with the author.

62. Meera Malik (b.1930), IFS 1954; resigned after marriage; author of *China the World and India*; her husband, Ajit Bhattacharjee, is a respected former editor of The *Hindustan Times*.
63. Darshan Bhutani (b.1933), IFS 1955; was secretary general of the International Control Commission in Vietnam; served as an ambassador to Indonesia and high commissioner to Australia; author of *A Clash of Political Cultures: Sino-Indian Relations 1957-62*.
64. Jainendra Kumar (1905-88), influential Hindi writer of twentieth century; explored the human psyche in novels such as *Sunita* and *Tyagapatra*.
65. V.K. Krishna Menon (1896-1974), defence minister, 1957-62.
66. Jayaprakash Narayan (1902-79), Socialist turned Gandhian.
67. Pranab Kumar Guha (b.1921), assistant editor, publications division, Ministry of Information and Broadcasting; press attaché, Peking, 1955-58.
68. Morris Abrahm Cohen (1887-1970), a Jewish soldier and adventurer who became aide-de-camp to Sun Yat-sen and a major general in the Chinese Army.

Diary—1957

1. Nirad C. Chaudhuri (1897-1998), Bengali writer whose masterpiece, The *Autobiography of an Unknown Indian*, published in 1951, put him on the short list of great Indian English writers.
2. Teng Ying Chao (1904-92), wife of Chou En-lai; married in 1925; was on the Long March.
3. Mohammad Hatta (1902-80), vice-president of Indonesia, 1945-56; prime minister, 1948-50.
4. N.P. Chakraborty, first director of the Archaeological Survey of India.
5. Raja Hutheesing, husband of Krishna Nehru Hutheesing.
6. Adlai Stevenson (1900-65), American politician and diplomat.
7. Allen Dulles (1893-1969), longest serving Director of Central Intelligence (1953-61).
8. A. Mikoyan (1895-1978), first deputy premier of the Soviet Union, 1955-64; survived the 1937-39 purges; at one time in Stalin's inner circle.
9. Sushil Mukerjee (b.1923), art and music teacher at Scindia School.
10. Marc Ribound, French photographer, best known for his extensive reports on the East; *The Three Banners of China*, *Face of North Vietnam*, and *Visions of China*.

11. Graham Greens (1904-91), British novelist; friend of R.K. Narayan.
12. English monthly edited by Stephen Spender (1909-92), the well-known British poet; Spender resigned as editor on learning that the *Encounter* was funded by the CIA.
13. Mao Tun (1896-1981), novelist, journalist and cultural critic; minister of culture, 1949-65.
14. Kamala Lakshman (b.1934), Bharatnatyam dancer.
15. R.K. Lakshman (b.1924), regarded as India's greatest-ever cartoonist.
16. R.K. Narayan (1906-2001), best known Indian novelist; created imaginary town of Malgudi.
17. Charry (b.1920), IFS 1948; consul general in Shanghai; author stayed with him on his trip to Shanghai.
18. Ho Lung (1896-1969), one of the ten legendary marshals; participated in Long March; visited India with Chou En-lai, 1956; beaten up by Red Guards during the Cultural Revolution; a diabetic, he was denied medicines; died a very painful death.
19. Mei Lan Fang (1894-1961), was one of the most famous Peking opera artists in modern history.
20. Peng Chen (1899-1996), long time powerful mayor of Peking; Politburo member; targeted during the Cultural Revolution for being close to Liu Shao Chi; survived the ordeal.
21. Malthus (1776-1834), famous for his book, *An Essay on the Principle of Population*.
22. Marshal Voroshilov (1881-1969), chairman of the Presidium of the Supreme Soviet; participated in 1905 and 1917 revolutions; escaped death during purges in 1937-39; close to Stalin during the Second World War.
23. Deng Xiaoping (1904-97), Chinese revolutionary, reversed Mao's policies, set in motion economic reforms, which transformed China.
24. Fang Yu Lan (1895-1988), most well-known Chinese philosopher of the twentieth century; spent time at Columbia University, New York; degrees from Princeton, Delhi University.
25. Bo Yibo (1908-1997), finance minister 1949-53.
26. K.M. Panikkar (1895-1963) India's ambassador to China, France and Egypt.
27. V.M. Molotov (1890-1996), most durable of the Bolsheviks; premier at the age of thirty; foreign minister, 1939-49 and 1953-57.
28. G.M. Malenkov (1902-88), premier 1953-55; worked closely with Stalin during the Second World War; expelled from the party in 1961.

29. Lazer Kaganovich (1893-1991), son of a shoemaker; held powerful posts in Stalin's government; pensioned in 1957.
30. P.C. Mahanalobis (1893-1972), scientist and statistician; founder of the Indian Statistical Institute, Calcutta.
31. Ho Chi Minh (1890-1969), president, Socialist Republic of Vietnam, 1945-69.
32. Prince Sultan Mohammed, (1877–1957), Aga Khan III, died on 11 July 1957.
33. Yumjaagiin Tsedenbal (1916-91), prime minister of Mongolia, 1952-74.
34. Semyon Budyonny (1883-1973), Cossack; held important cabinet level posts under Stalin; appointed marshal in 1935; brilliant Second World War record.
35. Male-female in Sanskrit grammatical phraseology.
36. Raj Kapoor very good.
37. Manjit Singh joined IFS the same day as I did. He died in San Francisco in 1970.
38. Close friends of mine.
39. Former foreign secretary; awarded Padma Bhushan, 2002.
40. Kuomintang. Chinese Nationalist Party founded by Sun Yat-sen.
41. Peking University. Mao Tse Tung once worked here as assistant librarian. Peita is the most prestigious seat of learning in China.
42. Madan Atal (1886-1956), friend and close relative of Nehru family; first came to China in 1938 with the Indian Medical Unit sent by the Indian National Congress; Mao Tse Tung wrote to Nehru on 24 May 1939 thanking Nehru for sending Dr Atal.

Diary—1958

1. Abul Kalam Azad (1888-1958), freedom fighter, Congressman and first minister of education in Nehru's Cabinet.

Part II

Prefatory Note

1. S. Dutt ICS, 1928; foreign secretary, 1955-61.
2. G.L. Nanda (1898-1998), labour minister; home minister in Indira Gandhi's government; acting prime minister after the death of Nehru and Lal Bahadur Shastri.
3. Morarji Desai (1896-1995), chief minister of Bombay, 1952-56; finance minister and later prime minister, 1977-79.
4. Krishna Menon (1896-1978), leading light of India League, London, 1928-47; high commissioner to the UK, 1947-52; Defence minister, 1957-62. leader, Indian Delegation to the UN 1952-61.
5. Swaran Singh (1907-1994), longest serving Cabinet minister; foreign minister, 1964-66.
6. Jagjivan Ram (1908-1986), minister in the Cabinets of Jawaharlal Nehru and Indira Gandhi.
7. Hafiz Mohd. Ibrahim – minister in Jawaharlal Nehru's Cabinet, governor of Punjab.

Meeting with Vice-President Dr S. Radhakrishnan

1. Chang Han-Fu Vice-minister for foreign affairs.
2. G. Parathasarthi (b.1912-95), journalist and diplomat; vice-chancellor, Jawaharlal Nehru University, 1969-74; served as ambassador to China, Indonesia, high commissioner to Pakistan and permanent representative to the UN; close foreign policy adviser of Indira Gandhi.
3. Pandit Sundar Lal (b.1886), Congressman and freedom fighter from UP; led cultural delegation to China, 1951; author of *China Today*.

Finance Minister Morarji Desai's Meeting with Premier Chou En-lai

1. Dr. K.I. Singh (1906-82), arrested in 1951 for indulging in violent activities in Nepal; escaped to China, granted political asylum, 1952-55; prime minister of Nepal.
2. A decision was taken for the finance minister not to return Premier Chou En-lai's call.
3. R.N. Kao (1918-2002), IPS, 1940; on deputation to the Intelligence Bureau, 1947-68; founder of Research & Analysis Wing (R & AW); was chief security officer attached to Premier Chou En-lai during the 1960 visit; retired as secretary [R] in the Cabinet Secretariat; established R & AW in 1968.

Part Three

Prefatory Note

1. Kurshid Alam Khan (b.1919), minister of state for external affairs 1984; governor, Goa and Karnataka between 1989-1996.
2. K.R. Narayanan (1920-2006), joined IFS 1949; served as ambassador to Turkey and Thailand; ambassador to China and USA after retirement in 1976; elected to Lok Sabha 1984; minister of state for external affairs, 1985-86; vice-president, 1992-97; president 1997-2002.
3. B.R. Bhagat (b.1922), member, Provisional Parliament, 1950-52; member, Lok Sabha 1952-77; minister of state for external affairs, 1967-69; speaker, Lok Sabha 1976-77; minister for external affairs, 1985-86; governor of Himachal Pradesh 1993, Rajasthan 1993-98.
4. Shiv Shankar (b. 1929), lawyer of repute; Cabinet minister in the governments of Indira Gandhi and Rajiv Gandhi.
5. Konstatin Chernenko (1911-85), president, USSR (now Russia), 1984-85.
6. P.V. Narasimha Rao (1921-2004), chief minister, Andhra Pradesh; central minister in Cabinets of Indira Gandhi and Rajiv Gandhi; prime minister of India, 1991-96; erudite, used one word where two would do; wrote *The Insider*.

7. Brajesh Mishra (b.1928) – IFS 1951 batch principle secretary to Atal Behari Vajpayee.
8. S. Gopal (1923-2002), historian and former president of the Indian History Congress.
9. Richard Nixon (1913-94), vice-president, 1953-61; president of the USA 1969-74.
10. Henry Kissinger (b.1923), American diplomat, secretary of state, 1973-77.
11. K.S Sundarji (1928-99), chief of army staff, 1986-88.
12. K.P.S. Menon (b.1928), IFS 1951; served as ambassador to China; Foreign secretary, 1987-90.
13. A.P. Venkateswaran (b.1930), IFS 1952; ambassador to China, 1982-85; Foreign secretary, 1986-87; resigned when the Prime Minister Rajiv Gandhi humiliated him at a press conference.
14. N.D. Tiwari (b.1925), several times chief minister of UP, external affairs minister, 1986-87; chief minister, Uttrakhand 2002-07; at present, governor of Andhra Pradesh.
15. K.C. Pant (b.1931), son of G.B. Pant; member, Lok Sabha 1962-77, & 1984-89; minister of defence, 1987-89.
16. Buta Singh (b.1934), home minister 1986-89; Agriculture and Rural Development 1983-84.
17. John F Kennedy (1917-63), president of the USA, 1961-63.
18. Michael Foot (b.1913), leader of the British Labour Party, 1979-83; deputy prime minister 1976-79; well-known orator and author.
19. Nguyen Co Thach (1923-98), foreign minister of Vietnam, 1980-91.
20. V.N. Gadgil (1928-2001), member of parliament; later minister of state; Congress party spokesman.
21. Dinesh Singh (1925-95), external affairs minister; long time MP, Lok Sabha; water resource minister in Rajiv Gandhi's government.
22. Shankaranand (b.1925), held several Cabinet posts, including health and power.
23. Simi Garewal (b.1944), well-known film actress.
24. C.V. Ranganathan (b.1935), IFS 1959; ambassador to China; also served as ambassador to France; joint author of *India and China. The Way Ahead After, Mao's India War.*
25. Li Peng (b.1928), premier, 1988-98; chairman, Standing Committee of the NPC, 1998-2003.

26. MiKhail Gorbachev (b.1931), president of the USSR, 1990-91.
27. Qian Qichen (b.1928), foreign minister of China, 1988-98.

Prime Minister's Meeting with President Yang Shengkun

1. Gopi Arora (b.1934), IAS 1957; additional secretary to prime minister.
2. Ronen Sen (b.1944), IFS 1966; IFS man in PMO; at present ambassador to USA; hard working, won Rajiv Gandhi's confidence.
3. S.K. Mishra – IAS officer from Haryana cadre, 1956 batch; closely associated with making Haryana a tourist destination.
4. Sarla Grewal (b.1927), IAS 1952 batch; principal secretary to the prime minister; governor of Madhya Pradesh, 1989-90.
5. Pu Yi (1906-67), last emperor of China (1908-12); lived in Peking after many years in prison. The film *The Last Emperor* was about him.

The Climax: Meeting with Deng Xiaoping

1. P.N. Haksar (1913-98), principal secretary to Indira Gandhi; member of the IFS; outstanding civil servant; endowed with analytical and brilliant mind; had been a committed Marxist at one time.
2. Zhao Ziyang (1919-2005), prime minister, 1980-87; general secretary of Communist Party, 1987-89.
3. Ronald Reagan (1911-2004), president of USA, 1981-89.
4. Montek Singh Ahluwalia (b.1943), currently deputy chairman, Planning Commission.
5. K.K. Tiwari (b. 1942), MP, Lok Sabha 1980-89; minister of state for external affairs 1988-89.
6. Mani Shankar Aiyar (b.1940), IFS 1963; at present cabinet minister for Panchayati Raj; Rajiv Gandhi's speech writer.
7. Zhu Rongji (b.1925), prime minister, 1998-2004.
8. M.L. Fotedar (b. 1932), personal assistant to Indira Gandhi and Rajiv Gandhi; Minister in P.V. Narasimha Rao's Cabinet; resigned over policy differences.
9. Shiela Dikshit (b. 1938), minister of state in Rajiv Gandhi's office; chief minister, Delhi, 1998-till date.

10. H.K.L. Bhagat (1921-2005), migrated to India in 1947 from Pakistan; Cabinet minister in Rajiv Gandhi's government.
11. Vasant Sathe (b. 1925), imprisoned during Quit India Movement 1942; well-known trade unionist; Cabinet minister in the governments of Indira Gandhi and Rajiv Gandhi; author of several books including *Tax Without Tears*.
12. Bhajan Lal (b. 1930), chief minister of Haryana for total of fourteen years; Cabinet minister in Rajiv Gandhi's government; present leader of Haryana Vikas Party.

Who's Who

1. Chen Yi (1901-72): Military Commander and politician; one of the Ten Marshals; Mayor of Shanghai, 1949-58; Vice-Premier, 1954-72; Foreign Minister, 1958-72; Politburo Member.
2. Chen Yun (1905-95): well-known economist; survived Cultural Revolution; became confidant of Deng Xiaoping; Politburo Member; first executive Vice Premier, 1954-64.
3. Chiang Kai-shek (1987-75): Supreme Ruler of China 1927-47; visited India 1942, met Gandhi and Nehru migrated to Taiwan 1949.
4. Chu Teh (1886-1976): Marshal; Politburo Member; founder People's Liberation Army; Vice-Chairman – Central Committee, 1956-66; Vice Chairman – National Council of Defence.
5. Deng Xiaoping (1904-97): Supreme Ruler of China after death of Mao Tse Tung; General Secretary, Communist Party of China, 1956-66; Chairman, Central Military Committee, 1981-89; ushered in mantra of one nation two systems.
6. Chih-Pai Shih (1863-1957): greatest Chinese painter of the 20th century.
7. Chou En-lai (1898-1976): Prime Minister of China, 1949-76; Foreign Minister, 1949-58; came to India in 1954-56, 1957 and 1960; one of the greatest diplomats of 20th century; charismatic, astute, wise, cautious, daring, charming, and ruthless.
8. Edgar Snow (1905-72): American journalist working in China in the nineteen thirties; met Mao Tse Tung in Yunnan in 1936; immediately thereafter wrote *Red Star Over China*; well-known also to Gandhi and Nehru.

9. Ho Lung (1896-1969): one of the Ten Marshals; Long Marcher; close to Chou En-lai; visited India with Chou En-lai, 1957; badly treated during the Cultural Revolution; Politburo Member.
10. Kuo Mo Jo (1892-1978): major literary figure; Vice-Premier, 1949-54; Chairman of the Chinese Academy of Sciences, 1949-78; visited India.
11. Lau Sheh (1898-1967): one of China's leading novelists; best known for *Rickshaw Boy*; tortured during Cultural Revolution, committed suicide.
12. Lin Biao (1907-71): one of the Ten Marshals; Long Marcher; Politburo Member; designated Mao's successor during the Cultural Revolution; plotted against Mao; killed in plane crash while escaping to Russia.
13. Li Peng (b.1928): Prime Minister till 2003; held talks with Rajiv Gandhi; visited India in 1990.
14. Liu Shao Chi (1898-1969): Long Marcher; party theoretician; President of China, 1959-66; died after torture and denial of medical aid in 1969.
15. Mao Tse Tung (1893-1976): founder of New China; revolutionary leader; Chairman of the Party till death; unleashed the Cultural Revolution; eliminated colleagues who had worked closely with him for forty years.
16. Peng Chen (1902-98): long time mayor of Peking; joined Communist Party in 1926; imprisoned for twelve years in prison and exile; Deng Xiaoping rehabilitated him.
17. Peng Teh Huai (1898-1974): Long Marcher; one of the Ten Marshals; Defence Minister, 1949-59; dismissed from post and Politburo; died during Cultural Revolution after brutal torture.
18. Soong Ching-ling (1892-1981): widow of Sun Yat-sen; sister married to Chiang Kai-shek; close to the Communists; held important posts after 1949; became Vice-President; visited India in 1955.
19. Yang Shankun (b.1907): President of China till 1991; imprisoned during the Cultural Revolution; Deng Xiaoping rehabilitated him; held talks with Rajiv Gandhi in 1988 in Peking.
20. Zhao Ziyang (1921-2005): Prime Minister, 1988-89; met Rajiv Gandhi in New York and Beijing; removed after siding with Student demonstrator in Tien An Man Square in 1989.

Acknowledgements

I am deeply appreciative of the help given to me by Professor Mridula Mukherjee, director, Nehru Memorial Museum and Library and to her academic coordinator, Dr Bhashyam Kasturi. They gave me access to the papers of the late P.N. Haksar (1913-98), which are now with NMML Archives. I have, in the Appendices, included the record of the final meeting between Prime Minister Jawaharlal Nehru and Premier Chou En-lai on 25 April 1960, i.e., forty-nine years ago taken from the Haksar papers.

I am grateful to my friend and erstwhile colleague, Sudarshan Bhutani for refreshing my memory on some important dates and events. We attended Peking University together from 1957-58. His book, *A Clash of Political Cultures: Sino-Indian Relations 1957-62*, proved to be very useful. He is not given to diplomatic cachinnation. He is a man, who measures his words and phrases.

Index

1842 Treaty, 100-101

Acupuncture hospital, 24
Acupuncture, 24-25, 36
Aiyar, Mani Shankar, 136
Akbar, M.J., 135
All India Student's Federation, 56
Alley, Rewi, 60
American Prisoners of War (Korea), 48
Antagonistic contradiction, 41
Anti-China activities, 95
Anti-China lobby, 114
Anti-Chinese activities, 99, 105
Anti-Chinese propaganda, 98-99
Anti-imperialist demonstrations, 31
Anti-Indian feelings, 91
Anti-waste and anti-conservatives movement, 67
Arora, Gopi, 123, 136
Arunachal Pradesh, 86, 115, 124
ASEAN countries, 117
Asylum, 85, 95, 99, 105
Atal, Dr M.,78

Autumn Moon festival, 10
Ayyengar, Ananthasayyanam, 16
Azad, Maulana, 81

Balanese dance, 23
Bandung Conference, 7, 50
Barua, D.K., 10-11
Bator, Ulan, 68-69
Bhadkamkar, Ashok, 5, 24, 41, 74
Bhadkamkar, Medha, 13
Bhagat, B.R., 113
Bhutani, Darshan, 36
Bhutto, Benazir, 138
Birth control exhibition, 56, 59
Bofors Joint Parliamentary Committee, 123
Boldness, 117, 130, 132
Boxer rebellion, 44
Brahmanical astuteness, 29
Brasstacks fiasco, 117
British Foreign Service, 39
British-French-Israeli attack on Egypt, 31
Buddha, Gautam, 66

Buddhism, 62, 66, 69-70
Buddhist monastery, 70
Buddhist monk, 15, 20, 35
Buddhist temples, 62
Budyonny, Marshal, 71

Ceremonial welcome, 120
Chang, Dean, 9, 12, 14, 55, 65
Chang, Jen Min Shih, 56
Chang, Mela, 9, 65
Chang, Tung An Shih, 54
Chang, Tung An Tse, 49
Chao, Madam Teng Ying, 47
Chaudhuri, J.N., 16
Chaudhuri, Nirad C., 47
Chea, Chang An Ta, 13
Chen, Peng, 28, 59, 73
Chi, Chang Nai, 81
Chi, Liu Shao, 10, 17-18, 20, 22-23, 28, 32-33, 61, 63-64, 66, 73
Chin, Aksai, 100
China-India Friendship Association, 27
China-Tibet policy, 86
Chinese Culture Department, 62
Chinese hospitality, 52
Chinese incursion in NEFA, 86 *See also* Arunachal Pradesh
Chinese revolution, 11, 130
Chinese version of Kalidas's *Shakuntla*, 62
Ching, Wang Fu, 13, 55
Ching-ling, Soong, 18, 22, 64, 73
Chipp, David, 17, 22, 58, 74
Chun Shan park, 56
Chun, Chang Po, 81

Civil war, 31
Colonialism, 7, 130
Colour bar in Indonesia, 17
Commonwealth Foreign Service probationers, 4
Commonwealth Summit, 113-114
Confucianism, 126
Congress Working Committee (CWC), 118
Conjunctivitis, 18, 79
Craftsmanship, 25, 27
Cultural Revolution, 82, 122

De Pury, David, 39, 43
Desai, Morarji, 87, 97, 104, 107, 109
Dialectical materialism, 25
Diwali, 38
Dung, Cheng Feng Yun, 77
Dussehra, 26
Dutt, S., 85, 94

Eco-Zones, 124
Eid, 27
Eishenhower, 49
Ellis, Robert, 14
En-lai, Chou, 8, 10, 12, 15, 18, 20-22, 33-35, 38-39, 47-48, 50, 58-61, 63-66, 72-73, 78, 80, 83, 86-87, 89-92, 94-110, 114-115, 120, 130, 133, 135, 138
Ernest Hemingway, 26
Expansionism, 17

Fang, Mei Lan, 23, 59, 62, 72
Five Principles, 8, 86, 88, 94, 105, 108-109, 130-131 *See also* Panchsheel

Five Year Plan, 27, 31, 65
Foot, Michael, 116
Forbidden City, 6-8, 121, 124-125
   regal splendour of the, 125
Forster, E.M., 6, 35, 46, 58
Fotedar, M.L., 123
Freedom movement, 31, 96
Frightful disaster, 122
Fu, Chang An, 87

Gadgil, V.N., 118
Gandhi, Indira, 115, 122-123, 128, 136
Gandhi, Rajiv, 111, 113-114, 116-120, 124-129, 131-133, 137-139
Gandhi, Sonia, 119
Gandhiji (Mahatama), 20, 27, 53, 89, 106
Gentleness of conduct, 73
Gobi desert, 61, 68
Goodwill and friendship, 95
Gopal, S., 72, 114
Gorbachev, Mikhail, 121
Gorky of China, See Hsun, Lu
Great Hall of the People, 120, 122, 126
Great Wall, 19, 28, 33, 68, 123
Great Wild Goose Pagoda, 134
Greene, Graham, 53
Grewal, Sarla, 123
Grewal, Simi, 123
Guha, Panu, 51, 57, 65
Gujral, Satish, 26

Hai, Chung Nan, 72-74, 119, 125
Haksar, P.N., 126, 132

Han-Fu, Chang, 89, 104
Hegemonism, 128-131
Hegemony, 131
Heros monument, 69
Hindi-Chini Bhai Bhai', 25, 87@
Hitler, 17
Hong Kong, 3-5, 14, 23, 25, 38, 43, 72-73, 81-82, 124
Hotel Miramar, 3
Hsin Chiao Hotel, 5-6, 8, 12, 20, 53, 63
Hsun, Lu, 27-28, 34
Huai, Peng Te, 20, 61, 75
Humanism, 73
Hundred Schools of Thought, 14, 25, 35, 55
Hussain, Haider, 28
Hutung, Tung Sung Po, 63

Ibrahim, Hafiz Mohd., 87
Impassivity, 22
Imperialism, 90-91, 97, 125, 130
Imperialists, 20, 100, 105
India Gate, 12, 108
India-China friendship, 101
India-China relations, 118
Indira foreign policy
International Conference on Cambodia, 117

Jammu & Kashmir, 90
Japanese exhibition, 24
Japanese imperialism, 130
Jawaharlal Nehru's grandson see Gandhi, Rajiv
Jo, Kuo Mo, 14, 62, 72-74

Joshi, P.C., 10

Kaganovich, Lazer, 65
Kai-shek, Chiang, 34, 54, 100, 135
Kalimpong, 95, 98-99, 105-106
Kao, R.N., 108
Kennedy, John F., 116
Khan, Aga, 69
Khan, Khurshid Alam, 113
Kissinger, Henry, 115, 118
Kong La Pass, 89-90
Korean war, 44, 54
Kripalani, J.B., 17
Kuantung reservoir, 28, 33
Kumar, Jainendra, 36
Kumar, Jainendra, 36–37

Ladakh, 86, 90, 100
Lakshman, Kamala, 57-58
Lakshman, R.K., 58
Lal, Pandit Sundar, 93
Lama, Dalai, 50, 85-86, 89, 95, 98-99, 105-106, 109
Lawrence, T.E., 54
Legation street, 38
Line of Actual Control, 109
Lung, Ho, 58-59, 61, 73
Lung, Lo, 81

Mahabalipuram, 66
Mahanalobis, 65-66
Malenkov, G.M., 65, 67
Malik, Meera, 36, 62, 68
Malthus, 60
Mandy, C.R., 6
Mandy, Shaun, 11

Man-made flying objects, 75
Mao Tun, 57, 62
Mao, Chairman, 8, 18-19, 22, 28-29, 32, 34, 40, 51, 55, 61, 72, 74-75, 80, 98, 101-102, 106
Marshall, David, 21
Marx, 20, 60, 77
Masani, Minoo, 56
Mathur, Shiv Charan, 118
Maun, Bau, 48
Maxwell, Neville, 109
McMahon Line, 92, 95, 100-101, 105-106, 109, 124,
Mehta, Jagat, 72, 94, 97, 104
Menon, K.P.S., 115, 121
Menon, Krishna, 38, 87, 91-92, 100, 116
Menon, Lakshmi, 17, 20
Menon, Shankar, 123
Middle East crisis, 37
Minh, Ho Chi, 66
Mishra, Brajesh, 115
Mishra, S.K., 123
Mishra, Vinod, 118
Molotov, V.M., 65
Mukerjee, Air Marshal, 20
Mukerjee, Sushil, 51
Mutual acceptability', 120@

Namboodiripad, E.M.S., 10
Nanda, G.L., 87
Narayan, J.P., 57, 91
Narayan, R.K., 26, 58
Narayanan, K.R., 113
National anthem, 120
National Congress, 9, 23

National Peoples' Congress, 73
National wrestling competition, 71
Nehru, Jawaharlal, 85-87, 115, 117, 120, 123
Nehru, R.K., 58, 97
Nehru, Rajan, 6, 36, 80
New Global Economic Order, 131
New International Economic Order, 131
New International Political Order, 131
Nicholson, Harold, 79
Nine Dragon Screen, 7
Non-aligned summit (NAM), 114
Non-dogmatic Marxism, 73
Noon, Lady Feroz Khan, 34
North Atlantic Treaty Organisation (NATO), 8
Nu, U., 21, 35, 37

Okinawa, 91

Pakistan Embassy, 27
Panchsheel, 38, 86-89, 94, 105, 108, 120, 130
  relevance of the, 120
Pant, G.B., 94
Pant, K.C., 115, 137
Paranjpe, Vasant, 104
Parathasarthi, G., 92, 104, 114
Peng, Li, 120-121, 123, 128-129, 131, 134
Pepsi and Coke, 135
Philosophy of revolution, 31
Picasso, 40
Planning Commission, 65
Prasad, Jitender, 118

Prasad, Rajendra, 27
Prasad, Tanka, 15, 19
Pu, Wai Chiao, 9, 14, 51
Publicity on Kashmir, 53
Pulitzer Prize, 44

Qichen, Qian, 121

Radhakrishnan, S., 72, 89
Rajghat, 89
Ram, Jagjivan, 87
Raman, Radha, 33
Ramayana into Chinese, translation of, 42
Ranganathan, C.V., 119, 121
Rao, P.V. Narasimha, 114-115, 118, 121, 127
Rashtrapati Bhawan, 12, 28, 88, 92, 96-97, 108
Ratnaswamy, Vincent, 75
'reactionary government', 106
Reagan, 128
Rectification campaign, 64, 67
Red Square, 69, 71
Riboud, Marc, 51
Russian revolution, 75

SAARC, 133
Sambu, Shamsrangin, 72
Sanitorium, 52
Scott, Sir Walter, 55
Security arrangements in communist countries, 119
Security Council, 51, 53, 55
Sen, Ronen, 123, 136, 138
Seth, Aftab, 138
Shakuntala, 20, 62

Shankar, Shiv, 113, 135
Shankar, Uday, 23
Sharma, P.N., 10
Shaw, George Bernard, 7
Shengkun, Yang, 122
Shih, Chih Pai, 39-40, 48, 52, 54
Shimla Convention, 95-96, 100, 105
Si, Mao Chu, 40, 55
Singh, Buta, 115
Singh, K.I., 105
Singh, Sardar Swaran, 93, 100
Singh, Tarlok, 11
Sino-India
  border, 86, 90-91
  friendship, 132
  front, 139
  relations, 86, 110, 113, 117, 120, 130, 132
Sino-Russian border, 128
Sino-USSR conflict, 121
Siqueiros, David Alfaro, 25
Social justice, 77, 130
Socio-economic-political crises, 138
Soekarno, 15-19, 22-23, 62
Somerset Maugham story, 52
Sotto, Gossi, 4, 26
Southeast Asia Treaty Organisation (SEATO), 8
Southern border, 102
Spanish civil war, 26
Spring festival, 54
Sputnik, 74-75, 81
Stalin, 15, 49, 55, 69, 74, 77, 81, 118, 125
Steinbeck, John, 26
Stevenson, Adlai, 49

Suez Canal, 7
Suhrawardy, H.S., 27
Sukhe Bator, statue of, 71
Summer Palace, 20-21, 54
Sundarayya, 10
Sundarji, K.S., 115
Suyin, Han, 5-6, 10, 13, 51, 66, 73, 75, 81-82, 97, 121

Tagore, Rabindranath, 53
Taiwan, 10, 74, 128
Tang, Lou Shou, 21
Tea-totalism, 134
Teen Murti House, 107
Teh, Chu, 18, 22-23, 61, 64, 66, 73
Temple of Heaven, 121
Ten Principles agreed at Bandung, 130 *See also* Panchsheel
Tho, Chen Chen, 20, 23, 48
Tibet revolt, 100, 107
Tien An Man (Tienanman), 8, 15, 19-20, 119, 121
  parade, 19
Ting, Chen Pan, 39
Tiwari, N.D., 115, 126
Trafalgar Square, 12
Tung, Mao Tse, 8, 19, 25, 28-30, 33, 64, 73-74, 79, 101, 115, 119, 126, 128, 136
'Two-Chinas' policy, 121

UNO, 32

Venkateswaran, A.P., 115, 137
Vietnam War, 121
Vohra, Ranbir, 26
Voroshilov, Marshal, 61

Waley, Arthur, 54, 57
Waterloo Battlefield, 33
West Changan Boulevard, 28
Wimbledon, 35
World Agriculture Fair, 90
Worthy, William, 44

Xiaoping, Deng, 61, 73, 75, 117, 119, 124, 126, 129-132, 134

Yangtse river, 5
Yee, Lam, 4
Yellow river, 76
Yi, Chen, 23, 35, 37, 61, 73, 87, 89-93, 95, 97, 100, 102, 104, 108
Yin-Yang philosophical concept, 55
Yuan, Fu Tao, 76

Ziyang, Zhao, 128-129, 131

Also by the Author

E.M. Forster: A Tribute
The Legacy of Nehru
Tales from Modern India
Maharaja Suraj Mal
Curtain Raisers
Profiles and Letters
The Magnificent Maharaja
Heart to Heart

Made in the USA
Monee, IL
04 May 2026